I0614903

He pointed to the recipe, and when she reluctantly did as he'd instructed, he said, "Add the wet butter and milk to the mix and beat until you get rid of all the lumps."

"Too bad I can't rid myself of the lumps in my so-called life."

"You'll get them smoothed out." He slid in back of her and took her hand, demonstrating the motion, tempting her to nestle against his chest. His iron-hard chest. "Just keep trying, luv."

His being so near was torture. "Do I add the fruit now?"

"Aye, the cranberries. You can spot a bad one from the others because it shows a wrinkle." He picked out a specimen, displaying it to her on his palm. "See, not unlike the line you get between your brows when you're deep in thought."

She rubbed the bridge of her nose. "I do?"

He sent her an all-male grin. "Captivating, actually."

He wiped flour from her face with a dishrag and plopped some cranberries in her mouth. She bit down, the tangy sweetness thrilling her taste buds, the sexy man challenging her vow to stay clear of him. But the very act of his helping her spoon the batter into tins pulled her deeper into his center, a universe composed of his culinary magic and kindness. His large hands and strong arms made her feel fragile and protected from the outside world. She remained there, a participant in sensations, till the bells over the entrance clanged together like dropped silverware.

Undercover in Venice Beach

by

Melody DeBlois

Love Is a Beach, Book 2

Undercover in Venice Beach

Cover Art by *Diana Carlile*

The Wild Rose Press, Inc.
PO Box 708
Adams Basin, NY 14410-0708
Visit us at www.thewildrosepress.com

Publishing History
First Edition, 2021
Trade Paperback ISBN 978-1-5092-3702-9
Digital ISBN 978-1-5092-3703-6

Love Is a Beach, Book 2
Published in the United States of America

Dedication

For Larry

Chapter 1

O wild West Wind, thou breath of Autumn's being,
Thou, from whose unseen presence the leaves dead
Are driven, like ghosts from an enchanter fleeing.
                    ~Percy Bysshe Shelley (1792-1822)

Audrey intended to find the dog a home with someone to love him. She raised her cell phone and snapped a photo of the Boston terrier named after the famous poet. Percy was a compact, square-shaped, clean-cut, lovable pup. His black-and-white markings only added to his dapper appearance, but his eyes protruded more than usual whenever he got spooked—just as they were now. He tilted his head to the side and sent her an anxious *ruff.*

"Hey, buddy, how about a cookie?" she asked.

One perk of being five ten, she didn't need a step stool to reach the top shelf. A shake of the canister told her it was empty—ditto for the bag of kibble in the pantry.

She sat beside him on the braided rug. "Don't stress, bud. I'll fix this."

Sure, Percy had his flaws. But on the whole, he was a happy, affectionate sort who didn't deserve to be orphaned. She'd adopt him herself, but her landlord didn't allow pets. Against her will, sobs generated from all those places inside her she'd been keeping in check.

He whimpered a little, and she hugged him, knowing he was as glum as she. Getting through this afternoon had been murder, but she had to pull herself together. For his sake, if for nothing else.

She dried her tears and shoved her phone in her purse. The finishing touches for the media post on the adoption site would have to wait—till the day after never if she could help it.

"You hold down the fort." She covered her unruly blonde bob with a scarf and scooted out the door into the freak September storm.

Tourists flocked to Abbot Kinney, "the hippest street in Venice," even on a day better suited for ducks. She darted by the bright murals painted on the buildings with their laid-back, bohemian vibe. Palm trees, spaced along the sidewalk, bowed in the wind. A graffitied trashcan threatened to keel over, but she caught it midway and rolled it to safety. Then she plunged into the florescent lights of Guthrie's Market. She focused on the colorful mounds of fresh fruit and vegetables while James Taylor sang "Fire and Rain" from a store speaker. *But wait.* That blue-eyed, pale-haired rat in the floral department—what was her ex-boyfriend even doing here?

She backed away, praying he didn't see her, and smashed into a mountain of lemons, sending them tumbling around her. The unfortunate act brought him sniveling toward her with a handful of red roses. A lot he knew. She was the daisies sort.

"Audrey," he bellowed as if her tragedy were his. "I'm so sorry about your—"

The lemon she threw hit him square in the forehead. "No. You don't get to say it."

"Attagirl, mow me down. Knock me out." He tapped a finger on his jaw. "Do some damage. I have it coming."

Instead, she silently picked up the mess, bolted to the pet aisle, and hauled a twenty-pound sack of chow from the shelf, then chose the dog biscuits with care. Satisfied, she headed toward the checkout line.

Forget the shithead ex on your heels.

Soon, though, he barged in. "Let me help you."

She shook him off, gritting her teeth. "Why are you here? Did your muse dump you after I caught you in bed with her?"

He was one in a chain of two-timing ex-boyfriends with excuses such as "I was only drunk, too depressed, too in love," or as the rat had claimed, "I need more passion." Had that been only three weeks ago?

If she were her badass twin sister, news of his cheating would soar from the loudspeaker. His unfaithful face would appear on social media. An exterminator, reporting a snake, would swing down from the light fixtures.

"Audrey, come home. Think of *Powell's Review*. You can't run a newspaper from the teahouse, not when there's no Wi-Fi."

She released the dog food beside the cash register. "That's not any of your business. But front-page news, I'm done supporting you. And full disclosure, if I ever fall for another poet, it won't be in this lifetime."

His pretty-boy face contorted with sympathy. "I heard Percy was on the street, saw it all."

Her throat closed up so much she couldn't swallow. "Never you mind." She paid and stalked off with her groceries. "You know where you can go."

3

"You're blaming me for your past." He blocked her way. "Did you ever think something you do drives your men to stray?" He sank his teeth into his bottom lip. "Sorry. That was mean. Uncalled for, but just give me one more chance."

"Another chance? Are you kidding me? So long, Casanova. Come around again, and I'll have you extinguished." *Aha!* Dead on her twin. "And you'd better watch out for the assassin on the roof of the Chase Bank."

By the time she left him with his mouth agape, lightning zapped the boulevard. People scrambled for cover. Thunder boomed, and Audrey's feet tingled. *Oh no!* A terrorized Percy wouldn't do, not today of all days. She scurried along with her heavy bundles, her arms screaming with pain, then froze near the open door of the teahouse.

An action figure of a man sprang from the entrance. His close-cut, chestnut hair shone in the streetlight, his handsome face tense and purposeful. He wore a bomber jacket and tight jeans as he carried Percy against his muscled chest. The dog's legs hysterically pumped the air, pistons of flashing white.

"Is this your pup, luv?" the guy called out to her in a deep, sexy, British voice.

****

The raindrops sparkled on the woman's thick, dark lashes as she dropped her shopping bags, took the canine in her arms, and looked at Liam like he'd just touched down from Mars.

"What were you doing with Percy?"

Before he could answer, an alarm from within the teahouse stabbed the air with a throbbing yowl. She beelined inside, leaving him to follow. He flung her groceries on a kitchen counter and deactivated the earsplitting blare.

Still, her dog yelped. Coughing, she switched on the fans, her gaze centered on the smoking kettle he'd just taken from the stove. She opened the oven door and took from the rack a muffin burned to a crisp. By her expression, he would think somebody dear to her had just croaked. Part of him wanted to bail, but the pitiful sight of her holding that charred muffin caused him to soldier on and hurl open windows.

"The sign said 'Closed.'" He showed her the thin screwdriver he kept in his wallet. "But the smell of smoke and the dog barking made me resort to desperate measures."

She tugged off her black jacket and scarf, and her wavy hair sprang in a sultry profusion of gold and bronze. Her eyes, a lusty shade of purple, doubled her appeal. She had those classic looks that meant no makeup was needed to alter what God, in all His wisdom, had given. He enjoyed the very sight of her, but as if she felt his gaze sizing her up, she turned away.

To top things off, sirens pierced the night, bullhorns blasting. *Bloody hell!*

A fire truck hissed to a stop outside, the stench of exhaust clouding the air. The mongrel sprang across the sidewalk like a German shepherd on steroids, barking his fool head off. While the woman wrestled with her dog, Liam surveyed the expanding crowd of shopkeepers and tourists. He had to split before he drew attention and spectators started asking questions.

Against his better judgment, he emerged into the

downpour. "All accounted for here."

A female firefighter leaped from an open door of the truck, rain pinging off her helmet. "We had a report of a fire."

"A teakettle left on the stove," Liam said. "Not to worry. I took care of it."

"It's my fault," the lady called, the dog squirming in her arms. "Quiet, Percy. Quiet, boy." She shook her head. "I forgot to turn off the burner when I left for the market."

Her voice sounded so done over Liam ached to comfort her.

The driver slid across the seat. "Everyone safe?"

She nodded, squinting against the flashing lights. "Yes, sir. Thank you. Sorry, you drove out for a false alarm."

"No problem, but we have to check inside." He slid a steel-toed boot down and jumped from the vibrating truck bay.

After an exchange of comments and the dog's feisty barks, the team made their inspection, and the fire engine whisked away. The looky-loos scattered, soaking wet and running for cover. During the deluge, several good-hearted souls embraced the woman, rain slashing across their faces. "Sorry about it…we've been thinking of you. If you need us to watch Percy any longer, it's no problem. Is there anything else we can do?"

Folks in this beach town took care of their own. The woman avoided eye contact to the extent he'd gamble she didn't relish the limelight either. When the last shopkeeper had skedaddled, she motioned him back inside. There, the odor of burnt aluminum lingered.

She hurled the ruined kettle into the rubbish, yanked up her phone, then twisted toward him. "Thank you." Her face had flushed as if she'd just knocked out sixty push-ups.

"No worries."

Her lower lip wobbled a little. "You're some kind of wonderful, you know that?"

His actions hadn't been that special, but she acted as if he'd single-handedly brought down a Russian spy plane.

He dumped the muffin in the bin. "Glad to help."

"I owe you." Rainwater dripped from her chin-length hair and landed on her shoulders in hollow plops. Soon, a fascinating line formed at the bridge of her nose. "You're soaking wet. Do you live nearby?"

"I don't." Forged passport, driver's license, credit cards—he had it all to use.

"And you are?"

"Liam James." Better to keep his Christian name when choosing a cover because it was instinctual to turn at the sound of it. Even though his mates had nicknamed him Archie, after his surname Archer, he stuck to Liam. Besides, Liam James matched the doctored ID card he kept in his wallet.

She held out the hand free of her phone. "Name's Audrey. Audrey Powell."

"Audrey, quite the combination." Her cool, soft skin as they shook stoked an already growing fire. "Awe-dree," he repeated. "The double syllables hang on the edge of my tongue—a mixture of melancholy and hope before dawn."

"For real?" Was she about to clout him upside the head?

7

"I guess that sounded sappy." Humiliated, he shut his mouth. He had never been a poet. Quite the opposite. What the hell had gotten into him? He thought it crucial to avoid her stare. "What about you? Are you a native?"

"Born and bred. You can take the girl out of the freak pot, but you can't take the freak out of the girl. No matter how much polish I give myself, I still roll up my pant legs and head for the circus along the gritty, old beach whenever I come home."

"Home to visit your mum?"

"Yes, only she's not here."

Taken aback, he paused. "What do you mean?"

Ping went her mobile as, texting a mile a minute, she sank to a chair. "Her funeral was this morning."

He had to be thick as mince. A woman in proverbial black and the dizzy behavior he suspected was unlike her. The merchants' condolences. She was using her phone as a coping mechanism, which he recognized since he did it himself when things got rough. No, it didn't take a Sherlock to connect the pieces.

"I'm terribly sorry," he said.

Cripes, he had gone into the battlefield blindfolded. Her mother's death changed everything. Asking how her mum died would be presumptuous. She seemed so upset all he wanted was to help her, but he wasn't sure how. He settled across from her as she scrolled the messages on her phone. He leaned over the table and wiped a tear from her cheek with his thumb. Perhaps he shouldn't have. What was the protocol? If she'd been a teammate, he'd have grabbed her a pint or taken her to the pub.

"You joined forces with them, didn't you?" she asked, blinking back tears.

"Excuse me?" His pulse skipped a beat.

"I guessed it!" She slammed her phone on the table.

Did he dare ask? "What do you mean?"

"You're a member of the Cult of the Marvelous Past."

"The Cult of the Marvelous Past?"

"That's how I secretly refer to some of the clientele."

His mouth had gone dry. "Why is that?"

"The cult's goal is to make sure, in the computer age, poetry, especially the old-school sort, isn't forgotten."

He slid the fitness tracker farther up his wrist, out of sight. "Well, I suppose you found me out. I came here on holiday. It turns out I got acquainted with your mother." He'd accomplish this mission by using his initial slipup to his advantage. "I'd stop by to recite poetry."

A pause ensued. "And you like tea?"

"I am an Englishman, aren't I?" To be honest, he preferred caramel macchiatos.

She waved him into the other room and gestured to the shelves filled with gold tins. "I can make you a cup, although I'm kind of rusty at performing the ceremony."

Little did she know how much he needed answers. "I heard your mother traveled the globe to establish her imports." He recalled his notes. "Sri Lanka, Kenya, Thailand, the coast along the Black Sea, China, Morocco, just to name a few."

Audrey gave a rueful smile. "She did, yes."

He pretended to study the labeling on the canisters glimmering in the chandelier's glow. "You must have gone with her once or twice."

She popped open a tin, and a lush, flowery scent made her eyes water—or maybe it was nostalgia. "Have you ever been in the Himalayas where oolong and white tea grow at altitudes of up to six-thousand feet?"

He'd been on leave there once but instead confided a different fact. "I spent most of my boyhood in the wilds of Northwest England."

"Hmm." She bent to retrieve a cup, and the shadows all but hid her long, lean body. "The perfect environment to raise a technophobe."

"You're right."

She couldn't be more wrong about him.

His mission had been to observe Monroe Powell. But when headquarters formed the task force, they hadn't known she was a goner. The details were sketchy. No birth record existed aside from her growing up on a tea plantation in South Carolina. She'd married a poet who died young but not before starting a business and fathering twin girls.

The fifty-three-year-old Monroe's teas were legendary. Most likely, a guise. Had to be because top secrets exchanged on the premises threatened the UK's national security. Liam wanted to believe Audrey was oblivious to any wrongdoing. In his line of work, though, a man could get killed if he didn't suspect everyone he met.

He drew a circle on the table with his thumb. "I saw your mum sell one of her potions to a patron. Would you say her teas are—" How should he put it?

"—special?"

Her shoulders stiffened. "They are, yes." She sucked in a breath. "But my mother could get a fence post to talk. For example, there was an introverted lady. Mama made her a pot of *Jiu Qu Hong Mei*, and the two spoke—talked for hours on end. The woman returned for more beautiful black tea and…"

"And?"

"Olivia Ricci is now our mayor."

"The power of suggestion." A chill traveled down his spine. To steady his nerves, he looked out the rear windows that opened to an Oriental garden shimmering in the rain.

"Mama didn't just share her passion. She helped people reach their goals. I'd wished for a little guidance when I came across the last thing she baked."

"The muffin."

"I found it in the fridge. It was like discovering a Fabergé egg, and now it's gone."

Something in her words threatened to thaw the emotions he kept on ice. "Why did you leave tonight?"

She closed her eyes. "Percy was out of dog food."

"Ah, your mum's pet?" When she nodded, he added, "What are you going to do with him?"

The canine pushed his head between his forepaws. Emitting a long drawn-out moan, he looked up at them from the polished teakwood floor.

But before she could answer, the sound of a vehicle screeching to a stop set Liam on high alert. The hairs on the back of his hand rose as his fingers reached and curled around the Glock hidden to make it accessible if need be.

Chapter 2

"Hope" is the thing with feathers
That perches in the soul
And sings the tune without the words
And never stops—at all.
            ~Emily Dickinson (1830-1886)

When Johnny Spade showed his face in the teahouse, Liam pushed to his feet as if called to attention while Audrey vaulted into her uncle's arms, and the yip-yapping Percy danced around them on his hind legs in a jiggety-jig.

She laid her head on Uncle Johnny's chest, drawing comfort in the usual smell of bay rum and starlight mints. "I'm so glad you're home."

"Hey, girlie."

The small Amazon parrot, Kubla, who had taken up residence on Uncle Johnny's shoulder more years back than she could count, opened his bright orange beak. And gave her a raspy, "Hey, girlie."

"Have I got some yarns to tell," her uncle added in unison because it was how the two rolled. They were a pair—the bard and his bird, a crowd-pleaser of the highest order.

A well-built female Uber driver followed him. Her poppy-red lips turned up in a smile. "Oh, does he." She cupped a hand to his ear. "I'll take you on to my place."

"How about a raincheck?" He scratched the sweet spot behind Percy's ears. "It's Sunday night, so this joint's closed. Perfect time to visit my niece and my favorite sister."

Dread jabbed Audrey between the ribs. "About that…"

Johnny tipped the driver a handful of bills. He shook Liam's hand as he introduced himself, planted a kiss on Audrey's cheek, and strolled the deep cavern of the teahouse. His stare darted to the high-beamed ceiling and the Victorian décor with its Asian influence. He took all of it in as if starved to death for home.

A decade ago, silver had threaded through his blond, waist-length hair, but nowadays, a short ponytail hung just past his nape. Other than that, nothing had changed—same eyes, the color of the Arctic Sea, same half-moon dimple in his chin.

He slid an oblong tin from inside the pocket of his khaki coat and set it on the tasting bar. "I thought your mama might take a hankering to this hyssop green tea."

Liam turned the box over in his hands and inspected it as if suspecting it held something illegal. "If you don't mind my asking, where did you get this?"

"São Miguel, an island of the Azores," Johnny said with a wistful smile.

"São Miguel," Kubla repeated.

"In a tea garden near a turquoise lagoon lush with bright-colored fish." He unlatched the case of his portable typewriter and plopped a manuscript on the mahogany tabletop. "There, I composed the first draft of *A Spy in Paradise*."

Her uncle was a scholar who made life beautiful with his words and his words that were ballads and his ballads that were stories and his stories that were books. Who would suspect a man like Johnny Spade of writing under the pseudonym Constance Spring? He wrote about *amour, amour,* as he called it, flavored with chronicles of espionage during the Cold War.

To Audrey, he was a father since her own had died before she had any actual memories of him. Although they didn't always agree—often debating an issue until each grew hoarse—the last thing she wanted was to break his heart.

"I tried to find you," she said when he met her gaze.

"I spent the end of my stay on the island of Flores, the place for anyone who likes canyoning and abseiling down waterfalls the way I do. This paradise isn't all over social media. It's so remote I never saw a soul on hikes with the Portuguese beauty I met there."

"That's why you never got my messages." She didn't mean to sound so accusatory.

He removed his Panama hat and dropped it on the tea bar. "Where's your mother?"

She had practiced the things she'd say at least a hundred times. She needn't have bothered. Panic rose in her throat, making her afraid of breaking before she began.

"We have to talk." She swallowed down the urge to weep.

"What?" His gaze drifted over her shoulder. "Monroe?"

"She…"

Liam advanced toward the exit. "I'll go straight away."

When he got to the foyer, he grabbed the umbrella

he had propped there and disappeared into the violent night. Audrey wanted to stop him and lean on him for support. But the following conversation needed privacy, needed the right words. She had none.

Johnny frowned in bewilderment. "What is it?"

"Terrible news," she mumbled. With a trembling tongue, she moistened her brittle lips. Her dry mouth, clamoring heart, and sweaty palms found no relief. "Mama was in an accident."

He closed his eyes. "Is my sister...?"

"She didn't..." Her fingers itched for her phone, but the sight of it would irk him no end. "Mama didn't make it."

Without hesitation, he turned his back on her. "What happened?"

She inhaled a breath from her diaphragm. "A truck hit her while she was out jogging with Percy." Her voice shattered, and to her dismay, her tears escaped and burned like molten lava. "I wanted you here."

"Your sister? Where's Lucy Lou?"

Since she couldn't provide an answer, this was another dreaded question. "I haven't been able to locate her either."

His broad shoulders shook, the parrot's feathers stirring, and Johnny's towering frame toppled as if he were caving in on himself. He uttered a strangled cry. Kubla flew into the air. The dog crouched in a corner, visible tremors passing through his body.

"Oh, Uncle Johnny," Audrey cried and reached for him, but he broke away from her and ran outside. She shut the exit so the pets didn't escape, and tore through the rain after him. He ducked into the stairwell that led to his apartment above the teahouse.

She lurched into the musty passage just in time to detect the door slamming with an echoing thud. Her body halted. Tears dribbled from her chin as she centered her focus on the barricade that kept them apart. Weak-kneed, she clutched the banister for support.

Liam hovered near. "Your uncle needs to be alone."

How dare he assume he knew anything about her family? Who was this man to be giving advice? Just another damned poet, that was who.

Her brain formed the words, "Please go," but they died on her tongue.

He drew so close his breath warmed her neck in a sensation not altogether uncomfortable. "Audrey."

She feared he'd add more poetry in his hunky British dialect. "I have this under control," she wanted to attest. Hadn't she always been able to cope? Trying to function now without weeping was difficult. Although her mother was the one who had died, she felt her own existence dwindling. An enormous gaping hole had formed in her heart, a place where she still wore pigtails and denim rompers and helped Mama blend her specialty teas. A pinch of vanilla, bits of dried fruit, all those tastes lost to her now.

Giving in to defeat, she hung her head and leaned against Liam's side. "I don't want him to be all by himself."

She took out her cell phone but remembered Uncle Johnny owned nothing digital. If she knocked just once, then maybe he would respond. Her chest swelled with hope, and she climbed a step, then another.

Liam caught her by the wrist. "Give him a chance to deal with the shock."

More pearls from Liam, one of those struggling geniuses for whom Mama'd had a soft spot. Frustration settled in Audrey's bones. Her teeth chattered, and she rubbed her arms with her hands.

He shrugged out of his jacket and wrapped it around her as if he were her very own personal rainy-day hero. *Chivalrous*. The word drifted to mind along with a warm glow deep within her that made the cold bearable.

With a gentle tug, he took her from the stairs to the sidewalk. Lights reflected on the slick, wet pavement. Laughter and carousing wafted from the doorways on the boulevard. He snapped open his umbrella. They anchored underneath. She gazed from the mural of an elf balancing a stack of books while stamping his foot on a desktop computer to the upstairs window. The darkness there mirrored the clouds that had parted so a silvery globe of a moon shone—a moon for lovers, not for a woman scorned.

Liam pointed a finger. "Look, there's your uncle's parrot."

Kubla teetered across the windowsill that jutted out at an angle from the first floor. They checked on him, made certain of his safety, then called out to Percy, but got no response. They found him cowering in the kitchen. He crept toward them, his tail between his legs. Both Audrey and Liam stooped to calm the dog who wriggled, awarding each an appreciative lick.

"Percy freaks at the slightest provocation," she said. "My mother thought someone abused him as a puppy. He was around three when she brought him home from the animal shelter. In those days, if you raised a hand, he'd recoil like he was under a zombie siege."

He gave the terrier a last pat and got to his feet. "Well, he wasn't about to abandon ship tonight." He opened the backdoor and stepped out into the yard. "I'd better get on with it."

The Asian garden separating the teahouse from Mama's bungalow sparkled in the porchlight as if enchanted. Liam turned toward her, his darkly lashed eyes a lustrous bronze-brown. The wind whisked through his hair, his shirt flapping against his flat abs. With his biceps shining and wet, he made quite a statement. He was the man destined to make the cover of one of Constance Spring's hot-steamy thrillers.

Audrey slid out of his jacket, sad to lose its smoky leather scent. "Where are you headed?"

"I thought I might bunk on a park bench."

Was he telling the truth or hinting for a place to stay? "Most likely a lie," she blurted, then slapped a hand to her mouth. "Sorry, but I've had more than my share of dishonesty. The fact is I swore off ever becoming involved with another poet."

How could she not with her addiction to them? Her shameful flaw. But didn't she owe this troubadour after he had saved the teahouse, not to mention dear Percy?

The clothesline squeaked as the pulley jerked around as if an invisible hand had twisted it. A gust pierced the air, and it sounded like Mom's tomboyish two-fingered whistle.

What would Mama do?

Audrey had only to ask herself the question. "Liam, do you want to sleep on the love seat inside? That way, you could watch over Kubla. I know you'd be uncomfortable, maybe even sore, and—"

"You can count on me. I give you my word of honor. I shan't ever let you down."

****

The first thing Liam did was supply the parrot with banana slices, a shot glass filled with water, and a drop of rum for good measure.

"Cheers, mate." He leaned over to where the bird ruffled green feathers splashed with turquoise down his front and a dab of yellow around his eyes. "That should take the edge off."

"Take the edge off," Kubla echoed as he jetted from the windowsill and landed on Liam's left shoulder, massaging it with his talons.

Liam took a seat, inserted the earbud, and shifted his mouth toward the microphone concealed in the collar of his shirt. "Hello, Alpha, this is Tech. Do you read me? Over."

Alpha came back. "Tech, that's confirmed."

Alpha ran the base station set up in a hotel. When they landed forty-one hours prior, the team of six had descended and turned the rooms into living quarters.

Without moving an inch, Liam said, "There was a fire, but I have control."

Kubla mimicked, "I have control."

People outside moved by the window, and Liam slumped in his chair. Were they the men from his squad? Hard to tell in the rain.

"Alpha, acknowledge," he said into the microphone.

He pictured Alpha with a row of computers in front of him. "Tech, standby, standby."

Through his earpiece, he heard voices rallying in the background. Then Alpha returned on the net. "All call signs, cancel. Cancel. All signs acknowledge."

One by one, the task force responded to the radio check, and Liam caught a fellow operative's not-so-polite reply. "What the hell is going on? Tell us?"

"Wait…wait…" Alpha sounded under pressure as voices rose. "All signs, this assignment is abandoned. All call signs meet at LAX and board British Airways at 0530. Tech, dismantle the teahouse. I need confirmation."

Liam acknowledged. Some flack hit the fan in the ops room. Alpha was getting chewed out by his commanding officers. Next came the sound of laughter and guffaws. Operation Teacup sounded now like a bloomin' Mad Hatter's tea party.

Liam had planted surveillance equipment in the early morning when he figured the teahouse vacated. Because of Monroe Powell's beliefs, no modern technology enhanced the premises, which led his team to grumble. No computers, no modem or cables fed into a TV to proceed as usual. Placing landline phone taps and mounting recorders took hours.

By now he realized why she never showed. As he worked at removing the devices, he clicked on a recorder and eavesdropped on the conversation between Audrey and her uncle after Liam left. Halfway through, he sat back on his heels. Monroe hadn't died of natural causes. Had someone taken her out on purpose?

A task force ending without notice occasionally transpired. Who knew why? Maybe headquarters needed to rethink and regroup. Perhaps, with Monroe Powell out of the picture, her teahouse no longer held a threat.

From the beginning, the mission had seemed quite

bizarre. Who would link teas, believed mystical, to espionage? Far be it for him not to suspect her of collaborating with the enemy. A woman who could influence a political party, as she had the mayor, might very well support other secret affiliations.

He recalled her daughter so desperate she'd been ready to experiment with those clandestine infusions. Would have, too, if the cupboard hadn't been bare, which had sent her away and led him inside. What would happen to Audrey, who had stunned him speechless with her amethyst eyes? She couldn't have committed crimes against her country.

What was he thinking? Getting soft wasn't an option. In the end, the task mattered not a wit. There'd be another. Soon enough, he'd be flying over the States on his way back to London and his flat on the bank of the Thames.

At 0405, from the window, he spied the rental vehicle pulling up to the curb. He darted out with a crate full of electronics and was about to set them in the backseat when the parrot he had forgotten fluttered off his shoulder.

"I'm in control," Kubla copied, then disappeared inside the palm tree overhead.

No way did Liam plan to miss his flight back to the UK. No one expected him to go beyond the call of duty to rescue the runaway bird. Who wouldn't be knackered after forty-eight hours of following orders? Home awaited him with a warm fire and the promise of a day and night of uninterrupted sleep. He deserved a little R & R. Before depositing the box inside the car, though, he glanced at the upstairs window.

In his next breath, he said to the driver, "Go on to

LAX, and I'll catch up."

Spade had just lost his sister. Bloody awful to lose his best mate as well. Plus, how many birds had he saved from hunters' guns when he was a lad? He couldn't very well turn his back on the poor creature.

Besides, what was a simple detour? He would slap a pineapple wedge on his shoulder, call out in the dusky dark, "Here, commander. Got a treat for you." That was the plan. Only Kubla didn't stir from his position in the tree. Had he gone to roost? The approaching sunlight would wake him. *Hold on a moment.* Wasn't it a fact that most parrots got the screaming meemies at the break of day? Spade might hear and look down on the street below.

With no time left to lose, he scored a ladder from the shed where he had stuffed his spy equipment. Strange little bird noises drifted from the dense leaves. Success in this task depended on him keeping his cool. If he made the wrong move, Kubla might startle and fly off into the wild blue yonder never to return.

Climbing one rung at a time at a snail's pace and raising his hand with the bait, Liam called, "Kubla, Kubla Khan, come out, come out wherever you are."

A branch from above wobbled. Fronds sailed down and struck his upturned face. The parrot's wings flapped, and he snagged the fruit along with a nip out of Liam's finger. Pineapple juice dribbled from Kubla's beak as he regained his stakeout.

Liam remained unfazed. Didn't matter if the culprit had wounded him. A soldier kept his head in any condition. That's why he devised *Operation Lure* and downloaded an app on his phone that imitated bird mating calls. An ace in the hole that got Kubla so fired up he pulled strands of Liam's hair out by the roots.

Every quivering muscle in his body said to catch the damned parrot—stat. Some early riser stomped by, and Liam slammed a shushing finger to his lips, then shook his head with disbelief. If the foreign office got a look at him now, they'd send him off on some godforsaken mission in the frozen steppes of Siberia.

He spun around, but not without giving the bugger a tuppence worth. "Stay put, mate, or I'll leave you to the cats."

Minutes later, as a biker pedaled by, Liam stalked back into the yard. Kubla edged out on a shaky limb, cocked his head to the side, and eyed the molasses at the bottom of a small trash bin Liam had set on the grass. When the bird flew down inside the trap, Liam tugged a string, and the wire screen snapped over the top with a clanging bang.

"Hooah!"

His victory ceased when he spotted his watch— 0545. Crap, he'd missed his plane. He'd ended up stranded stateside, grounded without even a map of Southern California, let alone Venice Beach. *Bloody hell!* His location might as well be Siberia.

Chapter 3

Fair is my love, when her fair golden hairs
With the loose wind ye waving chance to mark;
Fair, when the rose in her red cheeks appears;
Or in her eyes the fire of love does spark.
                    ~Edmund Spenser (1552-1599)

Audrey rolled over and let out a groan as something wet and cold touched her hand hanging over the bed. She pressed her face into the soft feather pillow.

"Go away," she said, her voice muffled. She flipped onto her back, finding the room dark. "It's the middle of the night, for crying out loud. Have mercy, Percy."

When he whined, she stole a peek at her phone. Nine thirty!

"You've got to be kidding." She rolled over and pinched the window blinds. The sunlight made her wince. She clapped a hand on the mattress. "Come on, snickerdoodle. Up and at 'em."

He tried his darndest to climb but failed. She gave him a gentle boost, and his hind legs kicked the air before he landed on all fours. She rose to a sitting position against the propped pillows, and he yawned, then snuggled against her.

"What a dream I had." She didn't say it was about

24

Liam. In her sleep, he'd bent her backward under that black umbrella and had run his left hand over her lips and down her neck, and she had only to tell him to stop. She had done no such thing.

By ten fifteen, juggling two cups of Earl Grey, she exited the bungalow. Percy trotted ahead, twisting around to make sure she was still there.

"I'm not going anywhere, buddy."

She wore jeans and a shirt with *Little Girls with Dreams Become Women with Vision* printed across it. She'd found it hanging in the closet in the room she'd once shared with her twin. Whether it was her sister's or hers wasn't relevant. Mama had given them each one on their sixteenth birthday. Today she needed to keep those words close to her heart, even if she hadn't lived up to them. Not by a long shot.

When she opened the door, the sound of snoring drifted from inside the teahouse. Liam had probably stayed up all night composing anti-tech poetry.

"Not a dang care in the world." She rolled her eyes and set Liam's tea on a table in the entry. "Must be nice, but we owe him, don't we? Let's let him sleep a little longer."

Too bad she hadn't gotten his number in the rare event he owned a cell phone. She'd rather text him than talk. So much safer.

Percy padded up the chilly stairwell and uttered a bark of greeting. The door swung open on its hinges with a long, wallowing whine.

She cupped her hands to her mouth and called, "Are you okay?"

"Enter at your own risk." Johnny's voice cracked.

Daylight slanted through the blinds, illuminating

book-lined walls. Ordinarily, Audrey loved it here. It smelled like old libraries and ink. She'd listen to her uncle's clattering typewriter as she fussed over a newspaper article. Being near him raised the level of her writing. Because he always drove her to question her topics, she wrote better. But not today.

Today Uncle Johnny, who prided himself on his five-mile-a-day run, shuffled as if he'd aged twenty-plus years. He still wore his clothes from the night before. His bare feet poked from the hems of his jeans as he slurped down coffee, his forehead creased with pain.

He squinted over half-glasses. "You got Kubla?"

"He's safe." But was he? She should have checked the windowsill. Instead, she'd gotten preoccupied with Liam, who she never actually saw this morning.

Her uncle slipped Percy a chew toy and motioned to easy chairs on either side of a wardrobe trunk heaped on top with travel guides and periodicals. "I can't wrap my head around… What the heck happened?"

She inhaled a deep breath. "The accident occurred a week ago Saturday." The date remained forever ingrained in her mind.

"I am so sorry you weren't able to get ahold of me. You planned things all by your lonesome. Nobody should have to do that. How did you ever manage?"

"Mama once mentioned she wanted a graveside service. A burial, a plot next to Daddy's. A friend helped me, a Madison Gray. You haven't met her. She took me in and worked with me on the arrangements."

He lowered his gaze. "I'm glad you had someone to turn to."

Seconds passed as he seemed to ruminate on all she

had revealed. He got up, switched off his ham radio, and jimmied a photo album from the bookcase, then collapsed on the chair. "My era was an exceptional time to live. Such innocence. No cell phones. They weren't even a glimmer in an eye. No dangerous video games or gossipy social media accounts."

He was leading them down a path open to a heated debate.

"Let's stick to Mama," she diverted.

He opened the small gallery of his and Mama's childhood across his lap. His face darkened. "Where was I when that bastard hit Monroe?"

And there it was, his shame hanging like a body over a ledge.

"You couldn't have done anything," she said. "Nobody could have."

"That's the problem with the neighborhood today. Too many protestors wander around, their fists pounding the air, shouting, 'Agree with my beliefs or down with you.'"

Audrey sighed. "What do protesters have to do with Mama?"

He leaped to his feet, his voice rising. "Don't put your head in the sand, sweet pea. The demonstrators today are crossing the line. They're not the peaceful warriors anymore. No sirree. These days, hotheads will rip you apart if you don't support their cause."

"Oh, come on, Uncle Johnny. Mama might not have had free Wi-Fi in the teahouse, but no one was out to get her because of it."

"I shouldn't have left. I was her brother, the eldest by a year. I taught her to tie her shoelaces and took her back and forth from school. I kept her safe from every goldarn person who had it in for her."

Her temples pulsated. "You can't believe someone meant to hurt her. Why would they? All she ever wanted was to bring peeps together with poetry and tea."

"Did they catch who did it?"

She paused, afraid to answer. "The cops aren't sure. Whoever it was didn't stick around."

He wriggled his feet into his unlaced running shoes. "I have to go over the police report. We need some answers to—"

"Don't you want to hear about Mama's burial service?" Along with everything else, she wouldn't admit the officer had asked if her mother had been suicidal. Percy had lowered his head as if ready to run for cover.

Uncle Johnny looked at the dog and sank back down in the chair. "All right. Go ahead."

Principles were the quality that made his writing meaningful. Conviction, taking a stand, a willingness to fight for beliefs...it was the grit of heroes. But he sometimes carried his ideals too far. No protester harbored a grudge for her mother. No one had acted out of spite. As Audrey formed the thought, her head pounded, and she clasped her hands together at her knees.

"It was the kind of day," she said, "Mama would have chosen for her going away party. The sky was a tumult of thunder and brimstone. With the rain pelleting against the tent, the mourners huddled on chairs. The mayor spoke. Merchants praised her, including an editor from *The Tea Almanac*. Bookshop proprietors and art center directors mentioned how much she had done for the literary arts. Father Lawlor talked about her charitable work, her projects with Alzheimer's patients, the Christmas dinners for the homeless, and on and on. I gave the eulogy with a little help from Madison."

"And you had that beau, what's his name—a fat lot of good he probably did you."

"I imagined Mama looking down and nodding her head in approval." Running out of things to add and drawing a blank, she blurted, "And my former boyfriend wasn't there."

"What?"

"I caught him cheating."

Her uncle's eyes narrowed to chips of ice. "Of all times to be a dickhead. Where's the lowlife now? I'll break his ever-loving jaw. I—"

"Don't get all crazy on my account. I'm lucky the cheeseball showed his true colors. I was planning on dumping him, anyway."

"Were you?" He didn't sound convinced.

"Yes." She tucked her hair around her ear. "There's someone else."

"The Englishman I met last night?"

"That's him." Did she have no shame? She couldn't even think about Liam without getting all warm and smiley inside. She tugged the bill of her cap down to hide her guilty face.

"Are you okay?"

Nodding, she said, "I'm fine." She'd give up almost anything to quit thinking about Liam. "I'd like to see those Kodak moments with you and Mama."

Time passed with them flipping through plastic-pocketed pages. Her mother's girlhood in the South fascinated Audrey. Granny Stewart had been a wise woman, rumored to be a witch, with stories and anecdotes about tea. For Monroe, owning a plantation hadn't been enough. She'd longed to travel the world over to find the perfect cup of tea for each individual.

Then Mama had met the poet who swept her off her feet. She couldn't have resisted his charms when he wrote poems that melted her heart. They'd married and bought the defunct business they transformed into Tea and Poetry.

At one point, Johnny asked, "Did you meet the Brit when I was away?"

"I did." She curled her hand and stared at her bitten fingernails.

He patted her shoulder. "He's your newest flame, I suppose. I can only hope for your sake this one's not a poet."

She flinched. "That hurts."

"How odd I never saw him around." His forehead scrunched up. "His showing up now, of all times, is weird. A body can't help but notice a London tower like him, yet I can't place him before last night. Why is he hanging out here?"

She leaped to Liam's defense. "He's one of you Luddites." She readjusted her tense shoulders. "I guess you don't recall his name. It's Liam James." Just saying it out loud was enough to turn loose a net of butterflies in her stomach. "Mama knew him."

"Funny, she never mentioned him to me."

"How strange." No way would Audrey volunteer the fact she'd let him spend the night. Alone. In the teahouse. By himself. Her cheeks burned with mortification, and she closed her eyes. She was so weary she rested her head against the chair.

"Is there something the matter?"

She covered her telltale face with her hands. No more mooning over an Englishman whose beliefs she opposed. Still, she'd better check on him—now before it was too late. What did she know about him, anyway?

Anxiety had her jumping to her feet. "I'll get Kubla for you."

She navigated around the stacks of books devised in a purposeful order, designed for his ever-continuing research. If he adopted a laptop, he could avoid all the clutter, but she wouldn't bring it up. Now wasn't the time.

Her uncle joined her. "He'll need my coaxing."

She snatched Kubla's birdcage and dashed down the stairwell, her loafers clipping her heels, Percy darting past her. "Leave it to me," she called over her shoulder.

At the bottom of the steps, she hit that clean, ocean air. The sky gleamed an endless silver, beautiful to behold. Venice Beach, after the rain—how could anyone deny its brilliance? With the sun nearly blinding her, she almost missed the sight of the chartreuse and blue bird feathers scattered along the sidewalk.

****

After Liam secured the parrot, he had written Audrey.

Thank you for letting me crash inside the teahouse. I'll get out of your hair, but before I go...let me just say, "May the stars shine upon thee, may thee walk with giants and know that the magic of Tea and Poetry is within thee."

Liam

Kubla was sawing logs. All had ended well except for the fact Liam was stuck on foreign soil, his body ached, and he had a sore finger. Not to mention, he was sleep-deprived. The temptress's damn problems had messed with his head. The quicker he escaped Venice Beach, the better.

The foghorn brayed from the Pacific, calling to him. Because of all his troubles, he would love to lose himself at the circus along Audrey's beachfront. If he had a look at the boardwalk, he'd consider himself rewarded for this unfortunate turn of events.

Instead, he crossed the street and leaned inside a dark alley. Rubbish blew across the damp concrete, and cathedral bells tolled in the distance. Otherwise, the silence between the graffitied walls reassured him. What better cover for an agent who'd failed a mission? He took out his phone and rang London.

He said, "I am detained in the States by circumstances. I thought I'd remain for a while and see the sights. I must book a return flight to the UK."

The covert speech was a code to put off a casual listener. He couldn't fool any professional eavesdroppers, but all SIS needed to know was that he was in Dutch. No chance in hell would he reveal a dodgy bird had "detained" him.

The woman spoke in a monotone. "Very well. I will pass on the message. Do you have a contact number?"

"No." Too risky to give it out. "I'll ring you in an hour."

"All right. Goodbye."

He continued down the boulevard. At the next streetlight, a picture popped into his head of Audrey, dealing with her grief all by herself. He shut his eyes against the deluge of feelings rising to the surface. He considered dropping his phone down the storm drain—that way, no one could trace him.

Had he lost his mind? She might prove guilty of treason. *Never trust a woman whose troubles are worse than your own*—his motto. And he'd better take heed of it, or end up sleeping with the enemy. He shoved his mobile back into his pocket.

As he wandered, he deliberated over the events of the last fifty-five hours. Noting the sudden charcoal sky, he zipped up his jacket. Another storm was inevitable. But the pervading darkness allowed him to blend in to the crush of people on the lane opening to the coastline. He'd made it there. Yay him.

The joggers, bikers, and rollerbladers whizzed by, almost knocking him on his bum. A sword-swallower asked for a handout. So did a beachcomber after touching his tongue to the tip of his nose. Everyone, from mimes to jugglers to musicians, had a skill no matter how small or insane, each at the mercy of the tourists for their bread.

Liam passed under an arch and the buildings to his right, shops of bright colors selling everything under the sun. The aroma of outdoor cooking suggested those summers at Cambridge when he had been a carefree lad with big ideas.

He sauntered into a shack where retro surfboards covered the interior and ordered the Blue Plate Special. Soon he was scarfing down fish tacos, the jalapenos making his eyes water. The sauce kicked of sriracha and lime. Through a food-induced haze, he heard an oiled-up bodybuilder holler at him from the open gym.

"Hey, bro, show us what you got, why don't cha?"

"Not today." Liam tossed his empty wrappers in the bin. "Another time."

He placed a call, and a woman answered.

"PIN, please." He gave it to her, and she said, "Just a moment."

He waited on hold, lulled almost to sleep by elevator music. Minutes later, all went dead. He tapped the contact, and again the phone cut off. The problem was a mere cock-up. Wasn't it? But it might be intentional. Maybe, though, the reception here was poor.

A street vendor selling a memoir by a local drew him, and he had removed a twenty when a man snatched his wallet. Liam shoved through the crowd and arrived in time to see the thief and his partner in crime, a German shepherd, vanish around a corner. Liam's knees buckled, and he hugged himself to ease that hot-poker-in-the-gut feeling.

He cut through the grass past palm trees and staggered through the sand littered with seaweed, broken glass, and food wrappers. A wave broke and showered him. Soaked and shivering, he turned. This carnival upstaging the sea was Audrey's grand escape?

He got out his phone, put a call through, but this time no one answered. What the hell? Did the agency think he had refused an order? Did they believe he'd betrayed them? Were they cutting him off to deny they ever knew him?

Scenes played out around him. A bald-headed bloke wobbled on his hands across a bed of nails. To his right, an Alicia Keys look-alike banged a keyboard while crying a river in song. Inside a glass booth, a mechanical sultan peered into a crystal ball, his eyes lighting up like a red devil's.

So much for the cool SoCal vibe. Just Liam's hard luck. Before long, he'd most likely have to join this circus to score his next meal.

Chapter 4

She looked a little wistfully,
Then went her sunshine way—
The sea's eye had a mist on it,
And the leaves fell from the day.
~Francis Thompson (1859-1907)

"Liam, I was an idiot to put my trust in you," she said through clenched teeth. She stamped into the teahouse along with Percy to find the Earl Grey untouched and right where she'd left it. "How can you sleep after—?"

The dog let out a woof, then sat, chest lifted, eyes focused on a low table where a towel covered a lampshade. Those familiar snoring noises came from inside.

Audrey blinked in surprise. "Kubla?" She raised the terry cloth. "Phew. I don't know what my favorite, and only, uncle would have done if he lost you."

She'd just cajoled the parrot into his cage when she spied a note on the counter. Her heart flip-flopped at the sight of her name written in fluid cursive.

The way Liam strung the last letter of his words back to dot his Is with tiny circles pinned him as someone who couldn't let go of the past. A freaking Luddite to the core. When she read the ending, she drew in a slow, shaky breath.

...the magic of Tea and Poetry is within thee.

Oh, he knew how to woo a girl. Audrey found the mortar and pestle composed of dark-gray marble and used it to crush Kawal tea, inhaling the bright-yellow Indian spices. If brewed, it would prove warm, calming, and delicious, and it would heal just about any ailment in existence.

"Blessed power of tea," she said, "cure me of my fixation with sweet-talking poets."

When she was little, she'd clung to her mother's apron strings, learning stories about teas that went back five-thousand years. Tea had been her poetry then, the stuff of life, where mystery rubbed elbows with clarity and unexpected grace. Then puberty hit, and she formed her own ideas. She strove to prove to Mama that internet access would gain a more significant clientele. Folks would stay longer.

But her mother wouldn't have any of it. "We don't have a money-grubbing agenda. We have a people agenda."

Because of their differences, even though Audrey loved the teahouse, no way would she form a partnership. The strain made her strike out on her own. Soon after college, she founded the newspaper *Powell's Review* and had a clear vision of the success she hoped to gain as an entrepreneur. She sold her soul to promote the business. After catching herself at her worst on livestreaming, something inside her shifted. The job was no longer fun, and to be honest, she had lost interest in it. If she didn't have employees who depended on her for their salary, she would cut her losses and walk away. Too bad it wasn't an option.

Only one solution for the teahouse presented itself.

Teach someone to be a tea sommelier and another prospective hire to prepare the menu entrees. That Audrey had refused to learn to cook in her turbulent adolescence made the plan more complicated than it might be otherwise. She could figure it out, couldn't she? A few days max.

That afternoon, she scrubbed away the rest of the soot from the fire. Afterward, she spent the evening writing thank-you notes and trying to contact her sister. No luck on the latter.

To top it off, that Wednesday, the toilet overflowed in the restroom. She plunged until water spilled over and puddled the floor tile. For the remaining hours left in day number three, her time consisted of preparing the recipes on index cards. And for all her effort, she got pastries that tasted like sawdust.

Late that evening, she texted her employees.

—*Be back soon.*—

She resented the fact she didn't have a TV or a laptop so she could binge-watch her troubles away the same as ordinary people. Having no internet service made her want to scream.

Still, two days flew by, and she hadn't gotten the hang of running the teahouse. Each accomplishment led to some unforeseen downfall.

Wires unraveled, and when she changed a lightbulb, a spark ignited and singed the hair at the top of her head, leaving strands sticking straight up. The smoke alarm went off at odd times, like when she used the toaster or plugged in the electric mixer. The piercing blare drove Percy into panic mode, and settling the poor dog down took hours.

Meanwhile, her culinary skills failed to launch.

Homeless Joe, a former lightweight boxer, offered the sweet cakes she gave him to the terrier. Percy raised his snout and left the premises as if offended, for goodness' sake.

On the third night, her uncle entered. To cope with his grief, he had been working nonstop on his manuscript. Her uncle hadn't eaten or slept but was fortunate to disappear in a story no matter what was going on around him.

She wished he hadn't decided on now to come to the party. Flour veiled the entire kitchen. Eggs had hardened and crusted on the butcher-block island. Spilled sugar had somehow gotten wet and held a wad of paper towels like glue. Clam chowder bubbled from the stove with a nasty odor, and potato peels had clogged the garbage disposal.

Uncle Johnny's sigh ended with "What happened to Claudia Huggins, who helped during the dinner rush, and the boy who dropped in after school?"

"She and her hubby moved to an adult community in Phoenix, and Aiden graduated last spring and is at Brown University."

Struck with a pang of regret, Audrey didn't know how to comfort her uncle. To sell the teahouse had stolen into her thoughts at weak moments. If that came to pass, the apartment he called home would be history.

"Land sakes, I didn't realize things had gotten this bad. Your mama had a gift."

"I understand, and I am not her." Not even close.

****

Liam woke up, flung his arm out, and groped the air for his phone, believing he was in his bed in London. Only headquarters rang at oh-dark-bloody

39

thirty. He almost rolled off the bench on the boardwalk, trying to answer, his muscles protesting. His fingers closed around the mobile, buried in a pocket. He slid a finger over the screen and sat up.

A woman spoke. "You are to return today. Please acknowledge."

Still half asleep, he sputtered, "Can you repeat, please."

"You are to report to LAX and return today. Please acknowledge."

"Yes, I understand. I'm to return today, but I—"

The phone had gone dead, and he dropped it in his lap.

So what if the foreign office had summoned him back? He didn't give a rat's arse. For two weeks, the Secret Intelligence Service had left him high and dry. Out of the blue, they assigned orders he couldn't follow because he'd lost his identity when the wanker swiped his wallet. What MI6 also didn't know was he'd put down roots. He quite liked Dogtown and wanted to keep his present way of life.

He had gotten in the habit of working out each morning with some of his mates on Muscle Beach. A bloke had to stay in shape, especially when displaced and making plans. No one would recognize him. He had a beard and a little length to his hair, but at least he was eating. By a stroke of good fortune, he had stopped by The Funky Fish Joint and asked to do dishes for a meal.

The proprietor Miguel Lopez had said, "Gringo, too bad you can't prepare fish. My cook just quit."

Liam grabbed an apron. "I'll lend a hand."

He had experimented with food since his boyhood.

Even when he was prosperous enough to hire a housekeeper, he'd still cooked. Creating tasty dishes relaxed him when on assignment. At least, he could whip something up for others. Sometimes, he'd peek through the porthole in the door. The customers enjoying their meals contented him in the way the military never had.

Within days, he got used to the boardwalk. It was like a sunshine-filled action movie. The bright-colored characters and the gamut of guitars, banjos, ukuleles, keyboards, and drums fed his fancy. A reggae singer roller-skated. A dwarf stalked by on stilts. The mere act of moving animated the entire seaside. Throughout most of Liam's life, he'd walked the same straight line without deviation. Before that, he'd lived under his father's strict rules.

Now he joined the hub of skateboarders and picked up their moves. A clown taught him to make animals with balloons and to fold paper into shapes of the birds he had befriended in his youth. Sometimes he took off for the ocean and stuck his toe in the water. Next, he waded out to swim, and another day led him to get up on a surfboard.

But after dark, the Strand, a.k.a. the Boardwalk, got edgy. Shops closed up early, and mercury-vapor lamps lit up, some buzzing like an empty prison yard. Lucky for him, he'd learned to defend himself. *Bring it on.* He still occasionally longed for his London flat overlooking the river, but he'd had no actual downtime before. He had to experience it longer, see what might come of it.

The most pressing reason, though, for him to remain stateside was the threat to England's security.

He vowed to complete the mission, even if he had to go it alone.

****

Audrey's heart shifted into overdrive at the banging on the front door. When she saw who it was, she couldn't open up fast enough. Her identical image made drop-dead gorgeous swept inside as books fell from the shelves, displays capsized, and tea tins popped their lids.

"Where is Mama?" Lucinda tugged a wheeled suitcase as Percy chased behind and howled like he'd lost his best friend. And to be blunt, he had.

Trepidation rushed up, choking Audrey. "You didn't answer your phone."

Her sister froze. "No need to tell me. I already know."

"That twin thing." Audrey understood because of the connection they had. The phenomena of sharing things without speaking. How it worked, only God knew.

Her sister slid down the wall, her ermine hat toppling off her head. Crimped platinum tresses spilled over her shoulders, curtaining her face. Such gut-wrenching sobs emanated. Audrey dropped to the floor to embrace her.

Percy placed a sympathetic paw across the hysterical twin's lap, and she buried her fingers in his short, fine coat. "I hate this!"

Lucinda felt things more than others. She expressed herself in the free-for-all manner that Audrey never dared, but then two fireballs might be too much for one planet. Audrey would rather die than admit envying her twin's ability to express herself however she saw fit. And soon, she found herself in the role she'd adopted at birth. *Hold yourself together. Act as if you figured it out. Remember, you're the eldest by ten and a half minutes.*

"It's okay. We'll get through this…"

After a while, her twin dabbed her balled-up fists against her wet eyes. "The facts. I'm ready."

"A Ford pickup broadsided her on Main Street." Audrey shook her head. "The driver fled, and the detectives on the case are still investigating."

Lucinda sprang to her feet, a swirling hurly-burly of ivory satin cut down to her navel, transparent skirt, and pearly patent leather boots. "Let's get the SOB, Aud. When we do, we'll slice off his willie and feed it to the fish."

"Knock it off, Cin. Let the police do their job."

"That's the trouble with you. It always has been. You play by rules that deserve to go. I've got connections trained to act with discretion. No one has to figure it out."

Audrey gripped her sister by the shoulders. "Listen to me. I get your anger. I share it. But the way you're acting, the next time I see you, it will be in a mug shot. Besides, getting even won't bring Mama back."

Lucinda hung her head. "What are we going to do?"

She didn't have any answers, no matter how much she pretended otherwise. "We'll put our heads together and work it out, just you and me."

"Strange how the clock's still ticking, the light's burning. The teas are as fragrant as ever. Strange that everything goes right on as if it doesn't have a clue."

"Mama's correspondence is on her desk as if

waiting for her reply. And the pals who haven't heard she's gone leave phone messages on her landline."

Her sister visibly swallowed. "It's those little reminders, isn't it, that break the heart?"

"The world isn't the same. I already measure time with when Mama was still with us."

Lucinda stifled a sob. "I'm so glad this place hasn't changed."

"I wish I could agree with you."

"Excuse me?"

She led Lucina into the kitchen where her twin let out an earsplitting, "Oh! My! God!"

Audrey distracted a freaked-out Percy by engaging him in a tug-of-war with his pull toy. "There was a small fire, thanks to yours truly. Nothing's gone right since."

"I'm sorry to hear that—sorry, too, you weren't able to get ahold of me." Lucinda broke off a bite of muffin and plopped it in her mouth. She made a face, spitting out oats and downing bottled water. "Are you sure you followed the recipe?"

"You can't cook either, can you?"

"Only packaged ramen." Lucinda tossed out the disaster and set the plate beside the sink full of dirty dishes. "Isn't there anybody to come to our rescue?"

Audrey's mind tagged Liam, the man who looked like he could carry the world on his shoulders and never break a sweat. How often she'd thought of him these past days, wishing she hadn't frightened him off and kicking herself for her weakness.

Frustrated, she admitted, "There was someone. The guy might have been able to make some repairs, at least."

"Where is he now?"

Her breath stuck in her throat. "I'm not sure."

"What a shame." Lucinda fixed her with a stinging glare, then shut her eyes. "How was Mama's funeral?"

"There was a huge crowd." Nibbling her bottom lip, Audrey sat across from her sister. "Uncle Johnny was in Europe."

"Poor man, he's got to be out of his mind with grief." Lucinda's face darkened. "Neither one of us was here for you. If I had been home, I'd have insisted on a multicultural service. I think Bodhidharma has the right idea. We move on to another life-form." She gestured a hand skyward. "When I come back, I prefer to be a butterfly."

Audrey smiled. "You are already wild and free."

"You don't know the half of it. The cameras dictate my orbit. Whether to eat or to starve depends on how I look in a fashion spread. God help me, I'd give anything to scarf down actual food."

"You would?"

"I want one of Mama's maple-frosted thingies."

"I hear you." Audrey leaned back, stretching out her long limbs. "Mama and her wondrous creations. I've done everything short of cloning them. I studied her files and her notes, but so far, nothing's clicked."

"We're screwed unless we can discover how she worked her magic."

"And it's not only her recipes, but her teas—"

"Those potions that granted wishes and chased away illnesses," the supermodel concluded.

Audrey drummed the table with her knuckles. "Not to mention the joy and comfort she offered others with the tea ceremony."

"Sadly for me, I never got to experience that." Lucinda broke out in hives when she drank anything with tea leaves. "Why couldn't I be allergic to pollen or house dust like most of the population? I might have found Mr. Right too."

Audrey grimaced. "If you're talking about my last mistake, he's out of the picture."

"Don't tell me…what now?"

"The loser…"

"So on top of everything else, your man did you wrong." Lucinda covered Audrey's hand with her own. "I'm real sorry, baby." She leaned back and snapped her fingers. "Let's burn down his pad."

"No way." Audrey smacked the tabletop with a flat palm. "I've already got a new motto. Men are dispensable."

"You best believe it, but, Aud, this teahouse isn't."

"I hoped to clean it up and perhaps sell it."

Lucinda's eyes widened in horror. "Where will the poets go? And what about Johnny boy? You can't kick him out."

She hated to admit it, but Lucinda was right. Discouraged, she eased toward the open doorway. In the early evening, people trickled down the boulevard. Hikers with backpacks. Tourists with kids and cameras. Bicyclists with helmets and bright-colored attire. All that "let the good times roll" made her sigh. Only the Powell twins were blue.

She spotted a man on a skateboard, and the rest of the scene slipped out of focus.

Audrey jumped up and down. "There!"

From her vantage point, about seventy feet to her left, she pointed out Liam. He wore cutoffs and a tank top that read *It's all okay*. His hair had gotten wavy and sun bleached as it blew around his smiling face. A surfer catching a wave flashed in the tattoo on his brick-hard arm. He supported a hefty-looking backpack, but with ease, he wove in and out of the people on the sidewalk. If she had never met him, she'd believe he, too, was born and bred in Venice Beach. He had molded into the culture noted by some as the happiest on earth.

"There's—" His name wouldn't budge from her lips. "It's *the* guy."

In a cloud of punches to the air, her sister cried, "He's hot!"

No, you don't. This guy's mine, she wanted to lay claim but didn't. "I think he works out on the boardwalk."

Why say anything? What healthy male wouldn't prefer God's gift to glam?

Chapter 5

My soul is awakened, my spirit is soaring,
And carried aloft on the wings of the breeze;
For, above, and around me, the wild wind is
roaring
Arousing to rapture the earth and the seas.

~Anne Brontë (1820-1849)

Liam hadn't expected Audrey there on the boulevard. Her hair, kissed gold by the sun, spilled around her killing-me-softly face. The shadows beneath her eyes stressed their purple majesty. His lame prose stunk, but it was true—his truth when it came down to it.

He stopped, popping his skateboard from foot to hand in a single continuous movement. "Good to see you." He did a double take when he saw the replica of her in the teahouse's doorway. "Blimey! Is that your twin?"

"Yup," she said as if resigned. "You want me to introduce you?"

"Sure." He didn't falter—anything to get back inside his target. But Audrey seemed to mistake his motive for enthusiasm over meeting her sister.

Her twin was different in the looks department. She grabbed him by the shoulder. Mists of her perfume had his ears buzzing, and he pulled away.

"Liam James," he said with a slight bow of his head.

"Lucinda Powell, the other twin." It sounded like a dare.

Had she done something to her mouth? Her lips appeared an exaggerated version of Audrey's. Her cheekbones were just as pronounced, but her nose seemed narrower, perhaps an illusion, her eyebrows penciled in an arch. And what the dickens was she doing with all that white hair? Was it stripped of color? But why screw with nature's wisdom?

She pushed him into the teahouse. "We've got a problem, and we'd like your opinion. You might as well put all that brawn to good use instead of wasting your life on Muscle Beach. Who do you think you are, Arnold Schwarzenegger? Why hulk up just for your bros? Better to be a pencil-neck geek or a Buddha belly, you know? I mean, I'm willing to pay you big bucks to help us out here."

Her voice sounded the same as her twin's but with an edginess he didn't find attractive. Her eyes were shiny with a quality that said, "All right for you, bud. Do my bidding, or I will take you out."

Meanwhile, Audrey had disappeared into the woodwork. She must be used to occupying the backseat while her hubba-hubba sister took over. Wasn't she aware she had her own brand of sex appeal? True, tragedy had caused her to look peaked. In contrast, her twin appeared overdone. Another man would delight in Lucinda's flair for the dramatic—her stun 'em with dazzle.

It wasn't his thing.

He sought the more authentic version. "What did

you have in mind, Audrey?"

She fluttered a hand over the poetry written floor to ceiling on the wall of the foyer. "The writing has faded with time. Maybe we could repaint the letters to make the poems stand out. What do you think?"

He combed his fingers through his hair. "The entrance would pop by reducing the lot to a few choice selections."

Audrey's brows rose. "You mean we erase them and start over?"

As if needing to be in command, Lucinda slammed a hand on the service bell beside the crank cash register. "It took forever to fill that wall."

"That doesn't matter if no one can read a single poem," he said. "They all run together."

She tilted her head, crossing her eyes. "It's a jumble, all right."

Audrey added, "But our father wrote some of them."

"You asked my opinion." If Liam had his way, he'd start over at ground zero. "I am a minimalist—a believer that the simpler a thing, the truer."

"That's fine, but I can't see—"

"Hold on a sec. The dude might be right." Lucinda whisked around. "What else would you do?"

He scanned the room, mentally computing lines and angles, arranging and rearranging objects in his head. "Remove the flowery wallpaper. It's too busy if you ask me. The bookshelves, I would strip them and stain them a light elm. The bric-à-brac is too much. I'd hang on to a few pieces—the photos of famous poets, the ginger jars, and the folding screen displaying that red dragon, for instance."

Lucinda shuffled her booted feet. "I don't know. The Victorian mixed with the Far East is what makes the teahouse different. Abbot Kinney is famous for its uniqueness, its eccentricity. It's not Beverly Hills, not Compton, but somewhere in between. That's what draws the multitudes. You can't mess with that."

"Not at all," he said. "I say we keep the integrity of the original but heighten the mood of being near the sea."

"It would be cool if you knew how to cook."

"I work at a restaurant on the Strand, but I can give my notice if you need a chef." He was laying it on thick, but, hey, whatever it took.

Lucinda said, "Looks like we're on a roll, baby."

Audrey danced with wild abandon—her arms raised, hands clasped, hips rocking back and forth. A half-cocked-with-lust grin formed, and Liam fought it by maintaining the poker face he'd kept while dealing with an adversary.

He directed a little dig. "After your admitted animosity toward poets, I am surprised you'd want to be within five feet of me."

She stilled, tightening her shoulders. "I—we need your help. We could put you up in Mama's bungalow behind the teahouse." She nodded at her sister as if for reinforcement.

"You can take the daybed in the sewing room," Lucinda said, then stared at him with narrowed eyes. "But if you try any funny business, you'll find I pack a Dillinger under my pillow."

"Wouldn't think of it." He stared at Audrey. "You need me, a poet, to come to your rescue?" He couldn't resist pressing her, and he didn't know why.

Red-faced, Lucinda glowered at him. "The last thing she needs is another asshole poet."

"Lucinda's right," she said, giving him the evil eye.

He held his breath. Had he pushed them too far and lost out before he began?

But Audrey relaxed her posture. "Okay, as you can see, we're not doing well on our own."

That was all he wanted to hear. That very evening he told Miguel he had to quit.

"Guess you'll return to your country," Miguel said.

Liam shrugged. "Not quite yet, mate."

He didn't mention his new position was a ruse. Playing the chef would be a cinch. He'd produce many flavorful dishes and meanwhile infiltrate, and if high-ranking political confidences came through, he'd find out.

The next morning, Audrey, Lucinda, and he met in the teahouse with tools, coffee, and strong tea. The three hadn't been at it long when Spade joined them. As they primed the walls for painting, he described the plot of his latest novel.

The story involved the loss of a vital US manual. A flight by the hero to Lisbon caused him to fall in love with a beautiful embassy clerk. Together, they hunted for four terrorists who had left a trail of bombings and murder in their wake. Their investigation took them to the Azores and São Miguel, where they found their target planning to invade the UK.

His summary hadn't an ending. It had been a promotional tease. Liam was almost begging for more, but he brimmed with curiosity too. Hadn't anyone from the home office thought to link this chap's fiction to the goings-on in the teahouse?

"I'll have the last draft done soon," he said with Kubla nodding.

"I'm in control," the bird quipped.

Liam cringed, worried the blabbermouth would spout off something incriminating—a *this chump isn't who he says he is.*

As luck would have it, the front door hinges squeaked, and some regulars, or so they called themselves, offered to lend a hand. Several locals gathered until the place boomed with the sounds of hammering and sawing, arguing over politics, complaining about work and spouses. Liam, supposedly in charge of the project, disappeared to fix nachos and hot wings. Well into the afternoon, the beer flowed, and the dog hid under his bed.

"Don't worry, mate. We'll end up with a five-star review."

Percy stared up at Liam and snorted.

"You'll see. Soon, we'll be in business. Me. The others. Even you. Good Lord, make it soon."

He'd gone from chief honcho to errand boy. The volunteers were listening to Spade—well, of course, they were. The ladies gobbled up his bunk about running with the bulls in Spain and hunting buried treasure off Key Largo. The blokes gathered around Lucinda.

Meanwhile, to ease his stress, Liam took Percy out in the yard. He slapped his hands on his legs and said, "C'mon, boy. Let's play ball."

But the canine cocked his head as if he didn't understand.

Liam ran, whirled around, and went down into a crouch. "This one's for you," he called, throwing a florescent-green tennis ball.

Percy thumped his tail on the ground, ears pricked.

"Show me what you're made of, soldier. Go get it. Fetch!"

The canine lay down, his square, compactly built body quaking.

Liam retrieved the ball and dropped it in front of Percy. "This is the deal. I saw you in that fire. You've got balls. How do you not know that?"

By evening, Spade had uncovered the Spinet piano. He played along with a man on sax and a lady on bass. The music, low and rhythmic, held a pulse that shook the walls. He sang about mamas wallowing over papas and trains calling in the night, "Ah-whooie, ah-whooie." Residents and day-trippers alike fell under his hypnotic spell. Even Liam drank a pint.

All rational thought vanished the moment he spied Audrey on the other side of the teahouse, her body swaying to the seductive beat. His heart thumped, and he mustered up all his fortitude to resist the temptation to come on to her. He longed to disappear with her for a walk under the stars. Away from people so they could dance, locked together in a tight embrace. He'd kiss her neck. Then her face, that work of art. He was halfway across the room when he caught himself. Given another idle second, he would have caved. That wouldn't do. Not at all.

With all this mental pull and release, this war against himself, a week passed maddeningly by. The diehards remained. Some came out of the goodness of their hearts, some to recite Yeats and Whitman. Did any pass classified information? Who knew? Not Liam.

For him, even though he eavesdropped, he had

secured no intel. Neither the tea shipment imported from Singapore nor Tangier had produced a lead. The merchants he'd queried proved useless. *To hell with it.* Restraint, calculation, and above all, patience would pay off in the long run. He needn't get obsessed. He took a moment to print across the top of a memo pad *Potential Threats* but that was as far as he had gone with it.

At the end of a fortnight, the remodeling concluded, the night closed in, and Spade asked Audrey to prepare tea while Lucinda, who claimed to be allergic, chose Hennessey.

"Yin Hao Jasmine is the choice of James Bond," Spade said. "They grow this scented green tea in Fujian."

The teahouse had cleared of all but Spade, the women, and Liam. Spade, whose fingers played the keys of a typewriter with the same zeal as he had the piano, added, "Poetry, that history of the human heart, is beckoning me back to my garret."

Liam watched from the sidelines. "You slam soul into that Smith Corona."

"You can't sock emotion into a machine that does your thinking for you." Spade yanked the paper from the roller. "The computer age has led to a decline in creativity."

Bugger! Liam had unintentionally launched the big guns. "But being a writer," he said, his interest taking precedence, "you host a website, don't you? How else can you connect with your fans?"

"The same as any author worth his salt. I keep in touch by post."

Liam's head whirled. "I don't believe it."

"A written letter is more personal than an email."

"You're right, but what about the digital formats of your books?"

"They don't exist."

"Are you joking?"

"Paper is preferable to the harmful rays from an ebook screen." Spade arched an eyebrow. "I shouldn't have to explain myself to you."

Under ordinary circumstances, Liam would argue the point. He'd mention the app or the physical filter one might purchase if worried about the effects of blue light. He longed to give Spade an earful, but to do so would blow his cover. How would Liam react if he believed in computers corrupting society? He thought of his father, and he had the answer.

"The advantage of the typewriter is it eliminates distractions from the internet." It was true enough, but Liam's chest constricted as his conscious cried, "You're a lying bastard." That damned role, but if he came clean, things would go south really fast.

Audrey grabbed a stool from the tasting bar and sat between the two men. "I am not saying I go along with Uncle Johnny's stand, mind you. But he always pleases his fans."

Spade removed his reading glasses. "And sometimes I write a lyric, which is important in a world consumed by people who can't put down their smartphones. Poetry, prevalent and widespread throughout the ages, isn't as popular today. Here in Venice, though, it thrives, especially in Monroe's teahouse."

Liam quoted the sign in the entrance. "Tea and poetry served here."

Spade laid a hand over his heart. "The great masters fed the spirit."

Lucinda bent over the table. "In Delhi, a friend invited me to a *mushaira*, which is a gathering of poets held in the house of a young rajah. People turned out to hear him recite, just as here in Mama's teahouse. I became so homesick I couldn't stand it." She massaged her uncle's shoulders. "Would you mind showing off a little?"

"Anything for you, Lucy Lou."

"Nobody can spin a rhyme like Johnny Spade." Lucinda straightened and tapped her feet to an inaudible beat while her uncle went into action.

"There was a man who lived on a hill,
With texting and media, he had his fill,
So he found a picture of Brigitte Bardot,
And a poem, written by the tragic Poe.
He spliced them together in his mind's eye,
The nymph and the words in a lullaby…"

He ended with, "He was out of his head."

And Kubla concluded with a warbly, "Out of his head."

The threesome cheered like Spade had brought down the Syrian Army, and the bag of wind took a swig of sweet green tea. "Your turn, Liam. Here's your chance to shine. Let's see what you've got."

A challenge if there ever was one. Audrey implored Liam to recite. Although he had gone to battle and acted brave amid the thunder of guns and machinery, he couldn't fake the white heat needed to compose a poem on a subject of which he didn't agree.

"Liam?" Audrey tugged at his arm. "If you're not comfortable, it's okay. You look as if we asked you to commit treason."

"No biggie, dude." Lucinda thumped him on the back. "Not everybody can sock an ode."

Spade crossed his arms in front of his chest and scrutinized Liam with blatant distrust. What could he do? Fake it? No, to scam real art was a crime. The rhymes he had made up on the beach lay buried in the sand too far away for him to retrieve.

He had written about the skateboarders who flew, twisting and turning in the air, contorting their bodies, and landing to begin anew. He'd mentioned a bloke painted from head to foot in gold and a goddess telling fortunes in a tent by the light of the moon. He'd boasted of the hot-on-the-toes trek to the sea, when the weather was steamy, and surfboards in the rain and walking on stilts. But even if he could deliver his boardwalk rhymes from memory, they weren't good enough for this audience.

"I've nothing prepared," he stated like a lead bomb.

A muscle flicked in Spade's jaw. "Just as I thought." He had the resigned look of a special ops commander handing down a verdict of misconduct. "Time for me to hit the road before I say something to spoil the evening."

After the clatter of the tea crockery, the snatches of laughter—the sounds of celebration—the invading silence dispirited Liam. He'd just lost any hope of gaining Spade's respect. Not that it should matter, but Liam's anger with himself grew until his knuckles bleached around his teacup. He'd let everyone down. He hadn't measured up.

Cracking a joke might break the ice. Instead, Liam

changed the subject. "It looks like we'll be able to open the doors soon." He disliked stating the obvious. "Audrey, you must look forward to getting back to your tribe. You're counting the days, I'll bet." So was he and trying to deal with the fact she was leaving.

Audrey's smile didn't make it to her eyes as she texted away on her phone. "I can't wait."

"Stay here," he wanted to say. To voice it, though, would dash any hopes he had of them coming together—just as well.

"Time to go," he said.

Lucinda waved a hand. "Night, then."

Audrey nodded, setting down her teacup. "Liam, thanks for all your guidance. You've been a gem."

"Don't mention it." Was this her way of brushing him off?

He marched across the yard and into the bungalow cluttered with too much stuff. His crash pad was at the end of the hall—Monroe's Hobby Lobby. With every wake-up call, he rose to a myriad of pillows, lace, lavender, and goose down. It was like finding himself jailed inside a sewing box. Tonight, though, he had knowledge more relevant than his sleeping arrangements. Audrey was leaving, migrating back to her Olive Street apartment, and he couldn't do a damned thing about it.

Chapter 6

Lady Clara Vere de Vere
Was eight years old, she said:
Every ringlet, lightly shaken, ran itself in golden
thread.

~Lewis Carroll (1832-1898)

When the sisters were alone in the teahouse, Audrey poured each of them a shot of brandy. Time for a little twin fest. Long overdue. This past week, she'd stood by, watching her sister stare into space for no apparent reason. Sorrow and loss were synonymous. She understood only too well, and the fashionista looked cool and confident even on a bad day, but something was bothering her, clouding her face at odd moments.

As it was now, when her silvery hair made her look like a snow queen as she hunched over the drink she'd not touched. "Do you trust him?"

Lucinda didn't need to give "him" a name. Audrey got who her sister was referring to in such familiar terms, and it wasn't their kin.

"Liam?" She tried to buffer her feelings. "You mean, do I think the man's hiding something?" She shrugged, and loosening her shoulders felt good. "Nah, I don't."

"You realize Uncle Johnny would beg to differ."

"That's because he's trying to protect us."

"Protect you, Aud, from losing your heart to another douche bag."

She shook her head. "Uncle Johnny suspects everyone and everything. He can't help himself. He should have been a special agent. Instead, he writes about them."

"Hmm, true, but hasn't it occurred to you that Liam's overqualified?"

"He's a poet," Audrey said, as if that explained it all.

"Yeah, and there's no bard alive who doesn't want to be immortal, yet he clams up when asked to recite. You didn't question that?"

"He's shy is all." She was defending him again, couldn't help herself—just as she couldn't keep from checking her cell phone when things got nerve-wracking.

Her twin rolled her eyes. "It's a blessing you're going back to work."

"I'm not looking forward to it." Audrey never lied to her sister. They'd always been up front with one another. "My heart's not in it anymore."

A silence ensued as Lucinda regarded her with sympathy. And why not? Last April, she'd insulted Madison Gray on a reality show. The press had crucified her. *Powell's Review* had suffered, even though she and Maddie became best friends. People still talked shit about Audrey on all social media.

"Being me is not a prize." She threw back a brandy shot. "Try as I might, I can't redeem myself on any forum in the internet community. I am a damn disgrace."

Lucinda covered her hands with the sleeves of her alpaca sweater. "At least you get satisfaction from your job. Modeling makes me feel hollowed out. I can't grow as a human being. Fashion only cares about what's on the outside."

"But I'm proud of you. Insane schedules and long hours didn't keep you from earning those impressive degrees."

Lucinda looked up from her brandy. "The honest to God truth? I'll tell you why you weren't able to get ahold of me. I had ditched my phone and was searching for answers in the holy shrines throughout India. To swap my life on the catwalk for the path set down by the ancient sages became my number-one goal."

"Why?" Audrey's voice pierced the air with shock.

"I want to make a difference like Mama and you. Especially you."

"What the hell, Cin?"

"I am defined by how I look, and that isn't working for me any longer. A leave of absence seemed mandatory. Another day of faking it would have done me in. I'm sick and tired of being me."

Audrey hadn't ever seen this side of Lucinda. Her sister's misery hit her so unexpectedly she had to push to her feet and pace to keep from screaming, *but part of you has always been part of me. Why didn't I guess you were unhappy?*

"Don't go back to modeling. I want you here. Full disclosure? I need you to take over the paper for me." The idea had just come to her. So what? All at once, their trading places made perfect sense. Not only would she be in her favorite place on earth, but she'd discover if she could excel at the work she had always loved.

Her sister was sitting there, running her hands over her toothpick thighs. "Well, I'm not sure."

"Why not?"

"Do you think I can? I guess you could coach me, but how would my being a former model go over with your staff? Don't tell me. I already know. We're doomed."

Audrey licked her dry lips. "Not if everyone thinks you're me."

"You aren't suggesting... Remember when you broke your leg, and I appeared the next day in your clothes and acted like you?"

"Do I? People believed I had a miraculous recovery."

"No one knew. Oh, Aud, you think this stunt might work?"

"Well, I can't traipse off to New York. Cameras don't lie, but if you fill in for me, even for a while, I'd be able to find out if I have what it takes to run things in the teahouse. You'd be doing me a huge favor."

"Are you finagling this so you'll be alone with Liam?"

Audrey giggled like a teenager to hide the bundle of nerves forming in her stomach. "You caught me red-handed." She paused. "No, honestly, let's do this thing."

"Just familiarize me with the names I need to know and the routines to follow. I can wear your clothes and move into your place. My weight's a little less than yours, but..."

"But you just lost your mother. To drop a few pounds goes with the territory."

Audrey slid onto the piano bench and played a

half-remembered song about the two of them building castles in the sky. Her sister joined in, both harmonizing verses blustered by brandy and the call to adventure.

The next morning, she tagged along to a Beverly Hills salon where Lucinda's name got them entrance. Already the people on the palm-spangled sidewalk were ogling her supermodel sister as if they were trying to figure out who she was.

A few asked, "Isn't that Lucia?"

Lucia was how the fashion world referred to Lucinda, but that character living it up in the magazines wasn't her twin.

Audrey lowered her ball cap down over her forehead so no one would notice she even slightly resembled her sister. She pulled up the collar of her plaid flannel shirt and followed along the red carpet as a doorman bowed, and Lucinda stroked his cheek with the back of her manicured hand.

"I have arranged everything, Aud, so no stressing. Come with me to experience a piece of complete paradise."

"Let's get it over with." Audrey shook her head at a man offering her a frothy mimosa from a silver tray.

Lucinda swooped up the drink and set in Audrey's hands. "This is what you need."

"It's nine o'clock in the morning, Cin."

An elfin girl with a sleek, blue-black updo, who called herself Gigi, took their pictures with an instant camera. She handed them robes to change into before their date with the miracle workers. Afterward, she swept Audrey down a chilly corridor.

"Cecil awaits your presence, mademoiselle," Gigi

said with a stagy French lilt.

"Is it too late to sneak out the exit?" she asked, but the smooth operator had already opened the door to a station where a black-bearded rascal ushered her to a cosmetology chair.

He raised a finger. "Ah, such a challenge…" He pointed to the photo of Lucinda attached to the mirror. "To transform you into the woman you were no doubt meant to be."

Her shoulders stiffened. "I'm not sure this is such a dandy idea."

But after a mimosa and a shampoo to die for, her body went deliciously limp. She should have protested when Cecil mixed chemicals so intense they singed her nostril hairs. Instead, his train of dialogue mesmerized her. "No, not quite. A shot of bluing, bleach—ah, yes, this will do." At one point, Audrey caught sight of her reflection. She'd morphed into an aluminum-foiled lion. No matter. The mimosas were plentiful, and Billie Eilish's breathy voice floated in the background. While manicurists massaged her hands and her feet, she napped.

Not a single member of the staff spoke above a whisper—a plot perhaps, devised by the experts to keep her from bailing. The tranquility proved a natural state of being. Her sister must have handed over a fortune for this pampering. Well, it wasn't all bad. Those were her thoughts until Cecil twisted her around, and she faced the mirror. Her breath stuck like a hairball in her throat. All the privileged treatment in the world wouldn't have prepared her.

She was a dead ringer for Lucinda. "Wow-wee!"

Gigi turned up to deliver her to a dressing room

where Lucinda's attire awaited her like in a dream, the kind where Audrey appeared in public without her underwear.

"Wait," she yelped as the curtain grated across the pole. "You made a mistake."

"No, mademoiselle. You still need to exchange clothes."

Audrey cursed under her breath as she struggled into a bodice so tight she couldn't breathe. Used to relaxed-fit jeans, she winced at the tiny waistband in the full skirt. She might enjoy a trip with Madison to buy an outfit, but her clothes never said, "Attention, please." What would happen if she just upped and ran away? Too late for that.

Her sister had already torn open the drape. "You ready, Aud?"

She drew in a breath, and her eyes stung at the sight of her twin posing as her. The pair held hands and made their way to a full-length mirror.

Lucinda craned her neck. "Lord sweet Lord, I'm a dull bird."

Subdued, Audrey nodded. "And I am a peacock." In all her imaginings, she'd had no clue what being a style icon entailed. Still, she tingled as if her entire body were awaking after remaining in the same position for too long.

"We can't tell a soul," the newest edition of Audrey said.

"Not even Uncle Johnny?"

"No one."

When they left the salon, her sister hovered behind. "Turn your feet out, Aud. Throw your shoulders back, head erect." Now she was being Mama. The girls had towered over the rest of the kids, which never hampered Lucinda, but to Audrey it was a matter of not fitting in. Maybe she had slouched a little, but it beat being called The Amazon Twins.

All that teasing returned as people gawked at her.

Her sister deserved a gold star for her so-Audrey chin-length cut and unpainted face. The twig was pulling it off, her eyes twinkling like a girl on the Ferris wheel in Pacific Park.

The air crackled with energy, and a bundle of unleashed nerves shot up Audrey's chest. She tried to ignore them, but she soared above the crowd, pale hair untamed, her garb a flowing calypso of color.

People, beware, I do come unglued!

A man, rubbernecking, walked into a sidewalk sign while a few girls bounded straight toward Audrey. "Can we have your autograph?"

She focused inward and assumed Lucinda's confident posture, and with a fashion diva's grace, she lowered her oversized sunglasses, colorful bangles jingling on her wrist, and wrote, *Best wishes, Lucia.*

****

Being Lucia meant Audrey had to dress the part. And that meant the twins had to tackle Mama's bedroom. They focused on weeding things out until Audrey didn't know if they were making headway or drowning in misery. Their attempt proved to be no alchemist's snap of the fingers. The sisters boxed up Mama's possessions, Audrey oppressed by a sense of sorrow, but she remembered why they had begun. They must lay the groundwork for distributing Lucinda's wardrobe, thus carving the way for the big hoax.

The twins made small talk rather than dwell on

their loss, but something as simple as a piece of clothing or even a familiar object caused a standstill.

"There's so much of her unique style in these gypsy skirts and shawls, but my favorite is this gown. It's so marvelously dreamy, right?"

"I haven't seen these round-rimmed John Lennon specs in years."

"Here's that photo of her on a camel in Mongolia."

Finding all Mama's history and eccentricities was like running a hand over a cactus. Audrey pulled out the thorns and continued, but the sharp sting remained. To abandon the project would ease the pain. They might try again when stronger. Perhaps ten years from now or never. Just when the job appeared to overwhelm them, Liam entered with a reprieve. She didn't want to stare, but the sight of him with a tray poised above his head rivaled all her fantasies. Honest to God, nothing seemed as sexy as him feeding her something as luscious as a caramel eclair.

"Excuse me, ladies." He bowed, this prince with forbidden nectar. "How about a treat to lighten your spirits?"

The aroma wafted toward her, enticing her senses. Didn't matter that she was now Lucinda, who must count every calorie. Time to indulge herself. Audrey licked her lips, and, yes, the act bordered on the seductive. But in the spirit of her past beaus, Liam appeared only to have eyes for Lucinda. He lowered the tray so she got first dibs.

Then it dawned...they had traded places. A swoony, heavy-lidded look dominated Liam's eyes as if... Wait, what? Was he hitting on Lucinda but believing her Audrey? Her heart ping-ponged off the table. Match over. The damage was insurmountable.

How had she missed his apparent feelings for her, the boring girl next door?

She closed her eyes, her head pounding. *We don't know what we have until it's gone.* The story of her pathetic life, a tale of woe, but she should be happy. Dancing on the table. She had just dodged the bullet of hooking up with yet another stinking poet. Good for her. Praise be for the one she let slip away.

Her sister, emerging from starvation mode, devoured the éclair and licked her fingers. Audrey, when offered her share, took a bite, then clumsily tipped over the tray. All those warm, gooey tarts slid off and landed with cartoonish plops on the floor.

Liam collapsed in a heap of clothes on the bed. "Blow me down," he said while Percy, the shameless, nabbed a treat between his teeth and sped off.

What a fiasco, but she had to break the news. "Next week, Liam, it will be just you and me in the teahouse."

His face fell even more. "Hooray," he said but shut his eyes as if miserable.

Come Monday morning, Audrey walked out to her Lexus. "Time to get cracking," she said to her sister and winced at the fake hard-nosed tone in her voice.

She refrained from speaking like herself even when the two were alone. She always had to be on. It was exhausting. Whenever she slipped up, she got so flustered she went too far the other way and sounded scary. Audrey adopting her sister's personality was like a bad movie adaptation of a New York Best Seller. Gone were the days of getting by with towel-dried hair and a trace of lipstick. Everything she did to herself was a major production. Still, she appeared a parody.

No way would she give up, though. Her sister was killing it as Audrey. By using her degree in strategic management and the other in journalism, Lucinda worked out a plan to better circulate *Powell's Review*. Now she'd put it into practice. Today her attire boasted plain gray slacks and a crisp white shirt. She appeared both relaxed and professional. To be truthful, she was better at being Audrey than Audrey.

In the chilly ocean air, Lucinda started up the engine and opened the window. "I'm afraid," she whispered behind her nail-bitten hand. "What if I mess up?"

And there it was, the insecurity Audrey hadn't witnessed since they were sixteen and she had been aiding her sister in her flee to New York by loading suitcases into the trunk of a taxi. "I'm scared to death, Aud, but I've got to try modeling. Carve a niche somewhere."

She was so independent, and unlike Audrey, no dark stains blemished her past, no shame. Lucinda was no failure. She had to discover, for herself, she already had made a difference in the world.

"You'll ace this," Audrey said, swallowing down her previous doubt.

The goodbye marked the end of their time together. For who knew how long? They'd talk by phone every day, perhaps every hour, but it wasn't the same, and what did she feel after waving goodbye? She'd tried for a level of common sense. She'd done the right thing. The exchange wouldn't be forever, but back in Mama's bungalow, as she prepared Jejudo, a tea harvested from Korea and designed for morning calm, her belly twisted, and she realized this was for real.

She, seeking relief, sipped the sweet, mellow drink with its fresh hazelnut notes. *Ah!* Still, the jitters wouldn't subside. Oh, the leopard-print outfit with all its bling worked for her, but the mere thought of Lucia's lily-scented perfume soured her stomach. Who cared if she skipped it today? Just this once.

She didn't have to worry. Didn't matter if she was off her game. The only person who'd notice was Liam, and strangely, he wasn't keen on anything concerning Lucinda. No need to dwell on this. His disinterest was for the best. She held that notion key until, there in the kitchen doorway, he glanced at her.

His rock-solid shoulders sagged, and he squinted as if hurting. "Audrey's gone?"

"Yeah." *Keep it casual.* The door had shut, the window closed. And hooray for that. Still, her blood raced through her veins as it had all those times before. The difference? Now they were together with no one else around, and buried in the fine print—*she wasn't who she claimed to be*.

He shuffled into the breakfast nook wallpapered in grapevines and whip-poor-wills. Audrey squirmed but kept sipping. He had shaved off his beard and let it grow back with enough stubble to be a turn on. His hair fell in seductive waves over his forehead. But his sulky mood this morning represented the kiss of death. Anything Byronesque had always made her howl at the moon.

He threw back a protein drink, then gave her a second glance, his eyes widening. "I thought tea made you bloody sick."

She choked and raised her hand like a traffic cop.

Of all the ways to slip up, drinking tea when claiming to be allergic to it took the prize for stupidity. This was bad. She'd ruined things. How could she redeem herself—or was it Lucinda who needed saving? Maybe both of them.

Then she recalled a lesson from a science class. "The human body replaces itself every seven years. I wondered if I still broke out in hives."

"I don't see a rash." He frowned with clear disapproval. "You look more like Audrey without all your makeup, and what did you do to your hair?"

She had to get the extensions out of her face somehow. "A ponytail."

"I didn't peg you as the ponytail sort."

"It works for all that we need to get done." *Stick to business. No slacking, or you'll go down the drain and take Lucinda with you.*

He drew so close she could either die from lack of oxygen or inhale. His scent conjured up ancient woodlands and rocky cliffs. Were her eyelids fluttering? His nearness was like a shot of smack. He wore a shirt that did crazy-nice things to his eyes. She twisted away so he didn't see his effect on her.

"Did I do something wrong?" he asked with a shrug.

"I expect you're ready for our grand opening." Spoken with Lucinda's brand of attitude.

"I am." He rinsed out his glass. "But I'll teach you some recipes, in case you ever have to take over." He lowered his chiseled chin. "Unless you have something against it."

The subject of cooking bombarded her with memories of past disasters. "Dude, course not," she uttered a la Lucinda. "And I should fill you in on the art of tea."

"Not sure what's worse, having tea with the queen or making a mistake in the tea ceremony."

"Mama used to say, 'A good tea master brews serenity.' "

"Aye, a cluster of summer trees, a hint of the sea, a pale moon…"

Her cup dropped to the saucer with a loud clatter. "If we're to work together, I must insist that you're strictly a cook and not a—a—"

"A poet? Because your sister has an adverse reaction to them? And you just might too?" He appeared to be guarding against a smile. "And here I thought you were just allergic to tea."

"Don't mess with me. I won't have it, you hear?"

His hands jerked into the air. "Wouldn't think of it. Why do you always act as if Audrey's being near me cuts seconds off her life?"

"Her last weasel did just that." She settled on one of Lucinda's shoot-from-the-hip poses. "She's on the wagon, so keep your distance if you know what's good for you."

"Audrey hasn't found the right poet. The one that's different from the rest."

She tossed what she had left of her lukewarm tea at him, missing him by inches. "Better watch it, surfer dude. Come on to her, and I'll sic the dog on you."

Percy, the ingrate, wagged his tail and dropped his slimy rubber chew at Liam's feet.

Liam cleared his throat as if holding back a laugh. "Looks like we know where the brute would rather hang out." He bent to scratch Percy's back.

She got on her knees and dabbed a sponge on the spilled tea. Too bad she couldn't blot up the toxic spill of her emotions while she was at it. Okay, she didn't want Liam believing Lucinda was her and making a play. Talk about convoluted. She was about to fire him on the spot when his gypsy eyes met hers, and she fell under their spell.

"I've got a project I need to run by you," he said.

She straightened to her full height. "Does this involve what you've been doing while my sister and I have been going through Mama's things, fixing everything, and when we asked you about your day, you'd change the subject or fire off opinions about this or that?"

He staggered in mock despair. "What's a bloke to do when in the company of the double-trouble brigade? Men have lost their lives over weaker liaisons."

He was making fun of her again. But the corners of his mouth with their almost imperceptible quirks lit the cold places inside her.

"You have something for me to see?" she asked.

"I thought you'd never ask."

He insisted they head to the teahouse where the chandelier tinkled in the breeze from the door. Bowls and plates, painted Lifesaver colors and covered with poems, gussied up the tables. Origami birds of all kinds provided a party favor at each place setting. Inside glass vases stood paper roses with verses written on individual petals.

She picked up a plate and examined it with care. "John Keats." Her awe brimmed to the surface. "Somebody's been busy." Incredible handiwork and so unexpected. She didn't know what to say.

She attempted to sound tough. "And we will use all this how?"

"We open the teahouse with a poetry dinner."

She held up a plate. "But people can't eat off papier-mâché."

"No, no, you miss the point. It's allegorical, you see. You take the intimate structure of the dining experience to recite the classics."

"This just might draw some attention. Tell me more."

"People, seated at the tables, receive a menu of titles from which they can choose. The short poems are appetizers, and the longer ones, main dishes. The desserts and beverages can stretch any length we see fit. They make their selection, and the poets perform table-side."

"You've gone above and beyond…"

He must have worked day and night. And she'd almost let him go. Why? Because she didn't trust herself alone with him. Well, that was on her. Any man who could act with such unselfishness was worth—she couldn't put a price tag on him. He was—her eyes flooded with tears that broke loose down her cheeks.

Oh Lord. What now?

He looked horrified. "What's the matter with you?"

"When you said *project*, I—I never envisioned—" Of all the idiotic ways to blow her cover, to break into sobs. "I am not myself today."

He took her by the hand and studied her like he couldn't figure her out, and her head swam under his keen appraisal. He depicted a man intent on examining her under a zoom-in lens. Had he guessed who she was? This mess couldn't get worse. Needing comfort, she started for her phone and caught herself. His thumb massaged her knuckles as he escorted her to a table where art supplies and writing materials awaited her appraisal.

"What do you say we put our heads together and compose a menu," he said. "Are you up for that, Lucy Lou?"

Chapter 7

There's a sigh for aye, and a sigh for nay,
And a sigh for "I can't bear it!"
O what can be done, shall we stay or run?
O cut the sweet apple and share it!
                                    ~John Keats (1795-1821)

Liam took a seat and watched the woman across from him. She was stealing looks at him. With composure he didn't feel, he straightened a yellow legal pad. Something disturbing had just happened, and that something showed in the mascara streaked down her cheeks, showed too in the tremble of her lower lip.

Thrown off his game, he chose his words with care. "I guess you're missing Audrey."

More moisture sprang into her eyes. "You don't know the half of it."

Her meltdown affected him more than he cared to admit. He fished through his pockets for his pencil. At last, he found one and wrote in swift strokes like knife cuts. Soon, a poem from Emily Dickinson's *The Lightning Is a Yellow Fork* appeared, which caught her full attention.

"That's good for a start." She scribbled an entrée that was longer. *There was a lady loved a wine. "Honey," quoth she; "Pig-hog, wilt thou be mine?"*

"Now that would charm the pants off a swineherd,"

77

he said and created a beverage from Alexander Pope. *Flow, Welsted, flow! Like thine inspier, Beer.*

She touched her fingertips to either side of her head, and soon a dessert flowed from her pen in the poetry of Thomas Campion. *There cherries grow which none may buy, till "cherry-ripe" themselves do cry.*

Liam had to be dreaming. He'd thought Audrey was the only one who got under his skin, but Lucinda, as she'd admitted, wasn't herself. She was different. He had served shepherd's pie yesterday, and the fashion model had devoured it. Had she eaten before? He couldn't recall, but she must have gained weight. She no longer looked too thin. Why hadn't he noticed, and why had his pulse kicked up?

He liked her, damn if he didn't.

It caused him to dig deeper to please her. "And for the menu we use daily, we could name food and beverages after poets."

"Check it out. Gertrude Stein becomes Gertrude Wine."

He burst out laughing, and she sent him a warm smile—this woman who before today would rather bring out the artillery than talk to him. *She wasn't herself* was a bloody understatement. Try a bird of a different feather. At least planning the dinner gave him something to occupy his mind. When they finished their prospective menu, she rang the poets to find out if they were interested in taking part. He couldn't help peering at her, finding her camaraderie unsettling and yet thrilling.

After an hour, she set down her phone, and her eyes brightened. "Now that my mother isn't here to protest, I'll get in touch with an internet provider."

Uh-oh, this called for a little shakedown. "I expect I can do the PR for the event without computers." Like hell he could!

"I was afraid you'd say that." She massaged the top of her head with her elegant, fine-boned fingers—fingers most likely featured in magazines advertising hand lotion. "Nothing's worse than a dang technophobe."

"Right." God help him if she ever discovered his true identity. "Put me in charge." Good grief, had he just uttered that absurdity?

But she rewarded him with a victorious smile. "Having a partner means he can do all the dirty work."

At least Liam had his skateboard to aid him in hanging posters. Not to toot his own horn, but if the word ever got out about his true identity, his name would be as famous as hers. He had always worked undercover, been proud of it. Yet here he was resorting to exchanging his top secret recipes to the local proprietors for a space in a window.

Done with all the finagling, he passed out flyers on the boardwalk. When he'd finished, all the tourists and locals knew the location for the kickoff party. He played it up big, making the teahouse sound like the place to be on a Saturday night in Venice. Convincing was where his army experience came in handy. He could be persuasive. He even allowed radio stations to broadcast his voice, a risk on his part. If the wrong person recognized it, well, it mightn't be pretty.

With all his preparations, he needn't have worried. Still, when a cold-pressure front descended on SoCal the day of the poetry dinner, he stewed. Tonight was his chance to prove he could be an asset to the teahouse. He mustn't screw it up.

Then Lucy—Lucy was what he'd taken to calling her—entered. From the silver in her hair to her glittery toenails peeking from her strappy sandals, she dazzled. He didn't care for women like her, yet he couldn't cease his ogling as she took her place behind the tasting bar in her flirty maxi dress and the topknot bun. He wished, in her attempt to relax, she'd stop rolling her shoulders and circling her head.

Talk about illicit cargo.

Enough! The teahouse would open at any second. Those folks, huddled together in line because of the cold, would take their seats. The show would go on. So he mustn't dwell on his unfortunate crush on the twins and the fact he needed to have his head examined. He had other problems to tackle, one being to keep a lookout for a bad egg in a kettle of partygoers.

He was going about his business, snapping up twenty-dollar bills like pancakes and depositing them in the till, when Lucy replaced him with a friend of hers. She took his hand in hers, not without his quick intake of breath as she led him behind the Asian screen. There, instead of the privacy he'd hoped for, he found an assortment of people awaiting their entrance.

"Liam, these are the poets," she said. "They call themselves 'The Talking Tears.' "

"Not the Cult of the Marvelous Past?" he almost asked but stopped himself. That was Audrey's term. Plus, one never knew—a traitor might turn up here among the group.

She introduced him to Grace Gonzalez, a big woman with soulful eyes. The other, Amy Chang, had a red-gold bun and a defiant expression. The preppy looked out of place somehow. "Bennett," he introduced himself. "Bennett Browning." And wasn't he a rising politician? Yes, voted the candidate most likely to nail a seat in the senate.

"Good to meet you," Liam said to each with a shake of his clammy hand.

At seven, Spade revved up the piano in a rhumba welcoming the stream of dinner guests. The crowd cheered, and Bennett shook a gourd and danced over to a table. The other poets followed suit, Grace shaking a tambourine while the rebel-rousing Amy beat a drum. Celebration, their manner implied, and the mood caught on. Everybody was singing along and laughing. So far, so good.

The teahouse wasn't any Vegas night trap, and yet eyes brightened as if people sat around roulette tables. One redheaded bloke picked up a papier-mâché plate and frowned as if confused, but his date squealed like they had dealt her the winning hand at the sight of her party favor—an origami canary as bright as sunshine.

A sweet-faced old bird tugged on Liam's sleeve. "May I have a cup of tea?" she asked, taking him down to eye level.

The towel over his forearm slid to the floor. "Surely. Do you have a favorite?"

"You pick."

Him? What did he know? "Might I suggest a tea that transports you across the globe with each sip?"

"And that would be?"

He clutched at the sudden tightness of his necktie. "Allow me."

She turned him loose with a gentle pat on his arm. "Thank you, dear."

Swallowing to loosen the tightness in his throat, he crossed over to Lucy and asked for her help. In seconds, she'd identified the lady as Miss Sharp—a dear family friend—and chose a loose-leaf tea with a fruity aroma. He had made his way back when The Talking Tears threaded out to take orders. Now things were taking off. All would go as planned. Had to.

Moments later, Bennett's smooth voice rang out, silencing all the commotion.

" 'The Lightning is a yellow Fork
From Tables in the sky
By inadvertent fingers dropt
The awful Cutlery.' "

The performers slipped seamlessly into their parts. Liam observed matters, his hands locked behind his back. People chatted as menus flapped and fluttered. A lady took a plastic bag from her purse and passed out soda crackers at her table. A middle-aged couple stamped across the floor, their faces flushed. Bells clamored together over the door as they opened it and slammed it shut.

A man with a Brooklyn accent spoke loud enough for the entire teahouse to hear. "Hey, where's the real food?"

"Yes," a lady chimed in. "When do we get something besides paper appetizers?"

Liam exchanged an uncomfortable glance with Lucy, then held up the menu. "This is a metaphorical meal we think you'll devour," he said with all the enthusiasm he'd used to impress his fellow officers.

The man pushed out of his chair. "We paid for food we can't eat? What kind of money-swindling trick are you playing?"

Miss Sharp squared her thin shoulders. "You should have expressed your intentions plainly in your flyer."

"I apologize," Liam said. "I thought the meaning was clear."

"Not on your life," the agitated New Yorker said. And others added, "No meal. What a scam. Wait until the news media gets ahold of this."

Liam mopped the sweat from his brow with a napkin. More people got up and headed out. In all his scheming, he'd never pictured the audience staging a revolt.

"Please give us a chance," he said, but no one paid any heed.

Miss Sharp confronted him with a waggle of her finger. "These folks are hungry."

Spade struck his keyboard, chords thundered, and Kubla sailed into the air. The Talking Tears slunk into the empty chairs and hid behind menus. Liam wheeled to the register. He removed the cash and chased after the crowd, waving a handful of twenties.

"Here's your money back since you're not satisfied." He handed half to Lucy, and between them, they placed the bills into each customer's palm.

"Doomed before we begin," she said through her hysteria.

Liam's scalp tightened. He'd been a stupid sod. Trouble was he hadn't ever done any actual advertising. But he had to turn things around. Or else.

Summing up his nerve, he addressed those waiting in the line outside the door. "Please forgive my mistake. But this teahouse is where artists gather, philosophers, writers—a select few in a mad world. What we plan to feed you is more satisfying than mere empty calories. If you want a chili dog, go to Goodtime Charlie's down the street. If you wish for nourishment to last, stop in tonight for a feast to fortify your spirit."

Lucy grabbed his arm. "Look." She pointed to stragglers making their way back inside.

Spade straightened his sports jacket and hit the piano keys with a flourish. He added a style to his performance that suggested the magnetic Sinatra. The Talking Tears announced each title from the menu, and the audience made their choices. Guest poets, some of Venice's finest, stopped by and poured out their hearts as each gave a plentiful helping of a selected poem.

A few rhymes brought a throng of laughter, whistling, and clapping. One soliloquy made people break down and weep. A poor bloke forgot to mute his cell phone, and the audience shot him dirty looks. The dinner lasted a pleasant two hours.

A woman raised her glass in a toast. "To you at the teahouse for expanding our knowledge of poetry in such an inventive manner."

The tips were adequate, the praise genuine, and they earned a standing ovation and an encore. Although Liam had tasted a bit of success, the expression on Lucy's face made him feel he'd hit the jackpot. With her eyes sort of dreamy, she stared at him as if seeing him anew.

He had to quit looking at her. "We did it," he announced. "You and me."

"No, Liam, you did it." She rolled her shoulders as if to release the kinks. "You mentioned all the right words to draw the customers back inside. I couldn't have done it."

"We are judged by what we accomplish under pressure," Spade said. "You held your own tonight."

Touched by Spade's compliment, Liam thanked him. He then expressed his gratitude to the volunteers for their efforts. A crew needed appreciation. No more had he thought this than he spotted Audrey, and he beamed inside and out. She wore an olive-green skirt and a lightweight sweater that looked suave as she stood next to, of all people, Bennett Browning. Liam could hardly keep from sprinting across the teahouse.

As he approached, she pursed her lips together in a faint smile and nodded at him. "Hi there. How are you?" She turned away before he gave a reply. "If you'll excuse me, I am interviewing Mr. Browning for *Powell's Review*."

He directed a question to Bennett. "So you're planning to run for senate in the future while moonlighting here?"

"I am. Classic poetry has a prestige factor. The image of someone who appreciates the past while keeping in touch with the future is perfect for my campaign, wouldn't you say?"

Liam suspected Bennett of being a mole. "Did Monroe Powell converse with you as she did the mayor?"

Audrey met Liam head-on. "Mama did a lot more than converse."

Monroe no doubt kept contact with revolutionaries. Had she been playing everyone? Nothing worse than that. He caught his reflection in a mirror and grimaced. Wasn't he "playing" people as well? He who swore to love old-fashioned poetry when he hadn't given a jot about it before he became marooned across the pond.

"There was something Zen about Monroe," Bennett was saying. "From her, I learned the benefits of drinking tea. She was all about finding peace within."

"I'm sure he isn't interested." Audrey turned and sent Liam a glower that said, "Back off, buckaroo."

He felt her rebuff like a cold, hard slap. He should feel bad, but he found himself more interested in Browning's role in the underhanded plot. Had he infiltrated on the receiving end of collecting secret plans and activities? And how many other dignitaries flocked here pretending to champion poetry and tea?

Curiosity made Liam say, "I look forward to hearing you recite, Bennett."

Audrey skimmed by him with the political contender on the other side. "You will. He's a poet who never backs down from a challenge."

Her dig wasn't wasted on Liam. He'd been off base believing her attracted to him. That should have put him in a funk, but her rejection didn't bother him. Her leaving on Bennett's arm came as a factor he willingly accepted. On the flip side, it ruled out Liam's being infatuated with the twins, plural.

After they closed for the night, he accompanied Lucy through the quiet oasis. He picked a daisy, thinking it perfect for her, and tucked it in her hair. Percy chased after them with his ball. Liam threw it, and the dog took off and disappeared in the shadows. Liam loved this slice of the Far East with its pond reflecting the two of them gliding by—she the empress, he the big phony. If he had a penny, he'd wish for her to see him as himself.

Impossible when she was singing his praises, her hand brushing his as she stepped inside the bungalow.

This place belonged in the pages of a Jane Austen novel, not the trendy boulevard named after its founder. They moved together toward the hall, a dog-tired Percy dropping on his bed. The mantel clock proclaimed the midnight hour. Moonlight shimmered through the crisscross curtains, outlining Lucy's striking silhouette.

When had she quit being "Lucinda" to him? Maybe when she'd fallen apart after her sister left. It gave him a look at her soft side, a part of her so unlike the other he'd have thought the twins pulled a switcheroo. Fat chance of that happening. No, he was the only fraud.

Was that her trembling finger on his lips as they paused in the dark hall?

His heart rate sped up, and he grew ravenous for more of her. Would it be too forward to kiss her? A kind of delirium mixed with his blood and caused him to move in, toe-to-toe, his trainers aligned with her silvery sandals. She leaned close and rubbed her cheek against his shoulder, making him barmy with need, and he fought for a shred of control. But they knew each other better now. The kiss wouldn't be uncalled for, now would it?

Out of the blue, her phone gave its mechanical rendition of Cindy Lauper's "Girls Just Want to Have Fun." She moaned, then as if distracted, turned her head, and the next thing he knew, she was heading the opposite way down the hall.

"Hey, Aud," she said. "Not sure. We won't know how things fared until tomorrow's reviews."

Shot down, Liam pivoted around toward his lonely room. His spirits sank along with his hard-on. So much for a good-night kiss.

Chapter 8

Go and catch a falling star,
Get with child a mandrake root,
Tell me where all past years are,
Or who cleft the devil's foot,
Teach me to hear mermaids singing.
                                ~John Donne (1572-1631)

The shrill of the kettle competed with the clatter of Audrey's pulse as Liam appeared in the kitchen with the morning newspapers.

"I thought you'd be keen to read the reviews," he said, sweat visible on his brow. "Should I have the champagne ready?"

"Let's hope so." Impaled by his angst, she sat at the table and thumbed through all three tabloids to the entertainment section. The critiques were scathing, citing faulty advertising and dissatisfied customers, stating complaints such as, "We went away hungry." A reporter from the *Santa Monica Outlook* blamed the failure on Mama.

" 'Without Monroe Powell, the teahouse might as well close its doors,' " Audrey quoted.

"This is damaging," Liam said. "It's my fault. I didn't make it clear in my ads that the food was symbolic. I should—"

"I should have caught the mistake," she cut in,

"but, no, I was much too busy planning what I would wear. This is my fault, all my fault."

She buried her head in her arms on the table. A newspaperwoman proofread everything, for crying out loud. This mess was just another black mark and a superb example of why she shouldn't have hired Liam. Poets always had a disruptive influence on her.

Dejected, she tore open *Powell's Review* and skimmed through to the article. "The Teahouse Opens with a Fresh Concept." *A stroke of genius*, Nathan Ingles wrote and continued to list the attributes of the dinner featuring the "Romantics." He ended with, *check out the food on their new menu.*

Audrey turned the newspaper around so Liam could read it. "We did good."

He put in, "Damn straights, we did."

"The problem is…" She twiddled her thumbs. "The public will think Nathan's biased. They'll say, 'What else would you expect from a family-run paper other than rave reviews?' "

He shrugged. "We'll just have to fix this."

Her eyes stung with the lack of sleep. "What are we going to do?"

"Tonight, we serve Dante's hot and spicy breadsticks, Shakespeare's mutton hearty soup, and King Solomon's spinach and artichoke soufflé."

Liam wouldn't recognize defeat when it smacked him in the head.

"What if no one shows up?" She'd give him the facts, as sad as they were. "What if we end up tossing out all that food? We should just throw in the towel."

"What kind of wimpy talk is that?" He dropped a wedge of brie on the counter. "Where's the lass who packs a Dillinger under her pillow?"

Although unaware of it, he had sent her a wake-up call. Lucinda wouldn't go down without the fight of her life, and for now she was her Rocky Balboa twin. "You know, I could help a little—cook, even."

"If I give you those lessons we talked about."

"Maybe…" Maybe what? Somehow, she never dreamed she'd be packing a Dillinger—let alone dressed to kill with too much hair, too many jewels, and a big tendency to kick butt.

All disguises aside, though, she had a business to run. The poetry dinner hadn't been all she'd hoped for, but they'd made a small profit. The problem was folks flocked to coffeehouses and cafés so they could bust open their laptops or browse their phones. If Tea and Poetry didn't allow free internet access, they wouldn't attract the clientele needed to succeed.

"We're at a disadvantage with no Wi-Fi connection," she said.

Liam sorted through Mama's recipe box. He gazed from Audrey to the files as if deliberating. "Someone close to you didn't agree."

He handed her a tea-stained index card. She traced her fingers over Mama's handwriting. A spirit as vibrant as hers lingered on all she had touched.

Everyone is so busy, her mother had written. *It's important to put away the smartphones. That's what the tea ceremony offers. When we lose tradition, we drain ourselves and forget who we are.*

"Do you think I wasn't aware of my mother's feelings? She saw accepting computers as crossing over to the dark side." It had been their ongoing conflict. "She was wrong."

His forehead creased as if he were about to say something. Most likely, he was thinking twice about arguing—particularly after their near kiss. Good thing her sister had called. A relationship thrived when two people shared commonalities. They didn't.

Even with their differences, though, those October days fell into a pattern. She met with Liam at five each morning to eat breakfast together—some pastry from the night before, a little Greek yogurt. Afterward, she slaved to come up with schemes to gain the teahouse more recognition. Her mother had a looming line of credit that needed to be repaid. Audrey might as well be back at *Powell's Review*. Besides, Lucinda's troubles had become hers.

After one such afternoon, Liam gestured her into the kitchen. The scent as she entered came from a sauce so rich it appeared almost black.

He picked up a ripe, ruby-red tomato, nodded, as if that explained it all, then held a topaz-colored bottle of wine. "These gems make the difference."

"May I sample it?"

"Please feel free."

She dipped a spoon into the thick, bubbly mixture and blew as he watched her with passion in his eyes. His intensity betrayed that he valued the sauce to the measure of response it drew from her. He strove to be the best. The pots and pans scattered around the kitchen were a testament to his diligence. If he had stayed up all night perfecting this dish, it wouldn't have shocked her.

"This is fabulous," she said like a TV personality.

As she watched him immersed in cookery, the sight made her weak in the knees. The new kid on the block just kept getting more grounded in Venice's lifestyle.

He awoke early each day, slave driver he was on himself, and hit the beach running. He was so disciplined he could have been a soldier in a former life, a gunner firing off rounds the same as he shot pepper into stuffed tomatoes or chopped eggplant. But while at the ocean, he pointed out each bird species to her. When he had been a boy, he cared for a goose that was "a bloomin' dive bomber." His eyes, when he'd spoken, lit like gold aventurine. And he'd talked in such a dazed way, as if in recalling his youth, none of today was real.

Now, though, he was gathering up salt, baking soda, and a big blue mixing bowl. "How about we duplicate your mum's muffins?"

"Oh, I don't know." She didn't need another failure.

"The secret is in half a cup of spelt flour."

She frowned. "Are you sure?"

"Sift all the dry ingredients first." He pointed to the recipe, and when she reluctantly did as he'd instructed, he said, "Add the wet butter and milk to the mix and beat until you get rid of all the lumps."

"Too bad I can't rid myself of the lumps in my so-called life."

"You'll get them smoothed out." He slid in back of her and took her hand, demonstrating the motion, tempting her to nestle against his chest. His iron-hard chest. "Just keep trying, luv."

His being so near was torture. "Do I add the fruit now?"

"Aye, the cranberries. You can spot a bad one from the others because it shows a wrinkle." He picked out a specimen, displaying it to her on his palm. "See, not unlike the line you get between your brows when you're deep in thought."

She rubbed the bridge of her nose. "I do?"

He sent her an all-male grin. "Captivating, actually."

He wiped flour from her face with a dishrag and plopped some cranberries in her mouth. She bit down, the tangy sweetness thrilling her taste buds, the sexy man challenging her vow to stay clear of him. But the very act of his helping her spoon the batter into tins pulled her deeper into his center, a universe composed of his culinary magic and kindness. His large hands and strong arms made her feel fragile and protected from the outside world. She remained there, a participant in sensations, till the bells over the entrance clanged together like dropped silverware.

"Someone's here," he whispered.

"Imagine that. We're not even open yet."

Slowly, ever so slowly, he turned from her. "I'll just pop these into the oven."

The front door closed on some distant planet to which she was only now returning. "I need to see who it is."

The sun through the windows lit two teens sauntering toward her. With no other thoughts than boy meets girl, she reached for their hands to give a friendly shake but found the guests preoccupied with phones.

"Good morning," Audrey said, dropping her arms to her sides. "Welcome to Tea and Poetry."

The girl's eyes grew wide. "You don't have Wi-Fi?"

Audrey's spirits tanked, and she shot a glare in Liam's direction. "No, we don't," she growled. "Sorry," she added self-consciously.

Cafés with free Wi-Fi drew in all the teens, but not at Mama's place—oh no. She'd expected to fill the last empty chair with students hungry for discussions about literature. Well, newsflash, nobody cared about Keats, Byron, or even Shelley. How she had kept the teahouse from going out of business was beyond logic.

With a heavy heart, Audrey snagged some menus. "A table in a corner?"

Minutes later, she brought teas stored in a vine-covered caddy and a black bowl filled with cranberries. "Everything that pleases the eye," she could hear Mama say. "Be sure to light a candle on the table." Audrey cleaned each piece with a soft cloth. "This is my way of honoring you."

The couple appeared six feet under in conversation, one that was digital and therefore edited when needed.

"It's so nice, isn't it, to have a break to discuss tea?" Audrey asked like some tribal elder. "We prepare many varieties to please you. We have ocha—the taste of Japan. We have our imports—Russian Caravan, Czar Alexander—such romantic names, don't you think? This Turkish tea grew near the Black Sea and—"

"I'll just have a coffee," the girl dismissed her.

Coffee?

Just then, Liam burst onto the scene. "We forgot to collect your mobiles at the door." He shoved a basket under their noses. "It's our policy—absolutely no cell phones. Hand them over straight away."

Audrey's mouth fell open.

The boy slapped down some cash. "We're out of here."

Audrey let out her breath. "They're gone."

"I am so sorry." Liam shook his head. "I had no right. You must be really pissed off. It wasn't my call to make."

****

Liam must have been playing his part to the hilt because it was the only explanation that made sense. "I was totally in the wrong to barge in and do whatever I wanted."

Lucy's lips quirked, her expression bordering on mockery. Was he done for? He, who could fit chameleonlike into any local? Quite simple, actually, to blend. He was a coolheaded professional who had just blown his stack.

He looked up to find her slumped against the wall.

"You can't help being an anti-tech goober," she said in a low, sad voice. "It's what you do. Only I…" She nodded at the empty tables. "We're lucky if we bring in some of Mama's former customers. We need a draw to run a successful business."

"I thought our new menu would do the trick."

"Your cooking is to die for. That's not the problem." She paused, her lower lip pouty but provocative. "It's me."

"Pardon?" Was he hearing her correctly?

"Mama would have been able to coax those kids into putting down their phones." She lowered her head. "I tried, but I fell flat. I'm not Monroe, never have been."

"My God, Lucy, you're not chopped liver. You've coaxed girls into buying fashion trends for years. You rate starlet status, a—"

"Oh, you don't know a damned thing!"

"I seem to be mucking things up."

"It's ironic that—" She rolled her eyes. "You can't possibly understand," she said as if her looks were more a curse than a blessing.

At a loss, he backed off without the slightest clue how to handle her. Her body shook, even her voice quivering, probably the result of trifling with the terrible teens. In all the scuffle, her satiny blouse had fallen open. The flicker of the candlelight danced over her smooth, ivory breast. If she hadn't been so distracted, she might have seen the pleasure that he took in the sight of her.

He lifted his gaze. "We publicize the teahouse— I'm not sure how—perhaps grab a bullhorn. Stand on the rooftops. Hire a rollicking band. Parade down the streets. Or better yet, get—"

"What did you just say?"

"Hire a band, you know?"

She shoved away from the wall, a lovely display of satiny skin and flowing, silky clothes. "That's it, Brit!"

"Most of the rock groups I know are from England, but—"

"I can see it now. A parade—you're a freaking genius!"

"Aye." He'd forgotten he had mentioned it.

"And we kick it off with a festival—not a big one. Say, a weekend, but it would bring in hordes of poets, and maybe we snag a handful of those young misfits. We'd host it right here, get the art centers in Venice aboard. We'll sell food, give discounts at neighboring restaurants, the same for the local hotels."

Her enthusiasm called him to action. "I can see it now. Let's call it something like 'The Masters of the Classics Festival.' "

"We shoot for the first week in December."

"That won't work. Much too soon. There isn't enough time. How could we score the help we need? And the permits, what about them?"

She angled her lovely head. "Have you forgotten who my mother was?"

"Oh, that's right, the bloomin' godmother."

"You've got it."

Struck with ideas, he paced. "To get this production off the ground, we'd better hop to it. We advertise throughout SoCal. We'll need volunteers, lots of them."

"There are scads of poets. They'd be glad to lend a hand."

That evening, Liam couldn't sleep and took a walk on the beach. The darkness hid him and the dog tagging along with him. With the roar of the sea, Liam's mind drifted to Lucy. She'd felt so right in his arms this afternoon. He should take a break from her. His attraction to her was a dilemma of the first order. The mere scent of her, of fruity herbs and flowers—her teas—had almost derailed him. The image of her lips stained with quenching cranberry wouldn't budge from his head. He inhaled a deep breath. If he kept up like this, he'd spoil everything.

A grave loss of UK's security was transpiring right under his nose. He had to quit mooning around as if stuck inside a Brontë novel.

Percy sounded off with his usual sharp barks, and Liam pictured him saying, "You're all wet," as if the corker had read his thoughts.

Oddly enough, he grinned at the dog's imagined response, laughing in the dark as a wave plunged up with a *kaboom* and drenched them both.

In the next few days, he followed through on his commitment. His next moves were all about connecting to high-ranking politicians and even more about scoring life-and-death secrets sent to a remote server he had rigged up.

Olivia had the lithe, compact body of a gymnast and an Italian face with a disarming smile. Her designer suit looked pricey enough to suggest she had done well. She sat at a desk composed of polished mahogany. Her granting him an appointment offered the opportunity to charm the veneer off Ms. Ricci.

"Thank you for agreeing to meet with me on such brief notice," he said. "I've compiled a revenue-generating plan that will benefit Venice Beach. I thought you'd want to get in on the ground floor."

She sent him a sultry smile. "You're an Englishman."

His accent had its perks with the ladies. "I hope you find merit in what I offer."

She batted her long lashes and gestured him to a chair. "Run it by me, will you?"

He gave his thirty-minute spiel on the financial impact a poetry festival would have on the community. He hoped to combine their efforts with the well-established art centers in Venice. The event would bring in tourists and lure those with money, not to mention the media coverage it would get. It would be like having a sport's team, he claimed, but not until he brought up the teahouse did Olivia's eyes gleam.

"I wouldn't be where I am without Monroe," she said.

A hero in a Constance Spring novel would reach

for his weapon. "Time to be straight with me, luv. Tell me about your involvement with Mrs. Powell or share her same fate." But he wasn't in a potboiler or a Hollywood movie. So he settled on the truth. "Keeping poetry alive was important to her."

"Listen, you've got me interested. I'm already coming up with ideas. I'll get the ball rolling—for Monroe."

Good enough. Even though Liam hadn't gotten more than a verbal agreement, he had planted a bug in her cell phone when she stepped out to talk to her office assistant. Because of it, he'd hacked a chink in accomplishing his mission. For now it would have to do.

Chapter 9

No more, no more you'll freely soar
Above the grass and gravel:
Henceforth you'll walk—and she will chalk
The line that you're to travel!
                    ~Ambrose Bierce (1842-1914)

In the little bungalow, Audrey kept her distance from Liam. She longed for his support, more so now. But he, too, seemed guarded. They spoke only of the weather. They had flung the windows open wide, and the jade garden sparkled like jewels after the rain. The sun was drying the wet teahouse that glistened against the sky. Many of the eateries on the boulevard were serving supper, but Tea and Poetry had closed their doors today.

Liam stuffed the turkey while Percy supervised, his nose twitching. She peeled potatoes while keeping an eye out the upstairs window. By now, Uncle Johnny should have quit his writing. He'd get prepared for the holiday unlike any other. She didn't want to think of him dwelling on the subject better left alone.

"Are you all right?" Liam broke the silence.

How should she react? "Peachy."

"It must be tough to face—"

"No." *No—what? No, I refuse to talk about it. No, now shut up! No, remember to be Lucinda.* "I'm just uncertain what to wear."

He shooed her out of the kitchen. "Women and their fashion hang-ups, but what would a bloke do without them? Scram and don't return until you've figured it out."

By afternoon, she'd let down her long platinum tresses. This day marked a new beginning. She'd be not quite Lucia, not quite Audrey. The in-between, she called it, and she was trying it on for size. For what it was worth, she didn't think she looked half bad in glossy lipstick with a hint of gold.

She emerged from the hall in a simple, sleek jumpsuit and stopped to pose. "Well?"

He turned a seductive gaze. "It's brilliant. Especially the sexy bit of cleavage."

"You sly dog. You're not fooling me." She winked at him. "You just want to lighten my mood."

He swung her around to face him. "Perhaps, but I like what I see. I think you're the bee's knees, Luce the Duce."

Before she reacted to the dizzying current racing through her, the real Lucinda swept inside their much-too-cozy nest. The sisters touched cheek to cheek, then narrowed their eyes slightly. Audrey had dressed down, while Lucinda's nails had grown out a little. She'd added pearls to her gray chemise. And didn't Audrey detect a hint of eye shadow? If they weren't careful, they would blow their cover by outwardly switching back to themselves.

Uncle Johnny strode into the dining room with a festive mix of maroon chrysanthemums, orange carnations, eucalyptus, and sunflowers.

"I'll just set my bouquet on the table, so y'all can

get rid of those weeds."

Yikes! Liam had collected wildflowers for the centerpiece from "those lush vistas along the canals," he'd told her with pride.

"You know," she said, "it would be nice to make a spot for the turkey."

Her sister slid in as fast as room service to clear all the flowers. "I agree."

Now that the table had become a blank canvass, Audrey envisioned honey-crisp rolls, sage dressing, candied yams, and pumpkin pie. Her mouth watered for the all-American feast she'd always known. What would she expect from a Brit but a break from tradition? Just as well he opted for a deep-fried turkey, a recipe he had picked up in New Orleans.

Liam tried, he tried so hard, and Audrey adored him for it. Throughout supper, he kept the talk light and careful. "How's the bird? Do you need more red potatoes? Another helping of salad? More wine?"

Her sister took another roll and heaped it with butter. "What's happening with the poetry festival? Are you ready to bring Venice to its knees?"

Safe subject, and to her credit, she'd poured a fortune from her New York bank account into sponsoring the event. If not for her sister, they might not have been able to join forces with Abbot Kinney's annual holiday block party. The mayor had pulled a few strings, not to mention Bennett's influence. Hooray for knowing the right people.

"You should see the floats," Audrey added. "With Liam's talent for wielding plaster of Paris and the locals' input, the parade will resemble a Christmas Mardi Gras. Maybe it won't be as big, but it will prove just as amazing."

"I can't wait to get a peek," her sister said.

From the head of the table, Uncle Johnny said, "If Monroe were here—"

Audrey drew in a stinging breath. Her heart sank. She'd thought they'd make it over the last of the hurdles. The padlock had come undone, though. Those whitewashed walls had crumbled, and Mama's ghost roamed the house as free as dandelion seeds blowing in the wind. No going back now. They drank more wine, and the rain started anew.

"Remember the Thanksgiving your mother bought that whipped cream in the can?" her uncle asked.

Audrey nodded, laughing despite herself. "When she pushed the nozzle, it shot up all over the ceiling."

"Oh my God," Lucinda said, "it was too funny." She leaned against her chair. "I'll never forget the first time Mama took it on herself to feed the homeless. She invited the poets to recite, and they did. She served a green tea, which made people feel so good they didn't want to leave."

Audrey waved a hand. "And that event started the tradition of serving the poor on Christmas."

"It was her gift to the community," Lucinda put in.

Johnny said, "Do y'all recall the Thanksgiving your mama rescued Percy from the shelter? If she hadn't come along, it would have been—" He grazed his throat with his index finger. "—curtains."

The dog slunk into the room and lay down, resting his head on his front paws, his eyes two bronze orbs that surveyed the group. He uttered a groan that shook his entire body.

"Thanksgiving isn't Thanksgiving without Mama,"

Lucinda said.

Uncle Johnny cried, "How can we even celebrate?"

Kubla raised his beak and echoed, "Thanksgiving isn't Thanksgiving," mirroring the misery around the table.

Deep sorrow reduced Audrey to sobs, and her voice had stopped working.

All but Liam had lost any ability to control emotion. He rose and rounded up the water pitcher, saying with a soft British cadence, "I shall only be a moment. Carry on."

He appeared so kind and patient, as if he saw their unfortunate pileup with compassion. Audrey wanted to throw down her napkin and join him in the kitchen. She even made it to her feet and gathered up two wine glasses, and they clanked together. She held a knife and struck a rim, and the sound echoed throughout the gloomy room.

"A toast is in order," she said as Liam appeared with fresh water. "To our cook, who took over and provided us with a first-rate meal."

His grin warmed her. "My pleasure."

She added, "I also want to salute my sister, who has gone full speed ahead in publicizing the poetry parade and festival."

Her sister nodded with an actual blush. "It's the least I could do."

Audrey hadn't time to talk to her twin as of late. "How's everything faring at the paper?" They needed to keep the subject from drifting again to the unbearable.

"Never better."

"That's wonderful."

"Yes, on the anniversary of John F. Kennedy's

assassination, we featured a story about people remembering where they were when they heard the president was shot."

All at once, Audrey stiffened. "That isn't what we—you—usually cover."

The rebel waved her hand in the air. "It was a breakaway from the norm, but the news staff commented on how much they liked it."

And her sister threw her napkin across her table setting. Why hadn't she taken the time to check in on *Powell's Review*? She'd been up to her eyeballs in work. As she gathered up dinner plates, she mouthed, "You didn't discuss this with me."

Her sister followed her behind the closed kitchen door. "Oh, sorry. I shouldn't have my own mind," Lucinda whispered. "I'm supposed to just walk in your Birkenstocks."

"That was the general plan," Audrey muttered.

"Do you really think being ten and a half minutes older makes you fricking Einstein?"

"Don't be droll. Your readers are the millennials. They probably never heard the phrase, 'Where were you when President Kennedy was shot?' Let alone care."

"Why not market the paper to include a bigger audience?"

"Because most of the baby boomers are retired, in case you haven't noticed."

"I didn't know there was an age limit attached to the word entrepreneur." Lucinda fixed her hands on her hips. "Your target's too small. That's what's wrong with you. You never think beyond the box."

"Listen, Cin, you can pour every cent you own into

Powell's Review, but if you don't cultivate your brand, you'll fall flat on your face."

"Well, Aud, you can't even keep an established business afloat."

Audrey's temper flared. "Touché," she sputtered. "Then again, at least I never quit my job. Nothing worse than a quitter, is there?"

The door opening stopped their heated argument before they came to blows.

Liam carried the turkey platter to the sink. "Might I get the dessert while you both comfort your uncle? He's having a bad time of it."

They nodded, but neither moved.

"Is there something wrong?" He didn't hang around for an answer, and he probably didn't want one. The smartest thing for him was to hop a plane and head home. Then he'd not have to deal with their dysfunction ever again.

The sisters returned to their chairs. Audrey tried to rationalize their conversation, but a disruptive pain settled in her temples. She wanted her sister to be proud of her, and why had she been so damn obstinate? She hadn't meant it. Well, okay, just a little. She had tired of pretending to be someone she wasn't. Being Lucia was a full-time job. If she could end this farce, she'd do it in a heartbeat.

Liam arrived back with brûléed apples and ice cream, and she struggled to keep her hands steady. If he noticed her shattered nerves, he didn't say. He retreated to the kitchen only to return with a teapot.

Audrey played dumb to disguise her sudden dread. "What's that?"

Liam beamed. "Now that you're no longer allergic

to tea, I thought we could all do with a spot of Kukicha."

No, no, no. This terrible thing couldn't be happening!

"Ah," her uncle said after a sip. "This connects me with the person who plucked the leaf and with the soil, rain, wind, sunshine, and the moonlight. It connects me with the eternal—with Monroe."

With her uncle's words, she slipped back into childhood. She and Lucinda sat at their My Little Pony table. And Mama was saying, "Watch the bottom of your teacup for a floating forest that you both can enter."

To ensure her sister wouldn't get sick, Audrey drank both cups so they could travel to the place where they dreamed of castles and all the simple joys born of innocence. Of the magic their mother told stories about, those richly woven tales her granny had passed on to her—a ceremony that made tea more than a beverage. It was the stuff of friendship, sisterhood, and of caring.

A mist gathered now in her heart, not unlike the one seeping through the window, tasting of sea and salt and of a time that existed no more.

Too bad Audrey couldn't drink her twin's portion as she had back when life made sense.

If it didn't happen, the jig would be up. Wasn't that what she had wanted?

For a moment, Audrey's gaze met her sister's. No rage showed in her face, only anxiety. Those identical eyes staring into hers crinkled at the corners. And the lines between the eyebrows, when had they appeared? Maybe the result of working late into the night, of worry, and of squinting—all for *Powell's Review*. Her sister cared about the newspaper in a way Audrey never had.

As Liam poured tea, Audrey said to her down-in-the-mouth twin, "Didn't you get a call from work? Hadn't something gone wrong?"

Her sister's eyebrow quirked for an instant. Then she shoved her cup away. "Yeah, that's right. Sorry, all." Her breath came out in slight rushes. "I'd love to stay for Kukicha, but I have to run."

She wasted no time throwing kisses and bucking out the door.

Chapter 10

Some have won a wild delight,
By daring wilder sorrow;
Could I gain thy love to-night,
I'd hazard death to-morrow.

~Charlotte Brontë (1816-1855)

The parade was a brilliant spectacle that Liam stared at with an open mouth. Hollywood nymphs threw candy from floats that cut a striking contrast against the sky. Lasses flew by Liam's nose, their glitter and sequins and golden fringes so bright they could wake the dead. Santa arrived via police escort. Sirens and carols blared as kids climbed aboard the sleigh.

Olivia Ricci had kept her word, bless her. The mayor spent so much time at the teahouse he wondered if she shouldn't take up residence. She had explained that the Abbot Kinney Holiday Block Party started in the neighborhood a decade ago. The event grew more popular and drew day-trippers and vacationers here to spend the weekend.

This season, Venice kicked things off with a Christmas-themed poetry parade. The teahouse had hitched up with the local literary art centers, and now balloons popped and spilled out poems written by both modern poets and those long dead.

Being stranded in SoCal had worked out in Liam's favor. How else could he have rounded up such fabulous freaks? Here in Venice, he had joined the circus that never left town. He palled around with the clowns who now clip-clopped on stilts along the boulevard. This jolly good show just kept getting better.

Until, all at once, a news copter buzzed overhead. Cameras aimed in his direction, and he dove into the deluge of onlookers. Folks, standing too close together, elbowed him. A Chihuahua nipped at his pant legs, and he staggered over unwrapped, sticky candy. He had no intension of someone from back home spotting his face on the telly. With the sun beating down his neck, he broke loose and took refuge under an awning.

"Lucy," he said into a walkie-talkie. "Where are you?"

"At the end of the parade." She sounded breathless. "The emcee just announced our festival. We'd better get to the teahouse."

"Copy that."

People jammed the sidewalks and crowded the booths set up for the festivities. He edged toward the far side of the street to avoid the mob. Fancy his spotting the wanker who'd taken off with his wallet. The mahogany-skinned man with arrogant eyes leered at Liam and said something to his dog. If Liam didn't know better, he'd believe the two meant him harm.

As he neared the teahouse, he spotted Percy waiting out front. This spectacle attracted the news copter determined to fish out a story. The silly-looking terrier, decked out like a mob boss in a fedora and sunnies, fit the bill. Until now Liam had remained off the grid. Just his luck. He was out in the open with the doggie who was losing his cool in the pounding roar.

He bundled the frantic canine in his arms and ducked inside as if he were avoiding a nest of machine guns. A mere year ago, he'd been taking detours so that the enemy wasn't able to distinguish him, knowing he and others could die with a misstep. His mission at the moment was to advance the public awareness of poetry—an undercover maneuver. Still, he couldn't deny his hope to snag an adolescent or two and turn them on to the classics.

****

Audrey was too busy to consider the jitters in her stomach and too hopeful to care. Night plummeted in with colored lights twinkling up and down the boulevard. Holiday music flooded from speakers in the teahouse, not quite drowning out the cash register dinging with each new sale. Voices murmured and laughed, and flatware clinked against porcelain.

To their credit, they had scheduled a reading. Ten poets had volunteered to recite. By staging the event, they intended to kick off the poetry festival with a bang. The dining room was overflowing with customers. The food had sold out. Audrey, laurel wreaths in tow, squeezed in next to Liam, who was looking from one table to another with approving eyes.

"Your audience awaits you," she said, struggling to ignore the way her senses sprang to life whenever their bodies so much as touched.

He leaned against her. "You ready?"

She thrust out her chin to appear confident. "A piece of cake."

He threw his shoulders back and approached the pulpit. "Good evening. Welcome to Venice, 'the creative soul' of Los Angeles. I hope you enjoy our—"

The lights flickered out. Not another disaster! A chill skittered along Audrey's spine. Through the dimness, her eyes met Liam's, and he shrugged. Off to the side, Uncle Johnny reached for the electric switch. Nothing. Yet out the front window, the holiday lights along the block glowed invitingly. Folks were expressing their unease with exclamations and scrambling toward every available exit.

Audrey lowered the laurel wreaths and snapped on a lighter. She spied her reflection glimmering in the dark windowpane like the ghost of Christmas past.

"Please," she addressed the gathering, "we have enough candles to light Dodger Stadium. If you'd have patience, we can pass them out."

Liam, the eternal optimist, tapped her on the shoulder. "We'll get through this."

"Are you kidding me? We won't win any new customers this way. The electricity's out yet again. I can't believe it. Next thing you know, the toilets will back up, and..." She had dialed down to her "woe is me" zone. If she continued, she'd lose it. "I'll stop now."

"Over there," Liam said, "several diehards have elected to stay."

A woman, dreamy and exotic with her Cleopatra hairdo and eyes slanted up toward the temples, stood at the candlelit platform. In a whispery voice, she uttered erotic phrases, "caressed in light and ablaze in organdy," and "hot, scented, Turkish bath, cool, thin, silk."

Liam edged close enough to say, "Splendid way with words, don't you think?"

His sultry tone, the look he gave her, made her believe he wasn't speaking of the writing but of something more personal. She drank from a glass of water, moistening the dryness his nearness gave her. She couldn't afford to allow the imagery to distract her. Distractions led to mistakes. Mistakes led to failure— yet again.

She ground out a white lie. "Her style isn't my cup of tea."

The candlelight shone along his tanned face, giving him a hungry-man urgency as he met her gaze. If he composed a poem, it would be full of sexuality—hot, steamy, and alluring. A woman would most likely leave her convictions behind if he recited to her alone.

He raised a teacup and saluted her. "To you, luv."

While they toasted one another, lovers leaned close and exchanged endearments. The hour grew later. Just before midnight, the reading ended. Surrounded by tea enthusiasts and poets, she realized they were her people, always had been. They were the prime reason she fought like a mama bear to keep from closing the doors. The ache for Liam hit, and she pushed it away. Better to keep her mind on her goal than to wake tomorrow to regret.

****

The following Friday, Audrey psyched herself up to shop for Christmas by dunking into a bathtub heaped with bubbles. She'd no more let the warmth of the water soothe away her dread of still another holiday than thoughts of her mother yanked her back in time.

While being driven from place to place, the twins perked their ears as Mama fired off the first verse of a rhyme she composed. For the rest of the drive, they took turns adding more verses constructed on the fly—didn't matter how clever or illegible. A single line ensured a chance to win. While ordinary kids took in movies on in-car DVD players, the Powell twins wracked their brains for a jingle. Wordplay was their game of choice, their family bonding time.

Unexpected sobs bombarded Audrey. She dipped beneath the water and pushed to her feet as if experiencing a baptism. She forced herself to go through the motions, conjuring up a carmine tunic from the padded coat hangers. Red leggings and white boots completed the outfit. If she dressed for the season, maybe she'd fake it until she made it. Besides, although cautious, she had to come together with Liam if their newest idea had any hope of succeeding.

She found him parked in a desk chair and tapping his knee, then scribbling his thoughts on a legal pad. A man planning a revolt couldn't appear as committed. Yet decked out in a surfer shirt, jeans, red suspenders, and a Santa Claus hat, he might have been one of the Beach Boys composing the lyrics to "Little Saint Nick." She hated to interrupt, wanted to go on watching him till Christmas came and went.

He glanced up then. "Look at you." He tilted his head to the side. "Let me write a song to describe your fashion sense. Call it 'Lady in Red.' "

"It's overkill, isn't it?" Heat flooded her cheeks. She dropped a shoulder, and her purse thumped to the floor. "I should change into something less flashy, ditch the top."

"Ah, the lady doth protest too much." He took her nervous hands in his and whirled her under the chandelier in the lushly paneled room. "Come with me, and I'll take you to the land of Christmas light and eternal bright. Oh, carry me away, sweet lady in red."

She gazed over his left shoulder as they twirled. She wanted to yield to the moment. If she gave in to him, surrendered to his absolute maleness and the odd things it did to her, they'd never leave the bungalow.

She tapped the face of her wristwatch. "We'd best hit the road."

"Didn't we get your sister to play at being you today? Do you realize how lucky you are to have a twin? It isn't everyone who can trade places when they have the inkling."

"Yes, well…" Guilt stabbed her, the fake Lucinda, between the ribs. If he only knew. "We can't expect Audrey and Uncle Johnny to stay through the entire work shift. I told them we'd be back early. But Monday is my sister's busiest day at the paper, and my uncle won't admit it kills him to leave his writing when he's in the middle of a scene."

Liam shoved her onward. "Then let's get to it, Red."

In Santa Monica, they boarded the Expo Line en route to downtown Los Angeles. A mumbling hum settled, then an electrical murmur as the train slid out of the station. A woman sat surrounded by a brood of children climbing on her. She stuck a pacifier in the howling baby's mouth, rested her head against the seat, and shut her eyes. Daily commuters lost themselves in their online newspapers and cell phones. Adolescents with earbuds played video games. Watching this, Audrey dreaded interrupting these innocents conducting their everyday lives oblivious to what was about to transpire.

But after the robotic voice finished its announcements, from his seat at the front of the cab, Liam rose to his feet. "I have a poem to recite by Ogden Nash."

People, either shocked speechless or curious, stared at him as he began. " 'In Baltimore there lived a boy…' "

A teen had taken off his earbuds and elbowed his homie, and he did the same, and they were smirking—all smart-alecky—but listening. The kids stopped slugging each other. Digital devices lowered, although some remained in place. Sighs of irritation followed. Still, in time, several phones and tablets were forgotten as the passengers' attention ignited.

One boy's eyes, at least, had gotten as big as nickels. "Is this true?" he asked his mother.

"No, dear, it's just a story," she said and glared at Liam. But her kids had quit hitting each other and throwing spit wads at the other commuters.

The teenagers had returned to their video games when a gent with a shock of white hair leaned forward on his cane. "Haven't heard that poem since I was a small fry."

A businessman set aside his to-do list. "Why not tell us another?"

Liam's selection included the serious, sentimental, and humorous. A few Scrooges dismissed him, others were lukewarm, but the majority cheered him on. Anyone who'd ever worried about the future of literature in a media-mad era would have taken heart.

About fifty minutes later, when the wheels squealed into the Seventh Street station, several listeners had joined in reciting some of the verses. The

Luddite looked radiant. Clearly, he was having fun. He'd always been handsome, but now Audrey could appreciate him outside of work at the teahouse. He'd been the ideal person for this job, not only a daredevil but also perhaps a little crazy.

A bit misty-eyed, Audrey raised her purse. That's when she noticed the ten-percent-off coupons she'd forgotten to pass out. "Rats," she said, flipping the stack between her fingers. "I blew it."

"Doesn't matter," Liam countered. "We gave something money can't buy."

She caved in with a grin. "Point taken."

To walk among the others patronizing the holiday markets lightened her step. She loved the unique gift shops but had to watch her pennies. Still, she found a flashy key chain for her sister, who lost her keys daily. Thinking of her uncle, she couldn't resist slipping into the soft glow of a used bookshop where vintage books shone in their gold-tooled bindings. She picked out an exquisite volume of Dashiell Hammett's *The Maltese Falcon*.

So many things in the shops jumped from their glass cases, saying "Buy me," those items that shouted Mama. As she collected the book titles, she explained to Liam, "For my mom, the hopeless romantic. Matchmaking gave her the greatest pleasure—ask anyone."

"And you're buying these now because…?"

"Because I can't help myself. Some habits are hard to break."

As if sympathetic, he sprang for lunch at a delicatessen where the aroma of hot pastrami and spicy mustard wafted through the air. Audrey's mouth watered, and the soft, crusty bread hit the spot. They talked for an hour. She relished the respite from her hectic routine. They should do it more often. At noon, they emerged well fed and relaxed.

The wind of the morning had died, and although holiday shoppers populated the street, a white glimmer of sunlight cut through the clouds. It lit Liam and the setting in a Christmas-card scene. She'd follow him anywhere. That was until he topped things off with an unplanned excursion to an outdoor ice-skating rink surrounded by silvery skyscrapers.

She tried to protest. "We don't have time."

He took her hand in his. "You're safe with me."

"I've never skated in my life. I don't know how."

He watched her with a smirk she found both aggravating and irresistible. "You forget, I grew up in snow country. Not to mention, I taught a clueless lady to cook. Skating should be a cinch. Be a sport and let me give you a lesson."

"I don't think so."

"Someone wise once said, 'Life shrinks or expands in proportion to one's courage.' Might this not apply to you?"

He was clever with his one-liners, but so was she. "Yes, but you've heard of fools rushing in…buster." She just flunked her portrayal of Lucinda, who lived each moment to the fullest—the same as Mama had. Only Audrey broke the rule.

"I refuse to teach anyone I don't believe has potential." He twirled a finger in the curls near her cheeks that her flat iron failed to straighten. "You can do this. Just rely on that moxie I saw when I met you."

"It's still there." She struggled against the tingles

his touch gave her. "I prefer having my feet rooted to the ground."

He opened his wallet. When she shrank back toward the curb, he grabbed her arm. "You don't have to skate if you don't wish."

That "you don't have to skate" was a ploy to push her out into a sun so bright it made her head pound. She huddled in the corner. Obviously, Liam had grown up on the ice. Once her feet were moving, she was lucky to keep her balance. What had she been thinking to allow him to talk her into this? Her skates wobbled, and she worried she would fall.

Liam's blades sliced to a stop in front of her. "Put your hands in mine."

When she did, squeezing her eyes shut against the glare, he glided backward—the showoff.

"March forward a few steps," he instructed. "Now let your body glide."

"Here I go," she said, peering at him through half-lowered lashes. "If I can keep it up, I guess I won't meet with disaster."

"That's the spirit." His hair lifted in the breeze. "Okay, start picking up one foot as you skate."

She bit the inside of her mouth. "Okay, I'll try."

"Great. Next, march, then set a foot on the ice while you lift the other." He encouraged with a nod as she tried her darndest. "Good on you, Lucy. You're doing well. Now touch your heels together, slide your feet apart, then point your toes toward each other."

She studied him showing her the move in an hourglass motion. "Got it," she said through the sounds of people talking, laughing, along with the clatter and scraping of blades.

"Keep practicing until you can lift your skates off the ice in alternating patterns."

Given time, she performed the skill and dropped her hands from his. "Look at me," she insisted, jubilantly clapping. "I'm doing it by myself." She glided and luxuriated in the wind whistling through her hair and chilling her face. "This is fun!"

If she hadn't looked at the rink to marvel at her feet doing her bidding, she might not have tottered and toppled backward. Her heartbeat raced along with her floundering limbs. She tried to straighten, lifted her foot, and met nothing but space.

In an instant, Liam caught her and pulled her into his arms. "For a woman so tall, you're amazingly weightless."

He set her on the ice and pressed against her, body to body, skate to skate. His warmth seeped into her as she shuddered, the fear still so intense she arched her back and clutched his shoulders until her fingers dug into his flesh.

"There, there, you gave it your best, Lucy Ducy," he said.

Disgraced, she nestled her head against his chest. "I'm an idiot."

"No, I should have warned you." Liam raised her chin in his hand. "Never look at your feet. Always lean forward with bent knees so you won't—"

His lips met hers. His kiss was gentle, brief as the brush of wings. Audrey was no more able to stop it than she'd been able to prevent her legs from going out from underneath her. He tasted of candy canes and chocolate. She couldn't do a thing but mold her body to his. Skaters whizzed by, and the world kept on spinning and glimmering. He had ahold of her, guaranteeing her stability. No more spills. But what was more dangerous? Falling again, taking a worse tumble, or his rescue?

Chapter 11

Two lovers by a moss-grown spring:
They leaned soft cheeks together there,
Mingled the dark and sunny hair,
And heard the wooing thrushes sing.
~George Eliot (1819-1880)

Audrey and Liam got off the train in Santa Monica, and he suggested stopping at a Christmas tree lot. After his nonstop prompting, she dragged herself into the emerald maze. The fragrance of pine enveloped her, filling her with memories too poignant to recall without a box of tissues in tow.

"Look at these poor victims," she said. "Cut off at their roots. What a waste."

He pointed to a tall spruce tree. "Now that's a nice one."

She balked at the idea. "Too much trouble. Trees dry out and lose their needles, and the needles get into the carpet. You don't find them until you step on one. Then, *ouch*."

"What about the gifts you just bought?" As if he realized she needed to chill, he massaged her shoulders. "Where were you thinking of parking them? Come on, have fun with this, Red."

As if a conspiracy to soften her up further, Christmas music wafted out to greet them. Didn't anyone guess how much bringing a tree home broke her heart?

"No, nothing as commercial for me."

He puffed up his buff chest and tugged on his suspenders so he looked rugged and strong enough to haul lumber—and, yes, just oh so hunky. "You plan to fight me on this?"

She reared her back against the chain-link fence. "I can't afford it."

He shook his head, grimacing. "What is it, Lucia? Did you stash most of your capital in a Swiss bank account?"

How had she forgotten to be got-rocks Lucinda?

"Hmm, one might think you'd have a golden egg just lying in wait."

Now she was in for it. What choice did she have but to play a "poor me" card? "I made rotten decisions in the stock market."

"You did?" He sounded more amazed than shocked. "Does this mean you don't have two brass farthings to rub together?"

"It means I don't want to spend a fortune on something that will bite the dust come January."

"You're strapped for cash." He jimmied out his wallet. "Let me take care of it."

How could she tell him she didn't want a tree because it reminded her of past Christmases never to be again? She shouldn't have to express her discontent. He should understand without her voicing her opposition. He'd proved insightful at Thanksgiving. Why was he fighting her on this?

He was leading her to the very end of the lot. There he gestured at a lopsided green giant. "The pick of the litter. Imagine how it'll look in the teahouse."

"Now that's what I call a freak of nature."

"Where's your sense of spirit? Don't you get it? The tree's imperfection makes it special. It puts one in line with the First Christmas. Consider, if you will, the paradox of a king born in a stable full of braying animals and frigid temperatures. Incredible, isn't it? Such conditions served as the catalyst that transformed the flawed into perfection."

An employee approached as if he'd just stepped off his surfboard with his windblown blond hair and sun-browned face. "Have I got a bargain for you," he barked. "That tree, twenty bucks. What do you say?"

"Make it fifteen," Liam said, extending his hand, "and we'll shake on it."

Audrey rolled her eyes. "How do you suggest we get that Freakazoid home?"

"Don't you have your mobile?"

She tugged her phone out of the bottom of her purse, past the sad reminder of the coupons she had forgotten to use.

"Here's hoping your uncle can break away for a moment to lend us a hand."

The sun dropped, allowing the emerging night. The trio hauled the tree into the aroma of garlic and herbs from Liam's pre-made stew and the contented buzz of customers. They skirted the tables, set with white linen cloths and adorned with folded napkins and jars of fresh flowers, and relinquished the tree in the corner by the fireplace where a gas jet displayed a cheerful fire.

At the sight of them, Lucinda's brows rose and disappeared beneath hair that was more polished than Audrey's platinum mop.

"I've never seen such a cockamamie excuse for a tree," the twin who had pinky sworn to be Audrey said.

Liam shook his head. "Can't any of you distinguish the master plan?" And he once again went into his comparison to the Christ Child born in a manger.

When he finished, Johnny dismissed him with a brush of the hands. "There's nothing wrong that a dose of know-how won't fix. I'll just hang an old planter screw from the ceiling and attach the tip to the hook with string."

Liam bowed his head. "I suppose that will straighten it."

Audrey sensed he felt slighted.

It didn't stop him from including the customers in trimming the monstrosity. Handfuls of tinsel and cherished ornaments suggested the 1950s. Soon, folks were fawning over the old classic pine. Carols by Nat King Cole and Tony Bennett played from hidden speakers. With oohs and aahs, kids pointed out the colored water gurgling up in the candle-shaped glass. A man called them bubble lights. With a sudden lightness in her limbs, she smiled at the sight.

Had Liam guessed the value of her seeing the tree decorated? Was her delight what made him so persistent? Even Uncle Johnny broke out of mourning to deck the mantelpiece with the Old World Santas he and Mama had purchased on their travels.

Audrey turned to Liam. "You knew I needed this."

His eyes held a gentle gleam. "That tree had your name on it."

She gave in to helping him string snowflakes and hanging them so they danced and twirled in the windows. The songbirds with spun-glass tails lent an exotic touch to a wreath they hung there. Sugar plums and beaded berries stood out against the pine. Liam's easy camaraderie and subtle wit lifted her spirits, and she confided bits and pieces of her Christmases with Mama. She even admitted her reluctance to move on.

"Dealing with what happened to my mother is difficult for me," she said once she was alone with him and shutting the teahouse down for the night. "I'm trying to sort things out."

"Do you mean with the way she died?" he responded.

"Nobody has come forward to confess to the accident. It makes me crazy. I check the street for any trace. It was a white Ford pickup. I'm always on the lookout. One day I spotted a truck and chased it on my bike. Never caught up to it."

He met her gaze without flinching. "Do you think someone meant to kill her?"

"Why? You knew her. She wasn't the type you'd expect on a hit list."

"I'd say not." He shoved a plate in the cabinet. "Can you recall any event that might have led up to her death? Did she mention a threat or a disgruntled customer?"

She answered in a rush, "I've wracked my brain to come up with a reason. Nothing fits. And I don't buy for a second what the detective in the morgue implied. He asked me if she was suicidal."

"Oh balls, of course, she wasn't."

"That's what I said. Not with those words, but my mother didn't have a death wish." She swallowed hard, lifted her chin, and met his gaze. "She'd never take her life."

"Listen, I'm here for you." He patted her hand. "I hope you get that. If your mum had problems, we should delve into what they were."

Things were getting much too scary. Murder wasn't familiar ground. Since Mama's death, doubt blurred Audrey's vision, but they were missing something. A simple explanation. She felt it in her bones.

The more she mulled it over, the more she didn't want to commit.

"We'll see," she said.

****

Encumbered with shopping bags, Liam passed through streets bustling with pre-Christmas chaos. Gulls followed, wheeling around and causing disconcerting shadows, their squawks piercing the air like gunshot. He scanned the scene for any potential foes incognito. After Lucy confided in him last night, he'd sprung into action. With her protection foremost in his mind, before daybreak, he'd recovered his Glock. No holding back, not when it involved a possible killer on the loose.

Just as he set the groceries on the butcher block, a muffled voice drifted from the dining room.

"Here's the code. You've got access. Pass it on to your contact."

Leading with his weapon, Liam tiptoed, cracked the door open, and slipped inside. Through the shadows in the curtain-drawn teahouse, Spade sat with his back to him. What the blazes was he doing here? Apart from Kubla, no one else appeared to be keeping the chap company.

He replaced his gun and cleared his throat to

announce his presence.

"Hit those Christmas lights," Spade said, and the parrot shot Liam a penetrating gaze as he mimicked the phrase.

Liam obeyed the order, then scanned the dimness beyond the glow of the tree for any trace of movement, no matter how small.

"Sit a spell, why don't you?" Spade rearranged himself in the chair as if to get comfortable. He was the perfect southern diplomat, but when he smiled, his eyes were flat.

Liam obeyed, thinking of the rarity of seeing Spade downstairs before noon with his trembling finger poised over the bottle of Hennessey.

"That's better," Spade said, then went silent, watching. He kept grinning eerily. The severity of his mood grew more transparent. "I would give every book I own to talk to Monroe. She always had the answers. I keep feeling she's just out of reach. You know what I mean?"

Liam gave a polite nod. Where was this going? The sticky air thickened with tension. Would Spade admit a confession of guilt to the charge of espionage?

"My sister was nobody's fool. I've always known that. If I concentrate hard enough, I can imagine what she'd say. You may think she was mild mannered, but she could be as fierce as a lioness when provoked."

"I take it she and you had things go sideways before?"

"What the hell are you yapping about?" Spade spat, and Kubla staggered to the edge of his shoulder as if ready to spring to safer ground.

Liam couldn't recall seeing Spade so worked up.

Something terrible must have happened. Maybe now he would confess. He might even announce the fellow conspirator who just disappeared into thin air.

Spade poured a shot. "Let's quit tap-dancing around."

"Sorry?"

He polished off his brandy and lowered his chin. "My highfalutin New York publisher passed on *A Spy in Paradise*."

The reply was so unexpected Liam blinked. "Why?"

Spade's frame was as straight as an arrow. "Nothing you don't know. I refused to turn my print editions into ebooks. Nor did I use social media for marketing my work."

Liam's comeback was an instantaneous crack he didn't voice. *This is your own damn fault.* And he recoiled before uttering, *what did you expect?*

More relevant, his temptation to tell Spade off proved unbearable. He bit his tongue to keep from speaking his mind. Besides, why lambast him when he was so low? It had never won him any respect from his father.

"I'm sorry." Liam was unwilling, with this turn of events, to mention his suspicions. He headed to the bungalow to apprehend the single person able to calm the storm.

He found Lucy bathing Percy in the utility sink on the back porch. She'd do well to brush his teeth while she was at it, but that was neither here nor there. The sexy woman, fetching in pigtails, short-shorts, and a tank top, yanked him to attention. He'd swear, with her look, she could sell rank to a five-star general. No denying she took "going casual" to a new level.

"Your uncle needs you," he said, rushing in to help speed up the dog-grooming operation. "He's in a bad way."

"What's wrong?" She dipped a cup to rinse the trembling mutt.

He had no words to sugarcoat it. "His publishers have dropped him."

Lucy smacked the water with a fist, splashing it out everywhere. "I warned him! He was a fool to think he could keep refusing to play by the rules. He—" She broke off, beads of moisture making her hair curl around her stunning face. "Damn!"

She whipped a distressed Percy from the bath and dried him with a towel. Liam picked up a brush to lend a hand. His flesh prickled, being so near to her. With every thread in his body, he battled her magnetism. He couldn't afford any distraction, not now considering the danger in their midst.

Soon, the trio hovered inside the kitchen of the teahouse. Percy took to his bed while Lucy trudged forth to handle her uncle. Meanwhile, Liam doused the butcher block with flour, conscious of the white dust swirling in the angle of light. A few minutes later, he was kneading the dough. Spade had gotten himself canned—the fool. If only he had played the blasted game. The worst might have been he gained a bigger readership.

Liam struggled to take his mind off Spade by focusing on the problem at hand. He'd monitored every shadowy figure who entered the teahouse. By listening in on private meetings, he kept tabs on Bennett and other politicians. Only by unmasking his nemesis could he learn how much intel had already been leaked.

To make matters worse, he'd just overheard a treasonous conversation under this very roof. Yet no one had showed up except Spade. Was there a hidden access door? Or was Liam going mad?

Nothing made any bloody sense.

Anxiety rose through him, and his hands shook. He punched down the dough, glad for the job, but it didn't erase his unease. His guiding star had dimmed after he left the military. Ever since, he'd struggled to regain his self-worth. This disastrous mission was his last chance, as he saw it. He judged himself by his accomplishments. If he must impersonate a poetry-loving Luddite to get a lead, so be it.

He took pleasure in maintaining a high standard. Even with baking bread, he waited for the dough to rise before breaking and shaping it into rolls and sliding them into a preheated oven.

He puttered with the preparations for tonight's menu while thinking of Lucy. Last night, she'd opened up. To him! He felt privileged that she trusted him. Things might soon end, and he planned to go back to the UK where his real life awaited. He set down the measuring cup and breathed in the yeasty aroma. Although he had played several roles throughout his career, he fancied the part of Liam James more than the others.

Liam James was a bloke who recited poetry on a train. He would create a parade or take a lady ice-skating. Picking out a Christmas tree wasn't unheard of for him. This Liam knew nothing of lying low while enemy bullets whistled around him. He still spoke to his father because this Liam was full of understanding and goodwill.

And before he had a chance to change his mind, this Liam was plopping the fresh rolls into a basket that he carried along with a jug of milk and a slab of butter into the dining room. This Liam lit the fire and turned to see the uncle whose world had crumbled after his publisher's rejection. And Liam nodded at the woman he'd kissed only yesterday. Yesterday, when they decorated the teahouse in a manner Liam Archer found too fussy for his taste. But Liam James liked the fanfare. The more, the merrier.

And this Liam took a seat. "Have you given any thought to publishing your recent manuscript yourself?" he asked Spade.

"Are you out of your mind? How will I sell it?"

Lucy's face brightened. "You have a fan base. Appeal to them by mail."

"But I have to find an editor, someone I can trust."

"I'm a good proofreader." A strange thing for Lucy to say. It was as if she quoted the wrong line in a movie. She tapped a finger against her mouth. "It's just that I want to help you out. Audrey's too busy these days with the newspaper."

Liam retrieved the pad of paper she'd dropped on the table. "Let's see. I'm sure the name Constance Spring, alone, should improve your chances of another publishing house, maybe a smaller one, taking the manuscript."

Lucy shot him a grateful smile, gathered three more tumblers, and poured a hearty splotch of milk into each. "Let's drink to your success." She raised her glass. "To *A Spy in Paradise*."

Spade's face softened at the mention of his baby.

"We advertise here in the teahouse," Liam said. "Make a banner. Set up a display."

"And you can do a book signing."

"We'll have a release party, give it a go."

With a gesture of his hand, Spade silenced them. "The teahouse isn't drawing in the customers like it used to."

"We need more publicity to gain a bigger clientele."

Lucy beat her fingers along her temples. "I say we aim for the glittering circus lights or climb mountains—a huge spectacle to promote Tea and Poetry."

Spade shrugged. "Do it up big?"

"Uh-huh, I've got it," she said. "We hike to the top of Sandstone Peak, the tallest point in Santa Monica. Once there, we entertain the other hikers by reciting verse. This time, though, we don't forget to pass out our coupons."

"Not a bad idea." But Liam guessed she was hoping for their performance to show up on video. He balked at the plan. He mustn't appear in any footage that might show up overseas.

"Tomorrow's Sunday," Lucy reminded them.

Spade swished his milk in the cup but didn't drink it. "I can keep things going here."

She nodded at Liam. "That leaves just the two of us. What do you say? Are you brave enough to tag along with me?"

He experienced a small bolt of warmth when she included him. "I'll rent a car." He couldn't prevent himself from enjoying the thought of collaborating with her. "We need to get an early start. Pack a lunch."

Spade said, "I will call in Audrey to help me. We'll

keep things rolling."

"Okay." Lucy raised her glass toward the ceiling. "Here's to moving mountains."

Chapter 12

We walked amongst the ruins famed in story
Of Rozel-Tower,
And saw the boundless waters stretch in glory
And heave in power.

~Victor Hugo (1802-1885)

The next morning, Liam insisted on taking Percy. "It will toughen him up, and it's not summer. He'll be fine." He fastened a lead to the dog's collar. "We'll just bring lots of water, and I'll drive so you can tend to him if need be."

He marched outside with the hiking gear. The cold air hit him, the chill of it gnawing deep into his lungs. Clouds hung low, the weather gray and gloomy. The rented Jeep clipped along at a steady pace. Its tires hugged the Pacific Coast Highway, but a turn onto a swerving thread of road made Lucy hang on for dear life.

"Dude, this scene isn't working for me!"

He stole a glance. "Don't you trust me?"

Terror glittered in her eyes. "Not on this patch."

"Do you think I aim to drive off a cliff?"

"It crossed my mind," she snapped.

He turned the car in such a quick motion that rocks rained down the rugged slope.

Her knuckle-white grip on the quaking Percy

denoted her heightened anxiety. "How much longer?"

"Look at that view. We've gone from ocean to desert in just a matter of a few kilometers."

"I want to live." Her skin was ghastly pale. As Liam pulled into the parking lot at the trailhead, she let out a "*phew*," then set her mouth in a determined line. "Let's tackle destination, Sandstone Peak." She disappeared into the loo with an overpacked Samsonite.

Upon her return forty minutes later, Liam's jaw unfastened. His face grew warm, and he dropped his stare to his travel guide. "We can trek out to the summit and back for a quick hike or extend the trip into the longer loop."

"I say we go straight to the top," she said as bold as sin. "No messing around."

"I'm not sure." He had to stall her. "Most people recommend the counterclockwise circle. That adds more mileage, making the 505 meters elevation gain much more gradual. If we travel counterclockwise, we'll reach the crest in 7.2 kilometers instead of the 3.2 kilometers on the clockwise loop."

"I can handle the quicker stride." She sent him a narrowed, glittering stare. "Can you?"

He was gobsmacked, suspecting Lucy had never climbed a mountain in her life. She'd emerged from the loo dressed to kill. She wanted to impress, he figured. But sandals with wood wedge heels? He wagered she didn't own a pair of practical shoes. And hiking boots were not on her radar. But how could she conquer a mountain in those platforms?

She was wearing denim—he would give her that. But it was a tiny jean skirt. If the crazy bird had any sense, she would add a parka, not the shawl she whipped out of her tote. What was the lass thinking? They hadn't scheduled a helicopter to drop her on the summit so a photographer could snap her picture. He must dissuade her straightaway before she ended up breaking her ankle or worse.

Because of this, he measured his response. "I'm not sure I can make it."

The dog started ahead, adhering to the clockwise path—of all the rotten timing for him to break out of his mold.

A smile tugged the corners of Lucy's mouth. "Say your prayers, buddy boy. Percy the lionhearted is leading the way."

"Let's just hope we don't fall down any rabbit holes."

She lifted her sharp-boned face to the sky. The wind reacted by yanking tendrils away from her hairline, and she looked at ease. Her collar flapped open and offered a scandalous shot of heaven. Those sexual fantasies he'd kept in check surfaced with a vengeance.

He flashed back to last Friday, over the fact they'd gotten on so oddly well. The way they both jumped yesterday at the chance to be alone together. Now here they were, as isolated as Adam and Eve. He should stop her in her tracks with good lovin'. Turn this cock-up into a win.

The pooch didn't know how lucky he was, romping along at her side. Her moves were that of a dancer, with her strong shapely legs scraped by underbrush as her inappropriate shoes took to the path as if it were a model's ramp. A flock of geese launched with a clamor of wings from their grassy bunker, and she giggled while the canine drill sergeant barked.

As for Liam, gypsy guitars serenaded in his head. He struggled to drown out the distraction. Staying attuned to his surroundings was a must. A rogue warrior with any competence turned everything into a war game. Plus, he intended to stay close enough to catch her if she fell. And she could very well fall as quickly as ice off a dyke.

She picked that moment to call over her shoulder, "At least winter isn't the season for rattlesnakes on the trail."

"Thank the Lord for small favors." His stare darted from side to side. He had an aversion to snakes, not that he'd tell anyone.

From the trailhead, they headed north. The path climbed fast and was steeper than he'd expected. Her feet in those sandals slipped, rocks falling away. His heart gave a quick jerk as he caught her around the waist to steady her. Her scent, of seagrass and mint, clouded his brain with unsated want. He struggled to empty his mind.

"We'll be there soon," she said, sounding as chipper as a cactus finch.

Hikers were descending Sandstone Peak. He'd give his Glock to abandon the trail and pack Lucy off to where he could talk her out of this suicide mission. Given time, her feet would swell. He waited for her to complain. Her long-legged, hip-swinging gait in that short skirt drove him to grind his teeth with frustration. When she twisted around toward him, he noted no distress on her face. Only sex. Raw and primal. Just when he thought he couldn't contain himself, a group of hikers caught up with them.

A man nudged him. "What do you think of this?

No garbage, no traffic, no crowds."

Tempted to retort, "No crowds?" he sighed his displeasure.

More trekkers were joining them, but he'd planned for an audience. That's why they were here. To pump the teahouse, that was key.

When they reached the crest, both of them were breathless. In agreement, Liam collapsed with Lucy in the coarse grass, the boulders protecting them from the brunt of the wind. They enjoyed a cold beer from his backpack. The overcast day prevented the views they'd hoped for, but the sight of the Santa Monica Mountains with their smaller peaks here and there was still mind-blowing. The sagebrush and rock formations were so small against the vast grayness that he felt no bigger than a pebble on a giant's shoe.

He lay back on his elbows, and the cold penetrated through his jacket. Lucy sat forward, her chin on her knees, as if working up her nerve. Fear was not a trait he'd labeled her with when they met. After living with Lucinda for weeks, he discovered she often acted more like the sister who still existed in his head. She was Lucy, but she was Audrey too. This variance, he supposed, was the norm with twins. Identical genetic codes all spun together as if a single person. It explained why Lucy doubted herself, why she wimped out when he least expected it.

He patted her shoulder with tenderness. "If you put your mind to it, luv, you can do anything. You know that?"

She got to her feet, which did not appear to bother her. She inhaled the mountain air and executed an exalted twirl, her arms opening wide. She looked so beguiling he wanted to swoop her up caveman style and pack her off to a private hideaway.

"These views are amazing," she cried. "Worth every step of the climb."

"Ready for the big show?" He handed her the program he'd typed out on a typewriter.

They found the highest point on Sandstone Peak, crossed their hands over their hearts, and proclaimed:

"O beautiful for spacious skies,

For amber waves of grain,

For purple mountain majesties

Above the fruited plain!

America! America!

God shed His grace on thee,

And crown thy good with brotherhood

From sea to shining sea!"

Hikers wasted no time discovering them at the tip. If any clandestine villains existed among them, they didn't show—no lone figure in a trench coat. No one was peeping from the sidelines, quite the contrary. People flocked to get closer.

Liam watched as if his being here now on this day in December in America were a strange dream. They recited a poem about Pike's Peak in Colorado, and he unexpectedly yearned for Ennerdale Forest back in the UK. Homesickness zapped him, leaving him weak and breathless. Still reeling, he welcomed the cell phones when they rose to record the scene. It gave him an excuse to drop behind a boulder.

Lucy continued to work the crowd, her skin vibrant. Children clasped her hands, taking excellent cinematography to masterful. Something about her existed in a realm beyond words. She led the group like a vigilant saint there atop the mountain. He'd never forget the sight of her, so uninhibited and free of care— maybe because of the altitude or adrenaline or the beer. Maybe a spot of all of it.

More hikers gathered as she went into a poem, called *Up-Hill* by Christina Rossetti, words that depicted struggle.

" 'Does the road wind up-hill all the way?

Yes, to the very end.

Will the day's journey take the whole long day?

From morn to night, my friend…' "

She finished to applause, and as he passed out the ten-percent-off coupons, she said, "Visit us in Venice Beach, and you'll discover how tea and poetry can make the world a better place."

Minutes later, they started west, past Inspiration Point to the Backbone Trail that then headed north on Boney Mountain. Lucy talked as they descended the slope. Her canine sidekick bebopped ahead of them. Liam had never known her to be so pleased with herself.

It made him grin. "You were smashing, Lucy Lou."

"I led the people, and they were receptive. You're always the one, but today you let me take the reins. Thank you. I didn't know I could do it."

Had he been such a sod that he hadn't seen she needed her moment to shine?

"I'm glad you stepped away to give me a chance," she was saying. "It's the same as the Christmas tree. You figured out what I needed, even when I was clueless. I had to perform on my own."

"Righto."

The only reason he'd allowed her to go it by

141

herself was he didn't want anyone to take his bloody picture. He was a fake and a jerk with a king-size ego. She shouldn't give him a second glance, let alone any praise. If he were a decent human being, he would drop her off back at the teahouse and continue his spying from a distance.

"You're the best," she said, making things a hundred times worse.

"No. Wrong." His esteem had sunk below sea level. "I'm not even a competent poet."

"I wouldn't know. You haven't ever recited any of your stuff. Only the work of others."

His stomach turned. "Nothing I write is good enough."

"That's pessimistic coming from you." She had that signature line between her brows.

"I can't help it. Now quit nagging."

The weather grew so dreary he zipped up his jacket for warmth. Despite the cold, his hands were sweaty. Lucy butted her way against the western wind out to a smaller trail to the left across a stream bed that gurgled and roared.

He caught up to her and turned her around, wisps of her hair forming a halo. "I'm sorry. I don't know what's wrong with me."

She gazed at him, her eyes trusting him when she should have kicked him in the nuts. "That's all right. You're tired. You never sleep."

"Sleeping is a luxury I can't take." It was the truth for him. He had been a soldier with a steel helmet and a heart to match.

"You drive yourself too hard."

Now he felt so bad he dropped farther behind her.

His footsteps were dull thuds as they descended the trail. She was a better person than he'd ever be. She was always honest, uniquely herself. No wonder she'd been the toast of New York. They should have started out using her star power to promote the teahouse. Instead, he, the two-time loser, had insisted on taking the lead.

He was sneering, but it was at himself. To be frank, he didn't deserve to share the same path with Lucinda Powell.

Chapter 13

That it will never come again
Is what makes life so sweet.
~Emily Dickinson (1830-1886)

When Audrey and her sister switched places, they'd traded phones. That was why, when she got a call displaying Madison Gray's number, she held her breath.

"Is everything all right?" she said after a moment.

"Why haven't we gotten together lately?" the friend she hadn't seen in far too long asked with her usual pull-no-punches feistiness.

She wasn't sure how to respond. "Things have been crazy busy."

"I see your sister's back in town."

Audrey rubbed her forehead. From the beginning, leaving her bestie out had felt wrong. But she and Lucinda had agreed not to tell anyone. Had Madison guessed? Audrey hoped so. She hadn't known the true meaning of frustration until forced to keep a secret of such magnitude.

To make certain the conversation remained private, she snuck out of the teahouse and stood in the moonlight. "Is there something you want to ask me, Maddie?"

"Have breakfast with me next Sunday, and we'll

discuss it."

Audrey let out a gasp of relief. "There's nothing I'd rather do."

"Say around nine?"

A week later, at eight forty-five, she turned the Lexus she'd borrowed back from her sister into the driveway of the ranch-style house. Excitement tingled through her as she saw the wide windows, and beyond it, the sky—pristine, cloudless. The sea through the trees shone as sharp as glass—Santa Monica at its finest.

Before she could ring the bell, the front door opened, and Madison pulled Audrey into a warm embrace, both talking at once. Harley, more human than dog and able to see through the disguise, nuzzled her with affection.

She dropped to her knees and wrapped her arms around the big hunk of love, her mind straying back to a few months ago. She remembered heaving a suitcase on the double bed in the guestroom where the windows looked out at the sea, Madison and Harley taking care of her, even Brandon doctoring her with yoga. They had been so dear helping her out after her mother's death she'd never forget it.

Now Madison patted Audrey's ridiculous head of hair. "This is so not you, my friend, that it's laughable."

"Hold that thought. I can't talk about it on an empty stomach."

Madison's own silky, red hair shone luminously around her angular features. Effortlessly smart in trousers, a blousy top, and garnet earrings, Madison Gray personified fashion sense and excellent taste. More than all that, she was so healthy and happy

Audrey's heart swelled with gladness for her.

Madison escorted her beneath the glory of cathedral ceilings and rough-hewn beams. "Brandon had a yoga gig. He won't return for hours, knowing him. It's such a spectacular day I moved our lunch date out into the sunshine."

The terrace was where the trouble had begun. Audrey had spoken out of turn. If she could have taken it back, but it hadn't been a choice. Now, because of the switch, Lucinda had experienced the shunning of social media. Her sister had dealt with it the same as she did everything else. She'd stood up to the jeers and fared better than Audrey.

With a slight hesitation, Audrey stepped out on the terrace shaded by an umbrella. She broke into a grin. The view of the sapphire sea, swirling white caps, and the sky as blue as a robin's egg offered a visual feast. She slid down to the cushioned wrought iron chair at a tabletop set with ivory bone china, ruby glasses, and glittering silver.

Madison uncovered a casserole dish with a heavenly aroma. "I hope you like cheese soufflé."

"Yummy." In glee, Audrey shimmied her shoulders. "I can bake a chocolate one myself. You should try it. It's not bad."

"Used to be boiling an egg was rocket science. We shared that shortcoming, you and I. That is until I learned the skill."

"I've gained a little culinary wisdom myself."

Madison's long lashes lowered, and her jade eyes flashed with skepticism. "Girl, you've lost weight."

"Well, yeah. Losing your mother will do that." She feared she'd ruin the lightheartedness of the morning by breaking down and crying like a baby.

"You don't have to tell me." Madison wasted no time with the seating. "After your mom's burial, my sister and I went to Baja. We conducted a memorial service, just the two of us, on the beach near the spot in the ocean where my mother and father disappeared. You delivering your mother's eulogy gave me the idea."

"I'm happy for you and Harper. I still can't handle the fact Mama's gone." Audrey snapped her fingers, her throat throbbing with pain. "As quick as that, you know?"

"I do." With her eyes moist, Madison said, "How are things going with the teahouse? Have you sold it yet?"

Audrey forgot she had mentioned putting Tea and Poetry on the market. "No, we've been trying to make a profit. My sister's here, and I met a man who pitched in to help."

"A man?" Madison leaned forward, her elbow on the table, chin in her hand. "Tell me more. There has to be more."

"His name is Liam James. He was a friend of my mother's." Unwilling to cross the line into saying too much, she paused. "He's a—well, he's what you call a—oh, why am I beating around the bush? You'll find out soon enough. He's a poet."

"A poet?" Madison scoffed. "Jesus, I thought you'd rather be tarred and feathered than get involved with one of them again."

Audrey sipped water from a cut crystal glass. "I guess I am a fool, but it's strange. If he composes poems, he never recites, let alone shows them to anybody. I can't say with any certainty if he is shy, insecure, or what the problem is, but I'd love to read a single stanza."

"Have you told him?"

"Yes, and he claims his work isn't good enough. Because I've gotten bits and pieces of poetry from him, I can't imagine even a nonsensical jingle being worthless. I keep feeling his inability to express himself has to do with his secrecy."

"Is he a private man?"

"I'll say. In shedding light on his past, he's a miser. But he isn't stingy like the others I dated. He got me a Christmas present. I wouldn't have discovered it, but I spied him sneaking it under the tree."

Madison shook out a crimson napkin, dropped it across her lap, and grinned. "Perhaps the man has written you a poem."

"I wish." Audrey snickered behind a raised hand. "But I doubt it. He's been avoiding being alone with me."

"Did something happen?"

"Last Sunday, we climbed Sandstone Peak."

"That's impressive. What's it like at the top?"

"Well, here's the funny thing. I got a bunch of hikers motivated by reciting poetry. It felt so good to tempt folks to set down their cell phones and listen."

"I get what you mean. People are terrible about giving up time on their phones." Madison gave her a thoughtful glance. "You used to be that way if I recall."

"I was." Audrey shook her head. "I just tire of our customers missing out on the poetry and the tea ceremony because they're distracted by an incoming call or text message." She sniffed. "I sound like my mother. She all but forbade cell phone use."

Madison chewed her french-grated carrots, shaking her finger. "That's what I do. When I schedule a meeting, I stand at the door with a box and collect them. I'll be hanged if I'll allow my staff to engage on social media while I am speaking."

"Go, you."

"Before Brandon, I couldn't live without my phone. I resorted to hiding in a closet to stay connected. But if there's one thing I discovered, it's that I am more at peace with myself by using digital devices sparingly. I'm living a fuller life."

"As little as a short time ago, I'd have argued the point. My poor mother. Whenever we got together, I complained about her reluctance to step into the twenty-first century. That's all I did was make a stink. Even now I have no answers. My uncle's Luddite beliefs cost him his livelihood. I'll help him in any way I can because I love him. We're pushing his recent book, a novel he's publishing himself."

"So you're working full time in the teahouse?"

Audrey had let too much slip. "Well—no. I'm not."

"I think you are." Madison wore an enterprising grin. "When I was in the neighborhood the other day, I hadn't seen you in so long that I dropped by the newspaper. I met your sister masquerading as you."

Audrey's stomach dipped. "She told you?"

"Not on your life." Madison laced her fingers together and stretched them over her head. "I guessed halfway into her second sentence."

"Because she's so much prettier than I am."

"Wait, no. You two look alike. There might be a few differences. I can't tell. It's just that you don't think exactly the same. She has grandiose ideas, but that's not a hindrance when you're drumming up ways to sell the news."

Audrey's conscience got the best of her. "I apologize for not telling you."

"No, I am not slighted. I wish you would have trusted me on that account, but I'm your friend, and I get it. Your heart's in that teahouse." Madison arched a brow. "Plus, I can't help but wonder if a certain poet hasn't influenced your decision to tough it out."

Audrey lifted her chin and observed a sailboat pitching on the waves. She'd just as soon drown herself than admit how much she cared for Liam.

"I see," Madison said, patting the back of Audrey's hand. "You've got it bad, sweetie."

Lucinda and Maddie always saw through her. "I sense Liam's hiding something."

"And you're not?"

"Well, I…"

Madison's penetrating stare cut through all the crap. "Have you told him you aren't a model?"

Audrey shook her head, then relaxed her shoulders. "I never in my life dared to really be my sister until I stood my ground atop Sandstone Peak. I can only describe it as a whoosh of air, a whirlwind, and something inside me broke free. A bravery I didn't realize existed in me—a passion I must have kept under wraps. I'd tell you it was acting, only it wasn't."

"Hmm." Madison drew little zigzags on the table with her index finger. "We go about our lives, and then a situation comes along to force us out of our comfort zone. And voila! We discover who we were meant to be. Didn't Brandon elude to this last April?"

A sense of déjà vu rippled in Audrey's head. The terrace, this wooden deck standing on stilts above the water, took on a surreal quality, the sea sparkling as if it held all the answers, and the sky opened to undiscovered possibilities. The images boggled her mind, and she grew dizzy.

She fought it by saying, "Although twins, we're as different as coffee is to tea."

"And yet you two are identical?" Madison pushed her plate away. "Maybe you both assumed unique personality traits as a way of coping with life."

"Hmm, I wonder if this switch might prove a blessing in the long run."

"I'd say so."

The morning offered a break from Audrey's long workdays in the teahouse. Being with a friend and being oceanside loosened all her tight muscles. Three hours flew by.

When she was ready to go, Madison packed the backseat of the car with books on meditation and spirituality. "You can't find a healthy weight if you're locked in overdrive—I should know. Yoga will calm you down to the bone marrow. When did you last take a slow, observant stroll on the beach?"

"I run my mother's dog daily."

"How can you compare running to a Zen walk?" Madison paused. "I worry about you. You remind me of myself not that long ago. Are you aware, if something happened to you, the world would keep on turning? The key to happiness is to find balance."

"I promise I will." Audrey kissed her friend's cheek, handed her a tin of the fudge she had made, then slid into the driver's seat. "Thank you for everything.

The lunch was scrumptious, the company..." She choked up with sobs. "I don't know what I'd do without you."

"Me too, you." Madison stepped back and waved. "Now get going before we turn into a couple basket cases."

On the way home, with time to spare, Audrey stopped at the cheery yellow bungalow where she'd spent many happy childhood hours. Mama had made Christmas treats for people such as her close friend, Gwendolyn Sharp. The visit consisted of tea and comforting stories. Before Audrey left, Miss Sharp produced holly for decoration and a sprig of mistletoe that she told Audrey to hang in a special place—to inspire true love's kiss.

Such a foolish ritual, Audrey wanted to attest. One that couldn't happen to her. Not with any man she knew. Especially not with Liam, as standoffish as he'd been acting.

****

Liam heard the Lexus pulling up and met Lucy so she wouldn't have to unlock the door of the teahouse. An excellent move on his part because her arms were full, and he didn't think she'd have been able to scrape up her key.

"What do you know? Liam to the rescue," she said, unloading the boughs of holly on him, then bending to scratch Percy under his chin.

"That's why the ladies call me indispensable." He dropped the foliage on the counter in the foyer. "I've all the right moves."

"Is that so?" She tilted her head, hands glued to her slim hips. "When you've coordinated your actions to go along with your heart, let me know. That's the trick, or didn't your mother ever tell you?" Pain shot through him, most likely detectable on his face, because she stroked his jawline and added, "Sorry. I'm prying, and I've hit a nerve."

"No worries." He removed the ancient Santas from the mantel and strewed holly there before replacing them. "Even Mr. Claus needs a place to crouch down in case of an ambush. One never knows where the enemy lurks."

Her shoulders lowered. "You're always using military jargon. How long did you serve?"

"Long enough to realize it wasn't for me."

"You didn't answer my question."

He sensed her agitation. And why not? He'd have to give her more to appease her. Only, the less she knew of his past, the better.

"No secret. I was in the army based in London." He turned away from her, wanting to prevent any further discussion.

"Do you miss London?" she fired after him.

"Not when I'm on this smashing vacation." It came out without thought, and he laughed, realizing the ludicrousness of his comment, but it wasn't London he missed. Lately, he longed for the untamed country—the dark forests, those wide, empty beaches, and the reed beds just inland from the dunes.

"Your vacation is over," she was saying. "You better increase your workouts on the boardwalk because I plan to feed the homeless Christmas Eve dinner."

"I don't understand. You need the money, not to mention the potential regulars you could gain. I had plans. I thought we could make candy apples for the tree, sell them. And we—"

She raised her hand, stopping him in his tracks. "It's not about how much we make or building our business. I say we give those less fortunate a fabulous meal."

"But now is not the time."

"What better season to feed the hungry?"

"This is where we disagree. The holiday rush only happens once a year. Do you want our prospective shoppers to go elsewhere?"

"Quit being a Scrooge."

"I never took you as a fool, Lucy."

She drew in a breath, bristling from top to toe. "If you don't like it, bud..." She pointed at the door. "Your home country awaits."

This conversation wasn't going well. If Liam kept it up, he'd be back in London in time for Christmas, but he would have failed his mission. Should he fight her on this and end up with a one-way ticket across the Atlantic, or choose his battles wisely?

He allowed a nod in concession, turned on his heel, and left before he said something irretrievable. *Keep a level head*, he told himself. Still, his stomach twisted in knots over the reasons he should tell her the poor would take advantage. He was protective of her. Stupidly so.

And as if to prove his inadequacies, the cake he'd baked collapsed. The lettuce froze, and the wine sauce tasted like something the dog fell into. He cleaned up the kitchen and swore to learn from his mistakes. To fall for a woman while working undercover complicated matters. For two pins, he'd abandon ship.

But an hour later, he was sniffing things out in the dining room. He promised not to quibble over their earlier disagreement. Crap, he hadn't meant to sneak up on her. The ingrained habit made him swerve off course. When he spied her tucked in the alcove and oblivious to him, he halted and drew to attention.

Ten feet from where he stood, he caught a glimpse of her thumbing through old LPs. She had pinned up her hair, but the arrangement wasn't the same as when they first met. Back then, her dos made her a sophisticate. A New Yorker. Now, as if ill-contrived, strands of hair trailed down her swan's neck. It gave her a sexier-than-Bardot look. And her face, that photographer's dream, held a secret expression he, with all his knowledge, couldn't decode.

As he edged closer, his focus centered on a sprig of mistletoe that hung from a ceiling beam above her—the ladder she had used standing between them. The term "honeypot" came to him—a honeypot was a female spy trained to lure and destroy men.

Avoid a woman who uses mistletoe as a decoy.

But his entire nervous system went haywire over her. What would happen if he slid all those pins from her silvery tresses? He remembered when he'd bundled her in his arms, her body molding into his. He imagined her saying now, "I'm sorry I fought with you." And he'd wear her down with his apologies, as best he might. And she would cling to him.

This interlude was his chance to make up with her, maybe the only one he'd get. It would be a harmless act similar to the skating rink. He should abandon the idea because, frankly, he wanted her now, wanted her beneath the mistletoe, wanted her against the wall, on the couch, across a table, atop the tasting bar.

With a proper dry throat, he faked a cough.

Her eyelids flickered as she saw him. "Are you still mad?"

"Nah." He moved the ladder out of the way and pointed at the ceiling. "I admire what you did there."

Her gaze shot upward. "I didn't mean... Don't you go getting the wrong idea."

"Never," he whispered. Then, unable to stop himself, he cupped her chin in his hands and stroked his lips across her cheek.

He caught a faint whiff of her neck and the sensual layers of secret herbs and magic existing there. The fragrance, as familiar as the woods of his homeland, mesmerized him. He ran his tongue over her delectable skin. The softest gasp floated from her lips. The firm pressure of her fingers pushed against his chest as if she wanted him to stop.

"I don't want you to blame this on the mistletoe," she said in his ear.

"The mistletoe is—" He brushed his lips over hers. "—a British ritual. Aye, a lad planted a lavish kiss on a lass's unsuspecting mouth."

"Seriously?"

"According to tradition, it's bad luck to refuse giving it a go."

His brain signaled for him to stop, but his body refused the command. He took his mouth on an exploration of hers, discovering the mélange of flavors. Lucy didn't immediately grant him access, and he became passionate to break inside, tongue against tongue. He took great pleasure in sampling ambrosial morsels, and she was no exception. To study various seasonings improved his palate. So why would she deny him that warm, soft mouth of hers? He needed to hold her while her scent intoxicated him with its riveting vapor.

Liam had only to end Operation Mistletoe. He was still in control. He'd stop straight away. More time, that's all he wanted. He touched the tip of her tongue with his own, to take advantage of the full monty there. If only she hadn't moaned savagely. She fit against him too well, creating tingling sensations of mouth to mouth, and, no, it wasn't resuscitation.

Every woman he'd known before flew out the window. His pleasure with her was more profound and more precious than he ever imagined. His order and his discipline dissolved into air. He experienced a sudden blind desire that took his breath away. He had to have more and kissed her harder, deeper, intending to kiss her all over. Then she was drawing back, moving in a different direction as he tried to empty his mind of her.

Panting, he said, "I heard mistletoe is hallucinogenic in small doses."

Slowly, her body stilled. "Well, that explains it."

To change the subject, he motioned again at the holly. "A little elf's been busy."

"Christmas isn't just about decorations."

"Agreed." He fought to steady his rapid pulse. "Father Christmas' visits don't depend on bling. He grants them to those who do good deeds."

"I want to accomplish something on the same scale as my mother, you know?"

No, he didn't, and that was killing him. "Your mum was a giver."

"Thank you for understanding, Liam."

And with these emotions came his need to shove Lucy into that secluded alcove where the mistletoe still awaited them. Would her face ever be as amazing in its sincerity, her eyes as intense and as dark a purple as time just before night?

She tapped the table with her ruby-polished fingers. "Christmas Eve's around the corner. Don't you think we'd better plan our day of giving back?"

"You won't suggest fake snow, will you?" He was unable to prevent a grin.

She gave his upper arm a light punch. "Let's have ourselves a merry little plastic Christmas."

"Aye, with an electric Santa and a fiber-optic Frosty the Snowman."

She clapped her hands. "Now those two would turn heads. No, I want to make those candied apples you mentioned, pass them out to kids who have never tasted one."

"We've got ourselves a plan."

And he'd go along with her, for her sake, he told himself. The truth? He couldn't care less if they pulled off a miracle. It was for her—end of story. Unfortunately, his thoughts, as of late, had little to do with espionage and too much to do with Lucy Lou.

Chapter 14

What crowding thoughts around me wake,
What marvels in a Christmas-cake!
                    ~Helen Maria Williams (1759-1827)

Audrey sat down for a second and looked around the Tea and Poetry. Just for tonight, the staff would treat the homeless to a superb meal on an upscale block. The plan was for Audrey to work the tasting bar. Do-gooders were on hand to wait tables while Liam and his crew catered food fit for royalty. This big bash was happening in a community where talk circulated of building a wall to keep out the urban campers.

"Greed, that's what we have right here in Venice Beach," Uncle Johnny commented that morning as they set up cafeteria tables. "Our neighborhood is now 'Silicon Beach,' home to Snapchat and Google."

"Don't large companies mean more jobs?" Liam asked with his foot in his mouth.

"Tech money is dirty money," Uncle Johnny shot back.

Audrey rolled her eyes. "Don't get him started, Liam."

In her mad hunt for another subject, she discovered the gifts under the tree. "Uh-oh. One of our guests might get itchy fingers." Her glance landed on the new packages, and a shiver flew along her shoulders.

"Where did we get the gifts from Mama?"

"I can explain," Liam said. "Last night, the temperature dropped. In my hunt for a blanket, I came across these on the shelf of the closet. I apologize if I overstepped. I shouldn't have fetched them without asking."

Uncle Johnny kneeled at the tree. "Monroe started in January and picked up Christmas gifts throughout the year."

Lucy got down and caressed each foil-wrapped box, tweaking the bows, checking the tags. "It's like Mama's only in the next room getting ready for tonight."

"She might have suspected she wouldn't be around to deliver them." Liam couldn't seem to keep from saying all the wrong things this morning.

Uncle Johnny looked up over his glasses. "Now what do you mean by that crack?" And the bard's parrot followed with an encore.

"I don't know," Liam said. "Maybe the wrong sort—"

"Mama could have had a premonition," she suggested before Liam set her uncle off with more of his assumptions. Lately, he'd been full of conjecture. She'd only egged him on by voicing her unease a few weeks ago. He'd been uptight ever since.

And Uncle Johnny's cheeks had reddened as bright as Rudolph's nose. "Time for me to get out of here for a spell."

"Just so you're back for the Midnight Service," she called with a laugh.

"Sorry, no. I won't be going this year."

"What?"

"Y'all go on without me."

"Mama wouldn't—"

The phone rang in the entry, and her uncle, being the closest, answered. "Hello?" His hand encircled his throat as he listened to the caller, and he reached into his hip pocket and pulled out a handkerchief. While wiping his forehead, he turned and studied Audrey like she'd grown donkey ears. He muttered something she couldn't hear.

He set down the receiver, his eyes iced over.

"Uncle Johnny, what is it?"

"Nothing." His face had gone white. "Wrong number."

"Are you all right?"

He zipped up his windbreaker. "I need a run to clear out the cobwebs." He left by the kitchen door, saying, "I might as well let Percy tag along with me."

She'd have thought he'd gotten enough exercise after putting in his usual five miles. Strange, he never included Percy. That was her job. Before Audrey, it was Mama's. In fact, her mom had been giving the dog his daily jog when she—

"Uncle Johnny?" A sudden sick feeling invaded her, and she raced into the kitchen to find it empty aside for a peeved Percy whining at the door.

"Well, that's as weird as all get out," she thought aloud.

"Spade didn't take the pooch." Liam sounded just as baffled but added, "He'll come around." The latter most likely made for her benefit.

Since Mama's death, Uncle Johnny hadn't been himself. But how could she blame him? He wasn't feeling all warm and fuzzy. Neither was she when it came down to it. Odds were Lucinda wanted to skip the Midnight Service this year too.

By early afternoon, the poets were practicing the poems they planned to gift to those who might not ever hear poetry. Miss Sharp brought in homemade mince pies. Olivia Ricci stopped by and drank a rare experimental tea imported from China, directing the show all the while. Even Bennett Browning, spruced up in a Santa hat, traded the comfort of family for serving the less fortunate.

Most tent dwellers attempted to look presentable. They sat at the tables, eating their fill, while she, along with the others, ran full speed ahead.

All around Audrey the shouts and laughter grew louder. The door swung open and closed with the earsplitting crash of sleigh bells. Children chased each other into the tree, sending it toppling to the floor. Servers, avoiding the fallen debris, rushed around taking orders, and the poets' voices got swallowed up in all the commotion. Her Lucinda disguise—a Valentino red that turned heads—didn't do squat when a father bawled her out because his son didn't get a candy apple. They hadn't made enough. By eight o'clock, the turkey and ham dwindled down to scraps. If it weren't for Bennett bringing in more food and Liam whipping up entrees, they would have been forced to close their doors.

He nudged her when she entered. "I see you ditched your daily uniform for a dress to make mere mortals bow."

"Thank you, I think." She searched the kitchen. "Have you seen my uncle?"

"Not since this morning. But you needn't worry.

He probably disappeared for a pint to get him through the holiday."

"Right."

An hour later she asked Liam to help her get an arthritic, old woman out the door. They had gotten her into the bus headed to a shelter when they all but plowed into someone with a scruffy German shepherd. Because of the man's dignified stance, Audrey instinctively saluted.

Meanwhile, Liam shoved forward as if he were about to wring the man's neck. Liam's aggression caused the dog to utter a warning growl from deep in her throat. Gums lifted over teeth sharp enough to tear a person limb from limb, and Audrey pulled Liam back.

"Hold up," she said. "The dog's not happy."

Liam balled up his fists. "That crook snatched my wallet."

The man didn't back down. "I had to know who you were."

"You could have asked. It would have saved me a ton of shit. Just who the hell are you?"

The man's dog tags flashed in the light from the streetlight overhead. "Got twenty years before I retired—Delta Force, a K-9 handler. Name's Sgt. North—Samuel North, Sam to you and your lady."

Liam grimaced at Sam. "You haven't answered my question."

"Been undercover here, me and my partner, Cleo." With straight shoulders, he faced Audrey. "We see us a shitload of unusual suspects patronizing the teahouse."

Sgt. Samuel North and his military dog seemed unbelievably surreal yet completely plausible.

Liam leaned in close and whispered, "Rather than

dismiss Sam as off his trolley, I say we go along with him. One never knows when a shot in the dark will strike a bull's eye." He allowed Cleo to sniff his hand. "So you've been conducting a stakeout, Sergeant."

The vet unstrapped a duffle bag from his back and opened it, exposing a pocketknife, a can opener, a green tennis ball, clove cigarettes, and several notebooks.

Liam whispered in Audrey's ear. "What a soldier carries tells something of what's important to him. Let's see what floats his boat."

Sam showed them logs full of meticulous details on the teahouse. The texture of the wrinkled pages told her he'd been spying through rain and shine.

She gulped. "What does all of this mean?"

Sam tore open a pack of Black Jack gum. "There're insecure lines, enemies listening to radio chatter." He offered a stick to her, which she declined. "I got my info eavesdropping on the grid."

Liam motioned Sam to follow him. "Let's take this up in private, shall we?"

Was he kidding? "Don't even think of leaving me out," she called.

Cleo's fawn-colored body pointed toward the alley, nose quivering, head stock-still—a working dog sniffing out explosives like Audrey had witnessed on TV.

Liam lowered his voice. "Most likely, Sam got Cleo when age forced her to retire. Handlers, by law, get first dibs on adoption. But was he once with Special Forces? By the hard lines in his face, I'd place him at the far side of forty. He might suffer from mental illness. That would explain why he's on the street."

"There's nothing sadder."

"We've got to dash," Liam said, handing Sam some cash.

"No turning your back on me, soldier. That's an order."

"Get yourself some food and shelter," Liam said over his shoulder.

Sam caught up with them and slapped the money into Liam's palm. "Don't try to ease your conscience. You cannot buy self-respect, Liam."

Shocked, Audrey grabbed Sam's arm and couldn't help inhaling the clove scent. "How did you know his name?"

Liam rocked forward, hands fisted on his hips. "Because he stole my ID and passport!"

"You're damn straights I did," Sam fired back. "And I'd do it again."

Audrey tugged Liam several feet away. "We've got to figure out a way to help him."

"Kill me now. What do you want to do, Luce? Take him to the teahouse and coddle him with kindness? Reward him for being a bloody thief?"

She led Sam around to where people were cleaning up the kitchen. While she handed Cleo and Percy ham bones, Lucinda made a plate of leftovers and set it before him at the table.

She wiped her hands on a dishtowel. "Have any of you seen Johnny boy?"

"No, I haven't." Because of Sam's speculations, Audrey's stomach lurched. "Did you look around for him?"

Her twin shrugged. "Girl, I haven't had a second to call my own."

She and Percy plunged up the steps to her uncle's

retreat above the teahouse. She called out for him in the darkness, then halted when a throaty voice answered her, "Here's the code. You've got access. Pass it on to your contact."

With a flick of the light switch, she discovered Kubla bobbing his head from the perch in his cage. "Here's the code. You've got access. Pass it on to your contact," he repeated the words from the manuscript Audrey had been editing, and her legs threatened to go out from under her. Uncle Johnny wouldn't go off without his other half. Not willingly.

Her heart beat too fast, too hard. No one would want to hurt her uncle. The fact was he often preferred his solitude. He liked to stroll the beaches, more so when upset. He would be calmer and more even-tempered when he returned—if he returned. Mama had never returned. *Mama...!*

She hugged her arms together, struggling not to panic. Although the police investigators had no vehicle to examine, it didn't mean the driver committed murder. *So come down to earth, Audrey Powell. Uncle Johnny may be a writer of twisted plots that center on KGB agents and terrorists, but he deals with fiction.*

With a racing heart, she hurried back to the kitchen where she found her sister.

"We have to head out," Lucinda said, "if we want to keep Mama's tradition of ringing in Christmas with the Midnight Service."

She was about to alert her twin. But why get her sister aboard with her fear? Instead, she grabbed hold of Liam and asked him to accompany them. He agreed and comforted Percy. She got the dog settled and thanked the volunteers for remaining to finish up. The last thing she noted before leaving was Sam wolfing down his food. Just what was his story?

When she left the teahouse, slipping on a lightweight jacket, the moon shimmered like a sickle slung into the sky. The trio piled into her Lexus. The ebbing tide revealed the sweep of beaches, and Audrey squinted, on the lookout for any trace of her uncle. Seabirds flew, skimming the shore. A star fell in a streak of light through the darkness. Soon, the cathedral rose—a beacon glowing in the night.

The lamp-lit parking lot held the arriving cars and families walking, the congregation bearing down on the church. Voices rang out, neighbors greeting each other, falling into step as they made their way across the street.

"Audrey!"

Friends gathered around Lucinda, believing they were addressing the other twin.

"Merry Christmas," they said. "I've never seen you looking so well."

Audrey, as the femme fatale from New York, got a silent handshake or two. She approached the church and sighed. Why hadn't she appreciated her modest popularity when she had it? Another tale of not knowing what she had until it was gone.

Her twin stalked by her. "We're early enough to find a pew to fit the three of us."

A man handed her a program, and she thanked him. A rush of joy caught her breath at the sight near the altar—the Christmas tree ablaze with starry lights. Lucinda pointed and uttered her appreciation as only she could. All the talk faded when the pipe organ played. The music came from the loft above and behind them. The notes swelled, trailed out to fill the walls with a stamp so recognizable Audrey didn't need to turn to see the organist. She didn't have to look down at her program either. Only Uncle Johnny could play to a packed house with such style. Her sister grabbed her hand, Liam the other, as their voices raised in song.

"Hark! The herald angels sing,
'Glory to the newborn king…' "

As the hymn continued in all its vigor, Audrey recalled that the regular organist had been pregnant. Had she gone into labor? Could be. Perhaps a Christmas baby, but whatever the reason, Uncle Johnny had taken her place. This arrangement must have occurred when he'd answered the phone that morning.

Many gathered to celebrate the birth of the Christ child. For now Audrey let the absurdity of spies and traitors fade from her mind. Instead, she clasped her hands together in prayer. Perhaps spreading holly, hanging mistletoe, and even drinking tea were all part of some bigger and brighter picture.

When we lose tradition, we drain ourselves and forget who we are, Mama had written on that little index card.

By attending the Midnight Service, Audrey experienced a sense of not only who she was but of the value of ritual in her life.

Liam patted her thigh. "I told you your uncle would come around."

She nodded. "It looks like he's not the only one."

Chapter 15

She walks in beauty, like the night
Of cloudless climes and starry skies;
And all that's best of dark and bright
Meet in her aspect and her eyes.
                                        ~Lord Byron (1788-1824)

When Liam went to bed didn't matter. His body, used to the military, knew only to rise before civilians. He slogged into his workout clothes, his head drooping with fatigue, and summoned Percy on the way out. They dogtrotted by the shopfronts and alleyways snoozing at the break of day.

Soon, the sun shone on a sea rocking with white caps and dappled with an occasional fishing boat or a diehard surfer. The boardwalk was oddly quiet. Liam followed a cautious Percy down the deserted street. In Liam's exhausted state, his mind got stuck on last night's confrontation with Sam.

What about the salty veteran? Assuming Sam wasn't crackers, why had he contacted them? His notebooks could contain a goldmine of information, maybe enough to crack the case.

On the way back to the home front, Liam noticed a street sign that said, *Venice Beach. Your Adventure Awaits.*

Wasn't that the truth? Never a dull moment,

especially when the aroma of coffee lured him. What he wouldn't give for a slug of caffeine. Before he was aware of what hit him, he held a double expresso caramel macchiato in his hands. Eons had passed with him pretending to fancy tea. All that time, he'd longed for his number-one vice. Tiptoeing around the bungalow's exterior, he intended on savoring the drink this side of Heaven before hiding the empty cup at the bottom of the rubbish. He stole into the kitchen like a cat burglar, then froze when someone tapped him on the shoulder. *Shit!* Burning the midnight oil didn't prevent Spade from getting up with the chickens.

"I took you for a tea addict," Spade said.

"Aye. I am. Totally." Liam wasn't sure how to adlib, not with his heart jackhammering. "But today…" He came to a dead stop when he noticed the kitchen. "What the bloody hell?"

"I'm preparing a meal I got from the rooftop of the world."

Was that an explanation for the massacre from counter to tabletop? Potatoes rolled over chickpeas and beans, and the pressure cooker had shot some gooey crap at the ceiling. Sacks had spilled over with millet, barley, and buckwheat flour. A mysterious leafy vegetable hung limply from a colander. Apricots and apples, fresh and sun-dried, huddled around a block of cheese. Blood-red wine splashed on the butcher block after Spade had set down his glass with a little too much gusto.

"Are you cooking breakfast?" Liam asked as offhandedly as he could under the circumstances.

Spade stirred some brownish goo with a wooden spoon. "I am making us a Christmas dinner that comes straight from the hearts and souls of the people of Shangri-La."

Heaven help us, Spade has gotten his groove back.

"I see." This holocaust came from somewhere, but Liam found it hard to imagine it was Shangri-La.

"Whenever my expeditions in the 1970s come to mind, I have the urge to retreat to those dark, snowcapped rock monuments of Rakaposhi. Consider, if you will, the charm that exists in a society devoid of any threat. With the Hunzas, one feels free from depression, secluded from everything but the loving and caring civilization. There, where fear doesn't exist, and people live in peace and harmony, I met my first love. You can forget all else but not your first love. You know?"

Damn if Spade hadn't caught Liam's interest. "I do."

"This land existed on the borders of China, Kashmir, and India, which made it an easy target for recruitment operations. As in my novel *Palace of Gold and Treason*. I got acquainted with their princess, my heroine, while conducting research. She was a kickass beauty. You catch my drift?"

"Aye, I do." Lucy, Lucy Lou.

The morning passed with Spade cooking and Liam inching behind to clean up after him. Although he didn't consider himself a neat freak, he kept his kitchen in apple-pie order. By late afternoon they stuffed chapati, lightly smeared with ghee, with potatoes and chickpeas. He had just enough time to slip into a hot shower—which he direly needed—before mess call.

The twins showed up dressed like opposites. Audrey wore a neutral shade of green while Lucy titillated the eyes in a dress as fancy as a frothy dessert. Funny, Liam couldn't say with any accuracy when he'd developed such a sweet tooth.

As for the food, Spade's meal would have gained the respect of any gourmet's palate. They had plenty to drink and eat on a table crammed with bottles and platters. The informality invited everyone to chill, and the talk fell into a buzz of questions and answers.

As in Lucy's question. "How did the newspaper survive Christmas?"

"Fantastic." The other twin took a swig of champagne. "We did an article on traditions and what happens when we eliminate them."

Lucy's eyes popped open as wide as grapes. "I thought about that just last night."

Liam offered, "Great minds think alike."

No surprise there. The double-trouble brigade often operated from identical electromagnetic waves. A fortnight ago, the sisters had come up with the same "thinking of you" card for Spade after he got the boot. Who did that? Only the Powell twins, Liam suspected.

The journalist stared into her glass. "One break in tradition irks me to no end, and so I wrote about it. I consider it so lame when people post a single Christmas-card greeting on Facebook instead of bothering to mail a bunch out to friends."

Spade shook his head. "There goes social media creating lazy, self-serving SOBs. Is it any wonder people today are forgetting how to write?"

Lucy slammed her spoon down with such a clatter Percy jumped. "Print a story like that and you'll piss off most of the readers."

"Stop the presses," he said. "People can't take the

172

truth." He nodded at Liam. "What do you say?"

Caught in the crossfire, Liam hesitated. "I say…" He got to his feet, picking up his dish. "Now that we've finished eating, why not open presents?"

When everyone pushed away from the table, he knew he'd dodged the bullet, for the time being, anyway. Yesterday, they had brought the gifts from the teahouse to the bungalow for safekeeping. Because he wasn't family, he expected nothing. To his surprise, even Spade dropped a gift on the arm of Liam's chair.

He perked up with interest as they opened the Christmas packages he'd come across in Monroe's closet. Her choices might provide him with insight. But blimey! He'd have thought the book for Audrey about an overachiever should have gone to Lucy. Lucy was the twin who believed slowing down meant give it the gas. To confuse things further, Lucy received a title called *Jump* about skydiving. Didn't Monroe know her children at all?

He couldn't say as much. Instead, he removed the wrapping paper on Spade's gift to him. He found a slim, hardcover edition of *Chandler Before Marlowe.* A splendid choice—Raymond Chandler's early prose and poetry.

"I've always been keen on noir," Liam said, impressed and smiling. "Thank you, sir."

Now what would Lucy come up with? He got the feeling, by the shape of the gift, it was a book. She must have snuck past him when she purchased her uncle's rare finds. Sure enough, after he slid the Christmas paper away, he came upon, to his great joy, an early edition of poetry by Ogden Nash.

"Splendid," he said. "I can add this to my

collection." Before he went undercover, he'd downloaded everything he read to his tablet. Having a print edition was special, the smell of the pages, the classy look of the cover. "Thank you."

"I thought you'd like it." Her voice bubbled with glee.

"I adore it," he said, and the rest hung nearly off his tongue—*I adore you!*

She smiled the same radiant smile that had graced magazines. "Here's something special to me that I wanted you to have."

"What?" He cocked his head to the side, studying her glowing cheeks. He didn't even know what it was, couldn't guess. But if it were special to her, it would be priceless to him.

After opening the small box, he swallowed. "A pocket watch." It was plain and sleek, with a white face and black Roman numerals. Something he would have chosen himself for its simplicity. "Where did you get this?"

"It belonged to my grandfather. The Royal Navy in the British military distributed them to their sailors. The numbers were coated with radium so the soldiers could read them in the dark."

Audrey swooped over. "You'd better take care of that."

"Guard it with your life," Spade chipped in.

"It's the perfect gift for a Luddite," Lucy said with a mocking note in her voice. "Besides, you never know the time."

Liam pushed the packages he'd bought toward the Powells. He didn't deserve their kindness, he who lived in Monroe's bungalow under false pretenses. Running his thumb over the cool smoothness of the metal case, he recalled his father, and a rock formed in his throat.

"Lucy, may I use your phone?"

A single brow lifted. "You want my cell?"

"I have to ring someone. Be right back." He held up the timepiece, admiring the quality and craftsmanship. He felt so moved by her act of generosity that he choked out, "You shouldn't have. But thank you. I'll treasure this."

The foreign office had given him a wristwatch. A high-tech model that counted calories along with steps and doubled as a phone. It didn't come close to the thrill he got holding the smooth silver disk in the palm of his hand.

He stepped out on the lonely boulevard. The traffic light winked green. The sad wail of a saxophone drifted from an open window. Liam longed to relax with a few jazz numbers. Not in the cards, though. He listened to his footsteps on the asphalt. Sharp raps they were, as sequenced as a one-man marching band.

When he got far enough so nobody could see him, he inhaled a breath. His chilled fingers reached for Lucy's mobile and tapped in his father's number. He lost count of the rings, each ending in a slight hiccup. Hard to say if Dad's landline was working in the secluded country where Liam spent his boyhood.

The ringing continued. He kept listening, anyway. Did he want Dad to pick up the receiver and tell him how good it was to hear from him? Well, he didn't. Ten years had passed since he'd last spoken to his father.

On the way home, he thought about his mates. Did they ask themselves where he had gone? If he could connect with anyone from his old life—just a single person who would know his actual identity—it might ease that thorny nostalgia stuck in his chest tonight.

If he were still in London, he'd most likely still be seeing that woman. A physician from Devonshire belonging to a long line of ancestors who developed steel used in industry. No matter how hard he tried, he couldn't remember her name. Natalie? Lisa? In a flash, he knew the answer. Veronica. Had he forgotten? Or did he no longer care about any lass but the one who'd given him her heart in a pocket watch?

By the time he reached the bungalow, Lucy's sister had unwrapped the box containing the wind chime he'd made her out of sea glass.

"Oh, all the colors of the rainbow." She sighed. "I guess I should have gotten you something."

The twins might look alike, but they were worlds apart.

He had hunted high and low for the gift he found for Spade. The blank book was a leather-bound edition with parchment paper and gold-lined pages. "For when you write your poetry," Liam told him, to which Johnny nodded with apparent approval.

"Thanks a million for the incentive," he said, and it sounded like he meant it.

To pen Lucy a verse that belayed what was in his heart seemed audacious. It wouldn't please her. Besides, he must keep her faith in him as chief cook and bottle washer. So how did he keep his feelings for her from being on display? He bit back all desire and gave her something he thought would excite her.

"It's heavy," she said, her face full of childlike wonder.

"Yes," he admitted, "and you will love the color.

Guess what it is?"

"A doorstop to let in the breeze when I burn a meal?"

"No." Laughing, he shook his head. "But close. Guess again?"

"A gumball machine?"

"Wait until you see. You'll be so happy."

With a typhoon of wrapping paper and tissue flying about, she finally had undressed the box. "An electric mixer. Just what I always wanted."

He caught the forced merriment and the way her body had drooped. Moisture puddled in her beautiful eyes, and somehow, he didn't think they were tears of joy.

"Now I'll make the perfect cake."

"Aye, isn't it a beauty?" By the look on her face, he'd better sell her on the idea. "You can even knead bread. And don't you just love the sea-foam green color?"

"Yippee." She swiped at the moisture escaping her beautiful eyes.

Her sister was shaking her head at Liam with blatant disgust. And he didn't know why.

"Have I given you a dud?" he asked with a nervous shrug.

"I was hoping for something a little more personal," Lucy said, catching her trembling lip between her teeth. "Like a poem."

"I don't understand."

"That's the problem. You never understand!"

She ran from the room.

What the devil had he done? Even Percy had buried his head beneath his paws and let out a rattling moan as if Liam were the stupidest person alive.

Spade collected the discarded Christmas wrapping and shoved it into a plastic bag. "Didn't your mama ever teach you anything?"

"My mum died when I was quite young."

"Uh-huh, well, that explains it."

Liam slid the mixer back in its box. "I botched things up between us. She wanted a poem. I failed her."

Spade relaxed his shoulders. "Remember, words are free. And they last forever. Use them wisely when it comes to women."

He nodded and applied tape to close the cardboard. A half hour later, he was hurling the bag of wrapping paper into the rubbish barrel outside. How to handle Lucy, that was the question foremost in his mind. If she were a machine, he could figure out how to undo the damage he'd done. Computers made more sense than women. They didn't get angry when he pressed the wrong key. They didn't get hurt feelings when he made a mistake.

Determined to work things out, after everyone left, he marched into the bungalow and down the hall toward the closed door of the master bedroom. He wouldn't be able to sleep otherwise. He raised his fist to knock but paused midair.

Liam pictured her lying across the brass bed where, above on the wall, Chinese lanterns flanked a Dutch still life that served as a focal point. If he barged in, he'd have to weave around the many stacks of Monroe's books and periodicals along the floor. He'd wind up falling on his bum. And all for what? Lucy didn't want him. He lowered his hand and turned to go but dragged his feet. His room at the opposite end of the hall might as well be Tristan da Cunha—notably the loneliest island in the world.

The sudden sounds of Lucy's weeping welded him to the spot. This wasn't what he wanted. He had unintentionally injured her, and her tears wouldn't do. He couldn't take it another second.

His knuckles lifted again, but this time they found their mark. *Rap, rap, rap.* "Lucy, can we talk?"

"Go away," she said, her sobs stifled.

"I won't move from this door until you tell me why you're so upset."

"Leave me alone."

"Talk to me, Lucy Lou. I didn't mean to make you go boohoo."

"Stop it, you buffoon. It's too late."

"It's the magneticity of you that keeps me here…" He twisted the crystal knob and entered the dimness on the other side. "You, my love, are the disturber of my sleep, the catalyst of my dreams…you who walk the landscape of my inner world, I find I cannot yield to your plea…I must seek you or die from lack…you, my darling dear, are my everything…"

Her crying ceased, and he made his way through the dusky room where the lanterns cast soft rosy light. Her silhouette as she sat on the mattress was tentative, and he wondered if she would push him away, claim a headache—or that he was too stupid to live. He eased in next to her, hoping she wouldn't notice—that she wouldn't kick him in the ribs. As well he deserved. Gradually, she raised a hand to his chest and spread her fingers, neither resisting nor inviting.

He bent his head, his wavy hair falling over his cheeks. "I'll make you a featherbed in the dark of the forest."

Audrey lifted her chin. "Shut up, Brit."

He cradled her face in his hands. "If that's what you want." His mouth hovered over hers, then dipped to her jaw, her neck, and the softness along her shoulders. "I thought you wished for poetry." He was baiting her now, pleased that she shivered beneath the touch of his lips.

Her breath was already unsteady. "I don't want you to kiss me."

"Liar."

"The first time we kissed, you caught me when I was slipping all over the ice. I was vulnerable. You were a man, and I a dumbass. It shouldn't have happened."

"Aside from the skating rink and the mistletoe, I've tried to keep from coming on to you. I just can't help myself."

"Seriously?"

He could tell she was happy because she smiled at his folly. Did she feel the same level of lust he did? That idea made him crazy with need. "If we don't stop this in the next minute, I won't be able to prevent the consequences."

He had laid it on the line and waited for her to move. Only fair in love and war. When she didn't, his mouth covered hers, and nothing of the gentleness he used before surfaced. Holding back was off the table. He had never been a man to lose his head, and yet he was falling, his senses aroused, his need multiplied. Pleasure shot through him, making his hunger build with an urgency he'd never experienced before. Like a sensual tango, his tongue caressed hers, let go, only to begin anew. Each thrust deepened the taste of wintergreen and something richer, like crème de menthe, but more delicious. How long he had wanted her. Tempted by her from the start, unable to act. Until now.

With a groan, he eased away and broke off the kiss. They were breathing hard, and he removed his shirt as Lucy lifted and took off her chiffon Christmas gown. She moved her head back and forth in that funny little way she did when they had been baking all day in the kitchen and her neck had gotten stiff. She had always looked like a queen when she did that, and now here she was with her long, wavy hair swinging on her shoulders. He'd wondered all these months how she would look if he saw her behind closed doors, completely naked. He discovered, looking at her, real glamor went down to the bone.

Her skin was delicate and as fragile as velvet—that which she'd kept hidden from the camera lens, hidden from her adoring public. How did Liam get so lucky? Lucia—dear Lucy—in the flesh. Yet she wanted him, only him. The passion shown in her eyes as they darkened to deepest purple, in the press of his fingers on her breasts, and in the sexy way she let out that little purr in her throat when he slid them down her long, lean torso.

He'd grown rock hard, and it was all he could do not to take her. He slipped back some just to watch the woman who graced her presence on him each day, the woman he'd lusted after from afar. She gave reason to his new and shaky existence. She gave life back to him. He never wanted to lose her. He pushed aside the notion, knowing it was a dangerous thought, an inevitability. They had now. Forget tomorrow.

She touched his closed mouth, then reached for him and kissed him deeply. He was aware of the pleasures he'd imagined on many a day when the two sat thinking, planning another way to promote the teahouse. His partner—how many hours had passed when he wished to call her his lover? Now he wanted to make their moments together last. He thought she'd guessed he was holding back, kissing her lightly to prolong their lovemaking.

He took her breasts in both hands, squeezing gently, and it appeared to fill her with such unrestrained desire she cried out, and the sweet spot between her legs seemed to awaken when he touched her, making her quiver, causing her to say, "Oh no."

She couldn't go on much longer, and hearing her moan, he used his fingers, almost driving her over the edge. At the last possible moment, he plunged inside her, lifting her limbs around him and plummeting deep. Insecurity, doubt, it all dropped away. The earth changed its course, and the dark sky burst into magnificent, newly minted stars. He kissed her passionately, surrendering to unmeasurable pleasure. And when he exploded inside her, he shuddered, and so did she until, spent, they both lay still.

Chapter 16

O singer of Persephone!
In the dim meadows desolate
Dost thou remember Sicily?
~Oscar Wilde (1854-1900)

Unable to sleep, Audrey pulled away without disturbing Liam. She dressed, and with Percy acting as wingman, she ran into darkness blued with the promise of dawn.

By now she concluded that her former men were clueless about the female anatomy. During their lovemaking, Liam found places she hadn't known existed. Her body had become electric, her nerves circuits that turned on separately and contributed to the whole. She told herself his prowess in bed wasn't an issue. One blissful night didn't mean a happily ever after. A mere lapse in judgment didn't make them an item.

Memories, though, flashed through her head in a blur. She remembered meeting his gaze with hers, the sweet zap of seduction there. She had sworn off poets, believed she would live better without them. But for months, Liam had stuck around. During that time, she'd ached to hold him at odd moments—when he saw something that made him laugh, or when he took the phones from the tech-addicted teens. When the publishers dropped Uncle Johnny, and her rainy-day hero charged on his white horse, coming to the rescue yet again. Yes, his many kindnesses had sealed him to the center of her heart.

She hiked out past the boardwalk to the beach and yanked off her running shoes. She settled back on her elbows and slid her bare feet along the pebbly sand. As if aware of her meditative mood, Percy sat next to her and rested his head on her shoulder.

Together, they stared out to sea. The water was never such a fiery blue, the rising sun never as bright as it shot golden rods throughout the heavens. A surfer girl and her beau paddled out to catch a wave, the smell of suntan oil lingering on the breeze. The surf roaring in Audrey's ears caused a symphony of familiarity and insight.

Last night she'd initiated their lovemaking with her overwrought emotions. She'd put up such a fuss over Liam's gift—which was romantic when she thought about it in the light of dawn. Cooking, for him, was his happy place. He'd wanted to share his joy with her, and she'd turned on him. Big mistake. Her gut told her to go to him and fess up about her true identity. Show him all her weaknesses, tell him she wasn't supermodel material. She was only plain, everyday Audrey.

If they were to develop a bond, she didn't want any secrets between them. Love was about trust, and he'd proved himself to be trustworthy. So must she.

"Let's go, pal." She slapped a hand on her thigh. "Time to make things right."

She found Liam still in bed, munching on an apple while hunched over something he was writing. When she entered, he broke into a wide grin.

"Good morning, my love," he said with exuberance.

She dipped into the chair across from him, smacking her knees with her palms. "About last night..." She might as well get her news off her chest before she lost her nerve.

His face seemed to draw a blank. "Did something happen last night?"

She picked up an apple from the bowl and hurled it at him. "You!"

He caught it midair. "Hey, somebody's got up on the wrong side of the bed." He patted the mattress. "Why bother to get up at all?"

"Someone has to earn a living." A better opportunity to level with him might present itself later. "Have you gotten another idea on how to reel in the business?"

He shuffled through the paperwork on his lap. "I have me the hankering to see you dressed in cowgirl boots with spurs. Skintight jeans, a leather jacket with a fringe...we'll dance to a little bluegrass music under the light of the moon."

His words induced erotic images—the tease.

"Are you asking for a bruising, mister?" She sent some Lucinda snark his way.

"We have us a cowboy poetry contest, invite the locals, rustle up some grub complete with a blazing campfire."

She toyed with the idea, liking it but doubting its plausibility. "Cowboys? Here? We would need to resort to Hollywood stagehands. Venice is too urban, too full of beach hermits and hippie types. As far as an open campfire, they're not allowed."

Liam slapped down his pen. "Chucks," he said, like an Englishman imitating a Texan. "I still have a mind to see you dressed in nothing but a Terry Clark hat and cowgirl boots."

"Play your cards right, partner…" Now she exited her chair. Until she confessed she'd been an impostor, it didn't seem fair to bait him. "First, we decide the next best way to bring folks into this here teahouse."

"Hmm, let's think it over." Liam slid on the clothes he had shed the night before, clicked his pocket watch open for a peek, and moseyed into the living room. He set aside the Christmas records they'd been listening to yesterday and focused on another stack.

"I've got it," she said, choosing a title from Peggy Lee. "The Beat Generation."

"You mean beatniks?" He sounded incredulous.

"That's right. Like the literary clan from the 1950s." She remembered Venice's history—the "Slum by the Sea," which made the beachfront ripe for the counterculture. "It was a fascinating decade here."

"Well, I don't know." He slid a record down the spindle of the stereo, pushed *reject*. The arm lowered to the scratchy noises of a phonograph needle on vinyl. Soon, a woman crooned to the blasts of horns and the low rumble of bass.

"Think of it," she said, her hips in tune to the beat. "We can throw a party, advertise it. Tell everyone to slip into black clothes and berets."

He twined his fingers with hers. "I prefer the western theme."

"We dim the lights, serve wine and appetizers, turn the place into a bohemian shack. We'll clear out the tables. Toss big pillows and throws on the floor for people to sit on."

"That many pillows would cost you the moon."

She pictured the event in her mind and closed her eyes. "I picture black tablecloths along with drip candles in raffia-wrapped Chianti bottles."

"You and I will have to drink a lot of wine between now and then."

"Let's put up notices requesting each guest to write a beat poem. We give them a gift afterward of all the poetry submitted in a book. That way they won't forget us. A book can change a person, you know?"

"I love it when you get hyped about things." He traced her jaw with his finger, making her insides hot and quivery. "Your face lights up with such artistry I believe the good Lord hit the 'copy and paste' key after he created you."

She'd never mentioned who was firstborn, but she loved watching him adoring her. Loved the way his eyes clouded up, and how she became hung up on every little thing he said or did. If she weren't careful, they'd never get out of the bungalow. Plus, it was already after nine.

"How would you like some breakfast?" she asked, taking off for the kitchen.

"I'd like to have you for breakfast. Is that an option?"

She swayed to the beat on the phonograph. "Let's hear your plans for this happening."

"Sorry, all I can recall are the mods of the '60s. I'm not that fond of beatniks."

"Oh, I forgot. You were in the military. You're not in favor of protesters and rabble-rousers."

"I dig you, luv." He stroked her along the temple.

"Do you want me to keep my hands above the Mason-Dixon Line, or are you gonna let me go ape over you?"

"A girl can hope." A little Audrey Hepburn never hurt.

Somehow they ended up in the bedroom again where they began tearing off each other's clothes as if they couldn't get to one another fast enough. Her temples beat with adrenaline as his mouth crushed hers. He lifted his shirt and shrugged it off, and she ran the heels of her hands up his sternum and along his shoulders and found her urge to have him increasing by the second. Gone was any trace of their prior restraint or tenderness. They made love with a fever that led to an ecstasy of unanticipated delight.

Afterward, the two ate a breakfast of mixed fruit and fed grapes and oranges to one another, a provocative gesture. A slice of pineapple, a bite of an apple, each new edition topped off with a beat poet's line.

"Getting out of bed is a drag, man," he said.

And she snapped back with, "The future is a fake, Pop."

He leaned close, plopped an orange wedge in her mouth. "The race for space is a dead end."

She nodded, chewing. "There's blood on the moon."

And he quipped, "And that's a king-size drag, man."

She got so caught up with his playfulness this morning she didn't have time to worry about coming out of hiding. Still, because of the change in their relationship, she must come clean—fess up and tell him what twin he had just taken to bed.

Good sense, pipe down. Not now.

If she confessed to being Audrey Lynn Powell this late in the game, he might walk right out the door. Better to pretend to be Lucinda than to lose him forever.

Still, in that stored time capsule of her mind, her former weasel of a boyfriend drawled, "Did you ever think it might be something about you that drives men away?"

Well, she wasn't herself, now was she? She was Lucia—and living that life.

****

Liam coined the last Saturday night in January, "Cool Cats and Smooth Sounds." Just before showtime, he herded The Talking Tears behind the silk screen. The group, known for their radical thought, clamored to raise the roof with complaints against society.

What a scene. Guys and dolls sprawled at tables shoved against walls or lounged on floor pillows. Their beatnik getup, a consensus of berets, dark glasses, and black outfits, granted them license to snap their fingers—you betcha, Daddy-O! Blokes, a trio, played the bongos. Spade presided at the piano. A neon-green Kubla pulsed to the rhythm while couples draped their arms around each other and swung their hips in a sensual boogie.

Liam dipped into the epicenter of the body-shaking crowd, others so close they breathed down his neck. Unease sliced through him. To say he condoned antiwar poetry was a stretch, even for a man undercover. He battled the compulsion to snap and speak his mind, but as the music sank into his pores, it buffered most of his irritation away.

Bennett inched in. "This is your baby, Liam."

He had given Liam a first edition of the *Beat Generation Cookbook,* a rare tome with a hefty price. Grateful, Liam had added him to his list of mates. After all, who could find fault with a chap who booked a flight to Frog Eye, Alabama, to seal a deal on a cookbook? *Well done, Browning.* The recipes impressed with specialties created in the heyday of beatnikdom.

Liam waved his hand, and Bennett assumed a passionate expression as he stepped up to the mic and began his poem.

Lucy reigned over the tasting bar. God, he missed her since he hadn't seen her all day. Inky black tights showcased her long legs. A pencil skirt captured her slim hips, and a wide belt pinched in the turtleneck at her waist. She came across as that pixie in the bookstore, that undiscovered model. Her cat-like grace as she reached for a canister gobsmacked him anew. Those patrons on barstools swiveled her way, transfixed. Her devotion to the ancient tradition of serving tea earned her admiration. He couldn't take his eyes off her, loving all she stood for, and after falling under her spell, he found himself next to her.

"Promise me you'll wear that outfit later," he whispered.

"If you promise me a sample of your poetry," she answered in a liquid, sexy voice.

"Serve me tea, and I'll compose a bohemian rhapsody. Hell, I'd give you the heart of this British sod on a silver platter if it suits you more."

Before she managed a comeback, Samuel North appeared. Just the sight of the German shepherd, ears perked, sniffing the air, was enough to send the party goers far away from them.

"I don't want any trouble," Lucy said, "but no dogs are allowed in the dining room."

Sam crossed his arms. "You want no trouble? Let Cleo be."

"You're breaking the rules," Liam said.

Sam studied the crowd. "You want to catch somebody here with a weapon? Cleo was in Syria. Dual purpose. Patrol and explosive detection."

"Does the dog have superpowers too?" Liam asked. "Because that's what it would take to spot a terrorist among all these people."

"And you should know."

Stunned, Liam gestured for Sam to follow him to talk without Lucy overhearing. "I guess you've been stalking me?"

"If you count my watching you plant the surveillance equipment, dismantle it, and set it up again. Looked like you lost your mind."

"Whatever you say, Sergeant."

"I say the man at the podium flapping his jaws has never been deployed. He wouldn't know a grenade if a piece of shrapnel hit him in the ass. You and I are a different story, Liam. We know what it's like when an enormous explosion sucks the air from your lungs. When it takes all your willpower to keep your legs from buckling."

Liam waited for Sam to continue, but he went silent. "Sergeant, you okay?"

Liam turned and saw Sam's "thousand-yard stare." *Bugger!* He'd seen that look in the eyes of other soldiers, seen it in his own mirror. It meant the soldier wasn't in the present. He'd stepped headlong into his past, and that didn't mean an R & R in the Bahamas.

He reached out as if Sam stood on the edge of a skyscraper. But Sam glanced up as if he heard a plane, his face a study of desperate concentration. In his head, most likely, the ground concealed tripwires. To spook him would threaten the safety of others, so Liam hung back. His hesitation allowed Sam inside the worst place he could end up. The spotlight.

Once targeted, he dropped to his belly on the floor and crawled. He dragged his right shoulder, probably experiencing his flesh there rubbed raw by his strap that bore the weight of his gun.

Bennett slid in beside Liam. "I'll put a stop to this."

"Allow me. I've dealt with shell shock."

"Sam's my responsibility," Lucy said, moving toward him.

Both men restrained her. "Not so fast," Liam said, to which Bennett added, "In that hyper-aroused state, he's a ticking bomb."

Sam sat up and covered his ears with his hands, as if bullets were raining down, and as if all other sound was drowned out in the noise of artillery.

He cried, "We're all going to die!"

Crap. Double crap. The pillow dwellers were scattering like a flock of frightened crows. Sam shouted about a missile headed straight for his platoon. His body shook, and sweat stood out in beads across his forehead and upper lip.

Bennett squatted in front of North and clapped to snag his attention, and Cleo whined and licked her handler's face.

Sam's gaze darted over Bennett's left shoulder toward a crouching Liam. "Go back, Connor! We'll never get out of this alive, the bastards!"

Liam inhaled a breath to curb his anxiety. "Connor is somebody else—not me. You're safe now. The mates here are on your side. You're home in Venice, safe. The fighting isn't here. It isn't happening now. You're safe and sound…"

People murmured, some offering a helpful word, but most had split. Who could blame them? In these times, with so much insanity, they must suspect North would pull out a weapon. Instead, he returned to the present, his eyes clear and his features almost neutral.

Liam helped him to his feet. Although he'd rather shoo Sam out the door, in all good conscience, he guided him toward the back. Cleo stuck to Sam's side. Liam asked Bennett and Spade to take care of the orders of food and drinks, which had died off as folks dispersed, their discomfort a result of Sam's meltdown. Battle fatigue, or any label he gave it, scared the bejesus out of civilians. And rightfully so.

Lucy poured some water in a glass and shoved it at Sam.

He scrutinized her, running his tongue over dry, crusty lips. "So it's the uptown bird who took over her ma's teahouse. One I ran into on the street."

"Yep, and you're the army officer who has been spying on me."

Liam perked up. "He is, and he's got it all in a notebook. Remember? Would you mind handing it over?"

"That would thrill you." Sam wiped the sweat from his face with a napkin. "I'm bettin' you'd give a month's rations to get your hands on it."

"I suggest you cough it up. It's the least you can do."

Lucy bit her knuckle. "You just cost us big time. We're barely making it here. Tonight's gig was an attempt to earn some bread."

Sam uttered an all-done-in sigh. "Wish I could make it up to you, sis. I didn't mean any harm. Your ma used to mend me with tea and poetry when I got like that."

"She did?" Lucy sounded more curious than anything else.

Sam let out a long, raspy breath. "She wanted me, each time I stopped by, to show her a little something I had written."

"What did you write about?"

"What else?" His eyes clouded. "The Persian Gulf, Pakistan, and bin Laden. She enjoyed hearing about it. 'Tell me more,' she'd say. 'Describe the war in the desert.' By the time I left, after cups of tea she had called 'Tranquility,' I lost the nightmares. She had fancy names for what the herbs did. Said it targeted brain patterns. It worked like magic."

Liam suspected Monroe of helping Sam with his PTSD. "An enchantress with a mission," he commented with awe.

Lucy raked her fingers through her mum's recipe file box. "There might be a card."

Cleo laid her snout on Sam's lap, and he dug his chapped hands into her fur and buried his head there. Something in that brought a quick twist to Liam's gut. He'd been in Sam's shoes, trying his darndest to cope with the past—still did from time to time.

"You got to know," Sam said, "used to be I want to forget the war. Now I want to rip my eyes out so I don't have to see the things I've seen. Without my team, I walk this world alone."

Liam understood Sam's sense of desertion.

Sam added, "I was with Monroe the day she…"

"Died?" Liam, who'd been in sync with Sam, now supplied in shock.

"What?" Every curve of Lucy's body spoke defiance. "What did you just say?"

"I'd followed your ma. Somebody drivin' a rig tried to apply the brakes when she stepped out from two parked cars… 'Hang in there, Monroe. You'll be fine.' Used my shirt, tied it in a tourniquet, but she was losing too much blood."

Lucy batted back tears. Liam longed to stop Sam, whose eyes were also wet, but she deserved to find out what happened. Plus, Liam needed answers too.

Lucy shifted her weight. "Go on."

"Your ma was fading, saw that look in the desert. I covered her with my coat to keep her warm and held her hand. I kept talking to her so she wouldn't feel scared."

Lucy shoved away from Liam and gripped Sam's thin shoulders, leaning against him for support. "Did she say anything before she died? Anything about the goings-on in the teahouse?"

"She said, 'Sergeant, you keep writing your poetry.' "

"That's all she said?" Lucy shook Sam by the shoulders again, and Cleo growled a warning. "Do you know how lucky you were? I wasn't as fortunate."

Sam, being so agile and spry, could have broken

free of her and taken off, but he stayed put. "I'm guessing it's all in how you look at it."

She narrowed her eyes. "So how did you meet her?"

"She saw me one day in the rain and let me come inside." He removed his coat and rummaged through a pocket for a bundle of paper.

That's when Liam spotted the blood-stained lining.

"Here are the things I wrote."

Liam lifted a jacket from a hook by the back entrance and switched his with Sam's. "Well, you were privileged to have Monroe to encourage you."

Sam nodded. "She was the only one who gave me a hand. In turn, I watched out for her. Her brother traveled off to do his thing. That left her on her own. If I didn't watch out for her, who would?"

Lucy released Sam. "Sorry I got in your face." She lowered down and rubbed Cleo's shoulders. "We need some help around here."

Liam forced his body to relax. "I suppose you can help with kitchen patrol. In return, we give you a free meal, a little spending money."

"Why would you offer me work after I broke up your shindig?"

"Lots of reasons." Liam recalled Miguel giving him the job on the boardwalk. Why not help a fellow officer? He didn't mention any of this or that Sam had been there for Lucy's mum.

He took a long draw from a glass of tap water and stared out the window. His theories about espionage in the teahouse were unraveling. None of his hidden cameras or mics had produced a blessed thing. Still, Liam hadn't taken a look at Sam's files.

After everyone left and Lucy and he snuggled beneath the bedcovers, she broke down and wept.

He held her the same as he had the night they first met. This time, he rocked her. "There, there. Things will get better now. You treated the sergeant decently."

"You weren't so bad yourself," she said through her tears. "Talk about giving the shirt off your back."

"I didn't need that jacket." He kissed the top of her head. "I've got you to keep me warm."

Chapter 17

When to the sessions of sweet silent thought
I summon up remembrance of things past.
~William Shakespeare (1564-1616)

Lucinda yanked off the cardigan that used to be Audrey's and tossed it on the back of a chair in the kitchen in Mama's bungalow. The scent of talcum powder had replaced the wild lily perfume. She bore no hint of cosmetics. No notice-me heels or flashy jewelry adorned her jeans and sweatshirt. She pecked Audrey's cheek and plopped down at the table. Her eyes lowered in ecstasy as she inhaled the steam rising from the pancakes.

"You outdid yourself, Aud." As if to prove it, she plunged in, stuffing her mouth as if she just came off a seven-day cleanse. "I guess Liam is good for something." She licked her fingers. "Teaching you to cook."

Audrey grinned, taking pride in the fact she'd aced her culinary lessons. She spotted her uncle from the window and flung open the door. "Good morning, Johnny Boy." She went full-throttle Lucinda. "What's up, Kubla Khan?"

Uncle Johnny dropped a kiss on her cheek. "How are my girls?" He bent over the real-deal Lucinda and planted a smooch on top of her head. "A beautiful day, isn't it? Hard to believe after last night's train wreck."

And Kubla shuffled and screeched, "Who's a train wreck? You're a train wreck."

"Was it bad?" Lucinda had toned down the assertive inflection in her voice.

"Pretty much." A steel ball lodged itself in Audrey's chest. Her sister's temper combined with her uncle's passion held all the ingredients for a blowout.

Her sister plowed her fork into her scrambled eggs. "I don't think you invited us to breakfast to show off your cooking skills."

"No, I didn't." How to begin? "I, uh, have an update."

"Is this going to get ugly?"

Uncle Johnny finished off a pancake. "Afraid so, pumpkin."

Audrey doled out a part of the bitter truth. "Sgt. North suffered a flashback during our beatnik reading last night. It came on fast, and it was horrible. He was reliving the war."

Lucinda looked up. "You mean that homeless soldier dude who was here on Christmas Eve with his four-legged partner?"

Uncle Johnny gave a small nod. "The same."

Audrey allotted, "Liam jumped in to help Sam."

"And thank the Lord for that," Uncle Johnny said.

"God's poor excuse for a hero to the rescue," Lucinda said. "Who'd have thought?" When Audrey didn't respond, Lucinda closed her eyes. "Okay, so what aren't you telling us?"

"Liam and I have taken Sam under our wing... being that he stayed at Mama's side the day she— she..."

"Died?"

Audrey nodded miserably.

Lucinda shot out of her seat, the sunlight through the window haloing her face, the freckles she no longer concealed making her look way too young to be nearing the end of her twenties. "What did he say?"

Uncle Johnny rose from his chair, arms flat at his sides as he always did when he wanted to keep from coming unglued. "That's what I want to know."

Audrey forced out, "Sam said the driver couldn't see her because she came out between two parked cars."

"Fricking dipshit!" shouted Lucinda, flying into a rage, losing all traces of Audrey. "I went to the businesses near to where Mama got hit and offered money for a lead. I thought there had to be witnesses, and now you're saying there was one all along."

"Did the sergeant get the license plate?" asked Uncle Johnny.

"No, he didn't."

Lucinda punched the air with her fists. "Then what the hell good is he?" She gave in to her despair by folding her arms over her chest and rocking side to side.

"He was too busy taking care of Mama." Audrey let them in on the sordid details.

Her uncle's gaze probed her every word. When she got to the part where the vet tried to stop the bleeding, his face softened, and his eyes moistened.

Lucinda didn't budge. Gradually, though, the angry blush drained from her cheeks. She sniffed and glanced away as if to gain an ounce of composure. "Sam deserves our help."

"Liam took him to the VA hospital this morning.

He's hoping to get therapy set up for Sam, therapy and maybe a support group."

Lucinda rolled her eyes. "Why did he do that? And why have we taken him under our wing? Liam's not family. We don't even know where he wandered off to on Christmas when he disappeared with your cell phone—which, FYI, is not in keeping with his supposed anti-tech beliefs. He's a sneaky one. You had no right to give him Granddaddy's pocket watch."

"I didn't realize I had to check with you who never cared a fig about that timepiece. And FYI, because Liam served in the military, I knew he'd appreciate it."

"Here's the thing. Why is Liam working for peanuts when he's capable of bringing in six figures a year?"

"Because he knew Mama."

"Really? Did either of you see him in the teahouse? I didn't."

Audrey tried to tell herself Liam remained stateside because he'd fallen in love with her, but did the facts hint otherwise? "I never saw him," she conceded reluctantly.

"The trouble with you is you let yourself be bushwhacked by a poet yet again."

"Enough!" Uncle Johnny cried as if emerging from underwater. "Lucy Lou, quit taking out your frustration on those you love most."

Game over! The real-deal Lucy Lou wasn't the twin who fell for every Keats, Byron, and Shelley. No, that would be Audrey. She alone wore the poet-junky badge of shame.

The antique chair squealed as Lucinda dropped on it. "I apologize for not telling you Aud and I switched places, Johnny dear." She shot Audrey an apologetic shrug. "As earth-shattering as this may sound, it's not that I don't like Liam. He's grown on me like a pain-in-the-ass brother. I just don't want to see you hurt again."

"I get that." Audrey arranged her tea caddy. "The thing is I know what I'm doing." But did she? Her fingers shook as she clasped the tiny spoon.

Uncle Johnny set a steadying hand on hers. "When do you plan to tell Liam that the woman he is besotted with is someone else?"

Lucinda stormed inside their circle. "She can't. Don't you understand why? Working at *Powell's Review* is the biggest challenge in my useless life. The staff might call me bossy pants behind my back, but they see the growth in the paper's circulation and ask for new assignments. I can't return to being me, not just yet. Please."

Wow, and here Audrey had been tempted to tell Liam the truth. Good thing she hadn't. Audrey wished to reclaim her former existence—but reality check. As of late, she'd allowed herself a full-steam-ahead mentality. She'd gotten used to the limelight, had enjoyed it.

"We're committed to seeing this through," Audrey said. "And the truth is, Lucinda makes a better leader of the pack than I ever did."

He gave them a thoughtful arch of the brow. "You two are selling yourselves short. Can't you see? You both have what it takes."

****

Dawn broke as Liam lay still and watched Lucy Lou sleep. No, he wasn't on guard duty—even though he would guard her till the crack of doom, if that's what it would take to keep her safe. He owed her the truth.

But to open up went against his code. Secrecy was a habit as ingrained in him as saluting a senior officer in the Special Air Service. The SAS was a hush-hush force unit in the British Army. Its enlisted did not tell anyone, even after they weren't members any longer.

Unable to help himself, he traced the line of her million-dollar cheekbones. Her skin, as smooth as peaches, warmed his fingers. She quirked an eyebrow in her sleep, her lips lifting in a beatific smile. *A tuppence for your thoughts, my love.* All the tension in her face disappeared, and only happiness remained. He longed to stay with this woman, to grow old with her, but when she discovered the truth, all joy would vanish, and she'd show no mercy.

He dressed and tiptoed out of the bedroom. In the yard Sgt. North was drilling Cleo. Liam joined them later, blown away by Sam and Cleo's bond. Although retired from active duty, the German shepherd's workout included a tennis ball that represented caches of ammunition and roadside bombs. The canine who had once leaped from helicopters and parachuted from warplanes moved through the jade landscape in a manner swift, silent, and deadly. The very opposite of the scaredy-cat. Percy's tail *thump-thumped* the grass as if ready to live up to Cleo's example. Fat chance of that happening.

Sam cooed endearments to his dog after every successful retrieve. Who'd ever suspect the hardboiled veteran of coming off as sappy? His "Stay, pretty girl. You good to go again, darlin'? Seek. Bring it on home to daddy," cracked Liam up.

What would it hurt to take one for the team? Liam

rolled a tennis ball from the can and displayed it on his palm. "You see what I've got for you, bucko?"

Percy's ears perked up to the sky as his body wriggled. Could the dog change his stripes this late in his career? Aye, on the twelfth of never. They'd been down this road too many times before. Doubting anything would come of it, Liam swung his arm back.

Percy watched the ball like his squadron's survival depended on it.

He wouldn't yell, "Fetch," as he had always demanded before. Instead, he'd go with Sam's order. "Seek," he shouted as he pitched up, over, and out.

The pipsqueak sprang from his hindquarters, ponged across the yard, pounced on the ball, and clamped it in his jaws. He shot back and dropped it at Liam's feet. His tongue lolled out the side of his mouth in a goofy grin.

With a bolt of pure joy, Liam jumped up and down. "Attaboy! That's giving that ball what for!"

Lucy Lou busted out of the bungalow, her fists swiping the air above her long, slender body. She slapped a high-five against Liam's palm and collapsed to her knees in the grass.

Percy nuzzled her chin as she stroked him while gushing, "I can't believe it, punky. A milestone for you!"

He rolled over on his back and happily kicked, paws up, belly exposed. When he flipped over on his feet, he sniffed the ball and focused his elated eyes on her.

She tossed it all girlie, shouting, "Seek," and the terrier scrambled to recover it.

"It wasn't a fluke," Liam shouted, unable to

conceal his excitement.

She added with candor, "Whoever said you can't teach an old dog new tricks didn't know Percy Shelley."

Percy plopped the ball before them like he was born to wear a bulletproof vest. Liam didn't expect the kiss on his cheek from the woman with those ravishingly sensual lips.

She nibbled his earlobe. "You deserve a reward for your patience."

Sam grunted. "Christ sakes, you'd think your man earned the Silver Star."

"I've got something better," she said. "I didn't know whether to ask you to go with me, but if you want to—well, that's another story."

He imagined the two of them at the Santa Monica Pier—the carnival rides. Her holding on to him for dear life. The midway games...to call himself a crack shot wasn't a stretch. Fancy his winning whatever little trinket pleased her. A day off, didn't they deserve a break? Tomorrow they'd return refreshed and ready to take on his responsibilities. The best part, he'd spend the entire day alone with Lucy Lou.

"I want to be wherever you are." His stare dove into her God's-special-surprise bluish-purple eyes. "What do you have in mind?"

"A nursing home."

That messed with his head. And not in a good way. Had he heard her right? "Sorry?"

"My mother read poetry to Alzheimer's patients. I've never done it, but I thought it high time I tried since it had been so important to her."

"Isn't that a waste?" *Oh crumb, let her reconsider!*

She wove her arm around his. " 'The idea is to spark a memory,' or so Mama used to say." She squeezed his elbow. "Are you game?"

"I guess so." His guts knotted. He'd rather hit the reset button, return somehow to Pacific Park, make it a reality. Spending their one day off confined didn't cut it.

As if to rub Liam's nose in the situation, Sam said, "Try not to get too stoked, Liam."

The sign on the lawn in front boasted *Heaven Can Wait Adult Community. Home of the Best Care Facility Ever. Just ask them.*

Lucy Lou popped over to the desk, signed a guest book like she was at a party, and handed Liam the pen. He suffered an urge to reach instead for the hand sanitizer. Not that the premises posed a speck of dirt, with its lovely seaside decor. And the lady, all polyester and pink ruffles, couldn't have been sweeter as she escorted them down a corridor.

"You're Monroe's daughter," she yip-yapped where walls of cheerful Valentines competed with the reality of steel rails and the distant odor of bleach.

Liam glanced into rooms. Canned laughter wafted from TVs as oldsters napped or waved to them as they whisked by. These places depressed him. These poor souls no longer controlled their own lives. A fate worse than death to his way of thinking. Ms. Cotton Candy ushered them into a multipurpose room where nautical themes struggled to show themselves against daylight barely breaking through the window drapes.

"Your mother always requested we gather up the late-stage Alzheimer's residents. She didn't like to see them isolated from staff members and each other. She thought they should hear human voices and poetry."

These late-stagers, most elderly but a couple unflinchingly young, slumped on comfy striped chairs parked around tables. They had fallen down the rabbit hole—some more than others. One white bird of a lady mumbled to herself in gibberish only she understood. Liam's heart went out to the gent in a wheelchair near the back. His body had stooped with age. Only the military hat hinted at the glory of his former life.

Liam had been baffled when Lucy insisted they visit, but now he just wanted to bail. Today, he'd planned to collect intel from Sam. Liam didn't have time to waste with folks who weren't aware of what day it was, let alone find logic in a poem. How could they enjoy language when words eluded them?

Lucy unpacked her cedar-scented material as if prepared to teach a workshop. He must hand it to her for trying to live up to her mother's reputation, but she'd wind up nuked because she failed to rouse this over-the-hill gang. He didn't care for his arse to be on the line, but he hated it when she took a hit.

For a tuppence, he'd grab her by the waist and say, "One for the money, two for the show. Let's make a break for it. Now go, go, go!"

She smiled then with such cautious hope it undid him to his steely core. "I want to give these patients an escape from their muddled thoughts."

He bit his upper lip so as not to voice his doubt and nodded his acquiescence.

She opened her arms as if to embrace the entire room, then introduced herself and said, "With Valentine's Day around the corner, I chose some love poems to recite. If you'd like to join along, please do."

Even the bird lady declined to chirp. Unaffected by their doleful quiet, Lucy performed a Shakespeare sonnet.

" 'Shall I compare thee to a summer's day?

Thou art more lovely and more temperate:

Rough winds do shake the darling buds of May…' "

For all her effort, she received nothing in return but his surprised adoration. He could either just watch her—to thunder with the rest of them—or do his share. Man up and provide support for his lady.

He, with a gunner's speed, brought forth a Keats' poem associated with Fanny Brawne.

" 'Bright star, would I were stedfast as thou art…

And so live ever—or else swoon to death.' "

In conclusion, the call to action produced mutterings and scuttling in chairs. Not the expected response. The deadlock didn't detour Lucy from reading more. Most likely, all that poetry gleaned on her mum's knee kept her spirits from tanking. His military training couldn't compare. He didn't belong here. He saw no use for marching to destruction. A sinking ship couldn't change its course.

"I don't think this is working," he said without meaning for it to sound like it was all her fault. "We aren't getting a whit from any of these lost causes."

"Well, we can't just walk out and leave them high and dry."

She sounded a little desperate. Liam hoped she wasn't about to lose her cool, not when she'd been on the moon earlier. He didn't think he could take it if she became as defeated as he already felt. "Are these the same poems your mum recited?"

"Right now I'm not sure. I'm not sure about anything anymore." Sadness shaded her doomsday tone. "Maybe I'm expecting too much. I'm not my mother."

"Don't be ridiculous. With practice, you perfected the tea ceremony, didn't you? And, no, you're not your mother. You're you, Lucy Lou—the one and only. You got this, luv. You find the poem that shines a light in the dark."

She leafed through handwritten notes, pausing on a page her mother had bookmarked. "What about this?" she asked with doubt in her tone.

"Recognizable. A cinch this love poem will strike a familiar chord." But in all truth, he wasn't any too sure but added, "C'mon, wheels up!"

As Lucy read Elizabeth Barrett Browning, maybe out of exasperation, she shouted, " 'How do I love thee?' "

" 'Let me count the ways.' " The voice burst forth from the veteran huddled in the corner. With his arthritic hands on the sides of the wheelchair, he heaved himself to his feet and perched at attention.

" 'I love thee to the depth and breadth and height
My soul can reach, when feeling out of sight…' "

His delivery held no hesitation or mistakes. He ended with the poignant and eerie, " 'I shall but love thee better after death,' " then he lowered his chin to his chest.

A single clap broke through the barricade of fog, and Liam's pulse accelerated.

"Oh my God, Mama was right," Lucy was saying. "To memorize a poem is to eternalize it and take it with you forever."

Before Liam could talk himself out of it, he drew from the Mother Goose nursery rhymes he learned in the village school on the edge of the forest where he lived as a lad. " 'Monday's child is fair of face,' " he shouted. "Repeat it!"

A few of the late-stagers complied, " 'Monday's child is fair of face.' "

Liam nearly jumped out of his skin as he sent the second line out with fervor, " 'Tuesday's child is full of grace.' " When more people joined in on the next verse, he waved a hand toward Lucy.

A smile lit her face as she contributed with a lilt, " 'Wednesday's child is full of woe.' "

As one poem led to another, workers found their way to witness the feat and add a childhood lyric to the pot of gold. The goal was to bring back the past, and that united both caregivers and patients. In the late afternoon, the sun filtered through the curtains and illuminated the room. Time as linear ceased to exist, and just for once, everyone lived in the electrically charged moment. Liam never dreamed he would feel this incredible. Even if he rode the Sea Dragon in Pacific Park or busted a hostage free from a deadly foe, he wouldn't be as pumped up as now.

"Well, what do you think?" she asked after they had left and were driving on the highway parallel to the ocean where a sunset glittered like the queen's jewels.

"Our brains are a marvel," he said with awe. He didn't add to this. His sense of shock and wonder had rendered him totally speechless.

Chapter 18

The moon has become a dancer
at this festival of love.

~Rumi (1207-1273)

The cedar chest clicked open, and Audrey filled her lungs with its fragrance. If she possessed the luxury of an entire day, she'd go through everything. She longed to see each black-and-white snapshot and fading Polaroid, to explore all the sentimental mementos withering away. No, she didn't have time to spare, but the valentines so devotedly collected and stored in newsprint made it so she hesitated.

Next thing she knew, she was spreading the cards out on the carpet. Silk-fringe and lace-bordered paper decorated with cutouts of hearts, cherubs, and flowers. Some were held together with accordion-pleated hinges. Verses hid behind secret doors. Feathers, fabric, tinsel, and glitter added a nineteenth-century look.

Liam crouched on the floor. "Quite a collection that."

"Isn't it, though?"

"The calligraphy is an element sadly lacking in our computer-generated society."

"The sentiments of a true Luddite."

"This kind of poetry may have lost favor—the rhyming and sentiment—but it is beautiful, intricate, and it shouldn't be forgotten."

"I never thought I'd say this, but I couldn't agree more."

He observed the messages inside a card like a professor with a red pen. "Listen to this." A pause followed as he perused the page, then kissed the tip of her nose. "Do you mind?"

"Let's hear it."

"This is a poem from your dad to your mum. 'My love for you is such a quiet thing…afraid of your knowing…' "

" 'You'd be gone in a fling,' " she added with the total recall of an ardent fan.

Liam recited the next verse as if he'd composed it only for her, taking her hands in his.

She joined him for the final bittersweet line. " 'It takes two to find paradise.' "

A tiny beat pulsated in Audrey's throat. "The way you jumped in to help me with the poetry this afternoon, if it hadn't been for you, I wouldn't have discovered how valuable Mama's visits had been."

He embraced her, putting his arms around her and holding her tight. "Working together is always better than working apart."

"I love that you chip in even if it means you get your hands dirty."

"Didn't you know? I love getting my hands dirty." He glanced down again. "Your mum and dad did things in a big way. How about we use these cards to make Valentine's Day an affair to remember? I'm not suggesting we give these originals to customers. We absolutely do not. We duplicate them and hand them out. Fancy how it will go over."

"But we don't have enough time."

"It will be a team effort. Get your uncle involved, your sister, and get Miss Sharp to proofread. Bennett, Olivia, and even Sam will join in if we ask."

"Right, and we get the poets involved."

"And we'll hire people to help us serve."

The excitement welled up inside Audrey as family and friends joined to bring the scheme to fruition. If the project failed, it would mean they probably wouldn't have enough money to pay the taxes. She kept this to herself but suspected Liam had somehow guessed.

He ran a campaign of "A Two-for-One Deal." And he created a "Lovers Only" menu. With his ingenuity and his motto, "Love comes through the stomach," he cooked up a heart-shaped pizza. Also, heart-shaped sushi, not to mention his desserts. The names he gave the pastries made her laugh. "You're the Bomb!" and "Stuck on You" and "I'm Bananas for You," complete with banana cream filling.

A week ago, Bennett had dropped in to conspire with Liam on a plan. It involved a marriage proposal to a woman he'd known only briefly, a Rachel Bellamy. Audrey and Liam hadn't met her, which they considered odd. As the days went by, Liam acted cool whenever Rachel's name arose. That struck Audrey as strange, since Bennett had become "a dependable chum"—Liam's very British words.

Still, on the day when over a hundred million commercial valentines passed back and forth, having completed enough homemade cards to pass out to each customer was something short of a miracle. Love's Own Day presented a chance to preserve another dying custom.

Only on Abbot Kinney Boulevard in Tea and Poetry, where she had told Mama to modernize, Audrey was spreading rose petals across ivory linen tablecloths, dropping old-fashioned cards beside plates, and lighting red pillar candles.

To improve the quality of their food, she'd been working with local farms and growers to bring the freshest organic food. She was spending a little more and gambling her soul and praying for a gold mine. In Venice terms, a gold mine meant a spot on "the coolest block in America" as dubbed by *GQ Magazine*. And soon, the teahouse buzzed with a college crowd out on the town. Young couples entered for the fanfare, as did seniors holding hands.

She concocted teas to drink. Her intent was about that elixir of life—Romance with a capital R. Because of this, she came up with titles such as *Cupid's tea* and *Tea for Two*. She got so engrossed in her life's purpose she barely noticed her uncle leaving his piano playing. When he inhaled deeply of one of her blends, she leaned across the bar.

"Does it make the grade?" she asked.

"Ahh, yes." He smacked his lips. "Reminds me of a tea I had while sitting on a plush Persian carpet among cavernous sandstone walls in an underground restaurant in Kermanshah."

"Ahh," twittered Kubla Khan, "an underground restaurant in Kermanshah."

Even Sam wandered over on his kitchen break and looked out on the lovers. "I had me a good woman before I was deployed."

He appeared so sad Audrey said, "I'll make you a cup of tea."

The recipe Monroe had used for his PTSD was MIA. Audrey measured some Hawthorne for Sam's heart, a few rose petals to soothe the nerves, rosemary to sweeten his memories, and lemon balm for treating insomnia. The perfect balance of honey and milk added for taste. Her fingers tingled as she worked. Her mind slowed down—the planet tilted. And she could have sworn she heard Mama say, "Whatever you do, sweet pea, don't shove the mug across the bar. Instead, make direct contact."

Audrey placed the warm cup in his hands. "This one's for you, Sam."

He took a sip and let out a contented sigh. He drank again and broke into a smile big enough to claim half of his face. "You did good. This here is mighty fine tea."

She poured more from the pot. "Tell me about this woman you used to know?"

He stirred as if lost in the whirlpools inside the cup. "Back home, a long, long time ago. The girl there understood me. Understood what was in my heart. Love like that only comes around once." He glanced at her. "Am I making myself clear, sis?"

"Very clear." She studied him for a moment. "What became of her?"

"Don't rightly know. Her letters stopped coming." He took another swig of his tea. "I plan to take Cleo on an R & R. That canine deserves it after giving the best years of her life to the war on terror."

"She deserves more than a medal she can't wear. Besides, you could check on your lady, find out if she still feels the same way."

"Maybe so."

At eight o'clock sharp, Bennett arrived with his date—a classy brunette with a long, thin nose and humongous dark eyes. Lucinda had agreed to take the engagement photo for the newspaper. She hovered in the shadows, on the opposite end of the camera for once.

He, dashing in his charcoal-gray suit and tie, pulled out the chair for the future Mrs. Browning. She wore the bored expression of many of the new adults entitled to the world served up on a plate of gold.

"Happy Valentine's Day," Audrey said with a forced grin. Something didn't feel right. "I'll be your server this evening."

And soon, she wove in and out of their soiree. The lovely room, the soft lighting, the aroma of their mouthwatering spiced sirloin roast—all of it perfect. Just what the efficient Bennett had ordered. The bride-to-be pecked at the food as her future husband talked about feeding the hungry and housing the homeless. She seemed a woman spun from a posh linage, bringing to mind Frank Lloyd Wright's houses by the sea. Yale. Yachts and caviar. The ideal other half—or not.

Liam entered with the dessert, and Audrey's breath bottled up in her chest. The heart-shaped cake stood out, small but elegant. A rose-colored arrow harbored the engagement ring, the diamond throwing slivers of light on rich dark chocolate.

By the time the bride-to-be realized the significance, Bennett had dropped to bended knee. "Rachel, will you marry me?"

She raised her hands to protect herself from the flashing camera. "I hadn't planned on this. I had no idea you cared for me in that way. You've ruined everything."

"You don't want to be my wife?" Bennett sounded horrified. "Why not?"

She scowled at him. "I'd rather be shot in the head."

"What?"

She rose as if she believed she'd descended from royalty. "I'll take a taxi. Don't bother to see me out." She groaned the rest. "Get me out of here."

When the bells above the door punctuated her departure, Bennett got up from the floor, dropped in the chair, and rested his elbows on the table. "I've no luck with women."

Liam slid the ring from the cylinder. "Sorry, mate. You went into the battlefield, and you got tore up, but you'll bounce back after you think it through."

Audrey rubbed Bennett's shoulder. "He's right. There'll be others. You'll see."

"No, there won't. I don't deserve to be happy."

She couldn't stomach his hurt. "How can you say such a thing?"

Lucinda said, "You picked the wrong chick. That's all."

****

Liam should have straight up told Bennett the woman he hoped to impress wasn't into him. Her kind should come with a warning—*radioactive. Don't get close. Stay the hell away. Haul ass and go on the run.* Spying had its advantages. He'd discovered Rachel had too much time on her hands. Her affluence meant she had no limits. The party girl adored being hit on by ten other blokes. She also, just for sport, slept with the husbands of other wives.

Liam didn't report his findings. He didn't need detective work to know Bennett was a straight arrow. He'd graduated from Harvard Law School and taken a few years off to join the Peace Corp. He taught English classes in a Chinese college and also set up a resource center there for children. The fact that his mum died giving him life could explain his desire to better the world.

Bennett now staggered from the table, saying, "I'm gonna tie one on, get drunk off my ass."

Liam patted him on the back. "Don't go without me," he said, even though when he turned to look at Lucy Lou, his gut clenched so tightly he almost yelped.

The crystal chandelier cast her in hues of gorgeous. Her scarlet dress, minus the apron now, showcased bare shoulders created for cherishing. Rubies swayed and sparkled from her kissable earlobes. The resigned disappointment she directed his way made it so the last thing he wanted was to leave her. Valentine's Day was slip-sliding away from him, taking her into never-to-be-realized moments.

Those were his thoughts until Lucy's sister blocked the doorway. "Not so fast, bud," she said to Bennett, her hands on her hips. She had that take-no-prisoners attitude he'd witnessed early on in her twin. This one could also bark like a sergeant major when she had the mind.

"Haven't you ever heard of paying it forward, Browning?" she shouted.

He blinked, backing away from her attack. "Excuse me?"

She sighed the blues. "In case you hadn't noticed, the couple who set your plans into motion is the real deal. Don't you think they deserve their very own fabulous supper? This is the designated night for lovers. So why skip out on me when I need your help in the kitchen?"

He turned his head toward the nightlife outside the open doorway, then back at Liam and Lucy as if mulling it over. He nodded his decision. "I'm in."

Liam almost interrupted but realized Lucy's sister had detoured his mate from crying in his beer. Just as well. Distraction, the name of the game, turned out to be in Lucy's and his favor.

She appeared to get this too as she chose a secluded table. "Here we are."

Spade shimmied the 45 "La Vie en Rose," down the spindle of the record player and sang along to the lyrics as if he were in Paris among the cobbled streets and cafés. The parrot closed his eyes as if entranced, and the duo left into the night.

Édith Piaf set the tone. He and Lucy talked as they ate beef so tender a fork sliced through it. They drank a little wine and chatted.

All the while, he couldn't stop gawking at her mouth. Her lips shone carmine and were as lush as a valentine heart. Looking at her made his own heart sing and filled him with unshed poetry. Who would have figured he'd get hooked in a way he never thought possible for him?

Not with his past.

If Bennett had it bad growing up, Liam just might have had it worse. Now wasn't the time to sink into thoughts powerful enough to kill the mood. So instead of confessing his feelings for her, he joined in as she ruminated over the evening.

"The night went pretty well," she said. "We made the money to push ahead. Give us a king-size victory, and we're back on the map."

Hell, he didn't want to discuss the teahouse. "You're stunning tonight."

Her cheeks colored. "Thank you. You're not so bad on the eyes yourself."

"I've meant to say how impressed I was with the way you handled the Alzheimer's patients."

"And you came through like Superman."

"We made the A-Team, didn't we?"

"I'd say so."

He fell to the center of the earth just looking at her. Many had gone crazy for her around the globe, he recalled humbly. *Bugger!* If he weren't careful, he'd find himself on bended knee, begging for her hand with a "Will you be mine?"

This losing himself in her wouldn't do. "You have any ideas for our next function?"

Bennett served two crystal bowls heaped with chocolate mousse. The spring in his step spoke volumes for his altered mindset. Was the other twin responsible for this turnabout? If so, he owed her big time.

Lucy slipped a spoonful of dessert in her mouth, and her eyes narrowed into flames of purple fire. "I might have one last idea."

"I'm all ears." Actually, he was all hard. "Let's just hope you aren't thinking of putting on a beatnik jam again."

"Not anytime soon." She set down her spoon. "In Mama's notes, she mentions a venture that was a hit in the early 2000s called a 'Typing Explosion.' "

"Hmm, how does it work?"

"We collect portable typewriters. We'll find one on the desk and another in a closet. Uncle Johnny will lend his portable. That gives us three."

"Are we going to hawk them?"

"Not a bad idea." Her mirth spilled over in laughter. "Our mission is to dress up like 1960s secretaries and type a poem for each person who pays to come inside."

"You'll look smoking hot with big hair and cat-framed glasses, but I—"

"You host this blast from the past."

"An MC, I can live with that. This affair should be fun. Tell me more."

"The patron gives a dollar and picks from a file of subjects. Then a secretary takes a turn typing a single line before she passes it on to the next. They stop when they have written a satisfying poem."

"I like the concept." Liam fiddled with the saltshaker. "Each guest will leave with a personal masterpiece. Wow, that's better than fortune cookies. Even better than valentines. It might catch on."

"That's our aim."

He broke off a rose from the vase and secured it in the curls on the side of her head. The need for her, need to complete the night with lovemaking, struck him so sharply it robbed him of breath. Lucia. He had no trouble seeing the image of her tonight on billboards. New York's loss was his gain.

"Holy crap, I'm lucky." He brushed a fingertip along her cheek.

Sadly, he'd lose her after she found out the truth about him. How would he ever leave her? How could he not?

Keep focused. "Tell me more about the Typing Explosion."

"Three women sit at typewriters where we will have attached bells and whistles and horns. We decorate the teahouse as it would have been in the 1960s when there were typewriting pools. They have a set of laws they follow, which are not unlike pool rules. Here's rule number one. 'No talking to the typists.' "

"You're taking all the fun out of it."

"Plus, 'Please stand a minimum of a foot away while the poem is in progress.' "

"Again, no play, no fun." He laughed. "Can I get my dollar refunded?"

"Sorry, no. There's a no-money-back policy. Plus, there's no biting allowed, no shoving, no spitting, and above all, no horseplay."

"A bloody shame. I picture my part in this coming to a bad end."

"Typists reserve the right to begin and finish each person's poem as they see fit."

He shrugged. "What will happen if a chap doesn't comply?"

She bit her lip, as if struggling to keep a straight face. "If a behavior does not comply with these codes of conduct, your poem will be deemed void and duly shredded."

He mimed shooting himself in the head. "I'm done in before I start."

Chapter 19

When the grass was closely mown,
Walking on the lawn alone,
In the turf a hole I found,
And hid a soldier underground.
                    ~Robert Louis Stevenson (1850-1894)

The mercury dipped to sixty-seven. Rain dropped in huge splotches on the folks trailing in a line outside the teahouse. The Santa Ana wind roared down the boulevard without mercy, turning umbrellas inside out, whipping others from hands, and sending them skittering off down the sidewalk. All this atmospheric drama heralded the grand opening of the Typing Explosion. To Audrey's way of thinking, the storm marked the beginning of the end.

She no sooner entered through the back door than Percy looked up from his bed and barked. He didn't recognize her, which was understandable since Lucinda had hired a stylist to transform the women into the 1960s secretaries. Audrey's teased and sprayed hair resembled a beehive, yet not a strand moved. Her face bore so much makeup a simple facial expression seemed out of the question. When all this humiliation ended, she would need a palette knife—or a bulldozer—to remove the plaster.

To make matters worse, the outfit Lucinda chose

for Audrey didn't fit. Her suspenders slid off whenever she relaxed her shoulders. The Peter Pan collar scratched her neck. Her nylons bagged at the knees. Irritation thrummed through her, accentuated by the fact only she knew the Typing Explosion would probably be their last hurrah.

Another critical review and the teahouse would face bankruptcy. April loomed before Audrey like Rumpelstiltskin counting on her weakness. All Mama's gold turned to straw in her daughter's grip. In a matter of weeks, the big bad bank would score Tea and Poetry.

"Sorry, Mama," she mumbled as she took a seat at the rectangular table with the other two secretaries, the wistful Grace and the defiant Amy of The Talking Tears fame.

The clueless Liam winked at her. He wore a sky blue shirt with gray slacks that cast him as a hot-looking master of ceremonies. He threw a nod to cue Bennett, who then opened the windy entrance. People poured inside, and Liam tried to prevent the overhead screen that revealed The Code of Conduct from blowing over.

Didn't matter if his British voice held the chain of command in it as he directed the dripping wet participants to form a line before the three secretaries. Audrey's electric typewriter hummed like an Indy car before a race. Her fingers itched to end this fiasco once and for all.

Didn't anyone know she wasn't a lyricist? Her status rendered her a listener, a reciter of others. How had she let them talk her into this charade? Oh, that's right. A stomach bug had taken down the usual crowd. She was pretending to be her twin and praying to come off as a—*choke*—poet. A wannabe of the first order. Her Lucinda act couldn't help her now.

Just get me through this, please!

To her left, a card catalog contained hundreds of available titles and blank cards for participants to write their own if they chose. The initial person handed her his, along with a five-dollar donation. She zeroed in and plugged away, forgetting about all else but her current job. She typed a stanza. The man, a burly bear, bent over. "Can I see that?" he asked, and the trio blew their bicycle horns in his face, warning him to back off. Liam pointed his yardstick at The Code of Conduct.

"Talking to the typists is against the rules," he said.

Liam's soldiering would no doubt lead to their downfall. Their first participant would become fed up with the typists and tear off into the gale. But he just nodded good-naturedly and filed down the line. After all, these secretaries typed poetry just for him. The rest of the gathering remained politely mute as pounding keys clattered. A poem progressed from typewriter to typewriter until a typist deemed it complete.

The smell of the warm typewriter ribbon delighted Audrey. She sank her fingers into the ancient card catalog. Her mind fired off a new beginning. A seduction of sorts—the love she always felt for poetry made manifest. Her modest contribution to the whole proved worthy. She fell into the lure of clicking keys, punctuated by burping horns, chiming bells, the periotic whistle, and last, the wham of the official stamp—an assembly line of sound.

But did she believe at the secret center of this show lay serious writing? How presumptuous, yet each composition touched on the poetic realm she lived with all her life. Even a fractured phrase in her hands from another offered the spontaneity she'd known as a child. The energy in this wordplay, the sense of fun it gave her, now rocked her world anew.

Still undercover, the other twin adjusted the lens of a high-end Cannon. Taking snapshots rang her bell. She caught a menagerie of Venice's own forever. A Goth girl with silver studs in her ears and a nostril. A guy, his beard braided and beaded. The plastic gals from Beverly Hills. A dude with his neck loaded down by gold chains. A petite lady with a crown of braids, her bookish date.

On the other side of the dining room, Liam prompted individuals to read their poems aloud. Laughter and a sense of awe followed his call to action. Cookies arrived and were soon consumed, without a hitch. More folks lingered about to witness the result of the typists and to luxuriate in community.

After four hours, Audrey drooped over the typewriter, her fingers numb. They ended up having to turn people away. Liam insisted the group return on the following Friday. He promised the same secretaries would show up again. The talk dwindled as the gathering drifted off.

Liam picked Audrey up and swung her around like they were alone. "We did it!" he cried. "Everything went down without a problem. Nobody complained about not getting what they expected. The electricity stayed on. No one had a mental breakdown."

She laughed despite the cement on her face. "People didn't feel threatened to run for their lives. No hearts were broken."

The media called the Typing Explosion a collective

creation. The public clamored for more. As a takeoff on the '60s phrase "love-in," Liam came up with Friday's "type-in."

The sky was the limit as word of mouth spread, and each night saw poets fostered at the mic. The locals and the tourists packed the teahouse and ordered from the menu. Liam's recipes caused a stir. Audrey's teas provided cozy-in-a-cup, marking a pause in the day. For the first time since Mama had gone, Tea and Poetry made a substantial profit. Each triumph met with another. They hired an employee to watch the entrance and others to help cook the entrees. Sam saved so much capital he could afford to rent an apartment.

Meanwhile, Uncle Johnny self-published his novel. His enormous fan base purchased *A Spy in Paradise* by mail-order only and didn't seem to mind. Lucinda gave him an excellent review in the newspaper, and the *LA Times* followed suit. He held a book signing at the teahouse, which warranted him success. In a matter of weeks, a small press picked him up, and he swore his loyalty to them and became more productive than ever before.

As the teahouse continued to deliver, life got more relaxed—until one day at breakfast.

Audrey was looking over a wedding invitation she'd gotten in the mail when Liam started kissing her neck. He was making her melt like hot wax, and she reached up and ruffled his hair, wondering if it would ever be possible for her to settle down with this man she cared about—and a poet to boot, or so he claimed. He still hadn't recited a thing of his own.

"What do you have there?" he asked her.

She flattened the card on the table, enjoying the

way the embossed bride and groom felt under the side of her hand. "Madison and Brandon's wedding announcement. I am a bridesmaid. I haven't mentioned it to you because we've been so busy."

His immediate change of mood showed in his hardened jaw. "I don't know. The teahouse needs us to run properly."

His resistance annoyed her. "Did you hear me? I'm a bridesmaid."

"Fine. Then I shall stick around to facilitate."

"Are you kidding me? We've got employees capable of covering in our absence."

"It would be better if one of us keeps the fire crackling and the soup steaming here in the teahouse. Tell you what, I volunteer to stay back. I don't mind. The recent hires won't know how to put things right when it comes down to it."

"In my book, mister, the true meaning of 'put things right'…well, to 'put things right' means having a man I care about escorting me to my best friend's wedding."

He didn't even look at her. "The help can't solve all the problems that arise."

Audrey shot some tap water into the kettle for tea. Exact detail mattered to Liam. That's what she loved about him. His attention to dotting every I and crossing every T. Still, why couldn't she make him see how important his going was to her?

"Listen, I have to tell you…I don't want to appear single in the wedding photos." He wouldn't want her to either, would he?

"No worries." He sounded nonchalant. "You, my love, don't need me. I'm sure you'll be a knockout in the videos." He crossed the room to her, his expression all at once intense. "There'll be videos, will there not?"

"The reality TV cameras are filming 'the seaside bash' as Madison refers to it."

An instant of panic stole into his face. "Well, there you go."

"Are you afraid of being seen with me?"

"Of course not." He leaned forward, catching her in his arms. "Here's the problem. The universe is calling me to compose verse. Should I say no when life's sting is tearing my flesh down to the bone? Out of the question. I kiss the powers from above for making me the sort who'd give up even special occasions like a wedding to have a spare moment."

"You can create your poetry any old day."

"Writing isn't something I can stop when I want. Whatever I am, I can't lie to my calling."

She seethed with anger and humiliation. "You're full of yourself. I don't have a clue why you refuse to go, but I'll tell you this. I'm sure I can find some other man to accompany me, and it won't present a hardship for him."

She bolted past the kettle, blowing its cork, and into the yard without looking back.

****

Liam grabbed the kitchen counter with both hands so he wouldn't chase Lucy out the door. Besides, what would he say when he caught up with her? Rattle off, "I'm already beating myself up for my bad conduct."

In her way of thinking, he'd abandoned her. She had no clue his mug displayed on the telly would alert the paparazzi of his whereabouts. Plus, he could picture what headquarters would say.

Did you hear where they found Tech? Alive and well, taking up residence in a Luddite teahouse in Venice Beach. Undercover to the disastrous end.

He switched off the gas jet, and the kettle quieted. He should have invented a better excuse for not attending the wedding than an obsession for poetry. *Bugger!* He shoved his hands in his jean pockets, his shoulders at his ears. He'd let her down.

Percy sat at attention and stared up with imploring eyes. He tapped his paw, toenails making little clicking noises on the floor.

"No dice, mate. I can't go out so you can pretend to retrieve bombs."

The canine barked loud and clear. He didn't blink.

"You're killing me. Don't you see that?"

These last few minutes were already tough to endure. To watch Lucy in the yard by herself multiplied his guilt. He was used to seeing her tending to the herbs and the topiary, but after he hurt her, she slumped stock-still beside the pond. Usually, when they argued, she rang her sister, but today her shoulders shook. Was she bloody crying?

A minute passed before he could break loose from his self-recrimination, long seconds where his bare feet touched down on cool clover, thinking of all the hidden things he must reveal to be able to live with himself. He caught Lucy in his arms, his heart bursting against his chest. They were alone aside from Percy, who fled into the far corners and didn't return.

"Sorry," Liam whispered, kissing the scalding tears from her eyes. His face was hot with shame. "I'm such a freaking idiot."

"I—" she said, and he bent to plant kisses on her

sweet-tasting lips. The tremors of arousal struck him without warning. Her flower-scented body surrendered to his, and heat rippled under his skin as desire got the upper hand. He moved in to press his mouth against that super-sensitive spot along her neck. She shuddered in excitement. When she bit his earlobe, her breath whispery and steamy, he grew tempted to shag her right there in the emerald oasis. The fragrances of foliage mixed with her sultry sexiness drove him out of his head. If he didn't act now, it would be too late.

He scooped her up in his arms and, never taking his mouth from hers, carried her into the deep coolness of the bedroom. There she stripped off her sundress and thrilled him with the sight of her in her string bikini. A sudden temptation to tell her the real reason he didn't want to go to the wedding made him groan in her ear. The gouging pain in his gut drove him to fondle her breasts, to kiss them tenderly, and play with her nipples. The sensation of those hard buds on his tongue caused him to suck, and she cried out and arched her back. She pulled off his shirt and sculpted her hands over his biceps, exploring the muscles of his chest, stopping along his tight abs to remove his underwear.

With an apt hand, she pushed him backward on the mattress, and as seductively as a love goddess, she crawled on top of him and rode him. He moaned with abandon and later turned her over so he could lunge deep inside her. In ecstasy, she wrapped her long, lustrous legs around him. God, he knew every inch of her. She didn't keep any secrets from him. That's what he loved about her, her honesty.

More than anything, he longed to tell her his real name, blurt it out when they were both lost to euphoria.

But to confess could throw water on their lovemaking. Instead, he covered her with kisses and pleasured her until she screamed, her limbs weakening and growing slack. Given time, she gave him what for in her comeback as she mounted him again. Her face held that glow of good sex, and her eyes darkened to indigo. That awful feeling zeroed in again, to tell all that he concealed, and it built in him, climbed like a fighter jet on the wind, never to be contained.

"I…" He moaned as he felt his release—an explosion on a soundless battlefield. "Bloody hell, I'd go with you to the devil and back." What had he just said? The words had spilled out all wrong. How could he retrieve them?

She lay across the sheets, staring at the ceiling, tufts of hair like a silver aura around her face. "Did you say…?" She was panting from their lovemaking. "You'll be my date for the wedding?"

"I'm hardwired to give in to you." She was his kryptonite. He'd just have to make certain not to get his bloody picture taken. No videos. Above all, no TV cameras. "I'll accompany you to this extravaganza if you still want me to."

He kissed her lips, enjoying their slick, throbbing feel.

She switched over on her side and rose to her elbow. "My knight comes through."

He ran his finger around her nipples. "All the better to taste you, my dear."

"Talk dirty to me," she said with a throaty growl, and before he got to the third X-rated line flooding to thought, they were making love again.

A few days later, though, when Lucy had left to

have her bridesmaid dress fitted, he took stock of his side of the closet. Too bad he couldn't jet to London and choose a custom-tailored suit from in his wardrobe. A double life might work out better than losing his former identity altogether. He needed to spill his guts and get his past off his chest, but when? He knew the answer. When he was sure the teahouse posed no threat to world peace.

Liam had gotten Sgt. North to hand over his surveillance reports. "My observations," Sam said, "are coming from a vet who was in a bad place."

Liam flipped open a file and, lowering his voice to a near whisper, asked, "You no longer believe in your findings?"

"I believe I was on a high wire and seeing things below as distorted." Sam shook his head. "It caused me many wakeful nights listening for footsteps in the stairwell."

"Are you accusing Spade of something shady?"

"Nothing I can piece together. Occasional talk used to drift down from his apartment that gave me cause to question his loyalties."

Liam's chest tightened. He didn't want Spade to be the traitor. "Did you actually hear him mention infiltration into covert matters?"

"I thought I did at the time."

"And now?" Liam's pulse skipped a beat.

"Now I'm guessing I might have been hearing things."

Nothing Sam said sat well with Liam. The last person he wanted to believe capable of collaborating with the enemy was Spade. And Lucy? What would her uncle's disloyalty do to her?

"Perhaps you were mistaken." Now he was fishing, but he couldn't let it go. He remembered the inexpressible unease he'd experienced on hearing the culprit on the other side of the kitchen door.

****

On April first, the date of the dreaded wedding—April Fool's Day—Lucy left in the morning to take part in some girly tribal preparations at Madison's place. Thankfully, Liam found black oxfords of Italian calf leather to go with his dress suit. He took his time getting ready. His hair was perfect, and his shoes were spit polished to a mirror shine. He sought to make a statement—a man of impeccable taste. A good impression for Lucy's sake was all that mattered. These were her people, not his. He didn't know a soul.

After he gave instructions to the teahouse staff, he took an Uber to Pico Boulevard in Santa Monica for the wedding. His brain cranked into gear. He meant to stay clear of cameras of any kind. After he tipped the driver, he blended into the guests following the foliage along the sea-scented and bridal-decorated path. They passed a house and headed out toward the beach. For the first time in months, he wished to possess his mobile. He needed to do something with his hands besides fisting them. It made him look like a bloke with a chip on his shoulder. He tried for a pleasing expression, but he was sliding down the sandy hill.

For the record, the wedding spot couldn't be more perfect—beach melting into the cobalt ocean. The setup was all about nature-inspired staging—seashells, driftwood, starfish—with laid-back elements like the white-suited calypso band. These good vibrations gave the effect of a seaside vacation, with aspects of the

Great Gatsby thrown in. It was all going well until he ran smack into a TV camera.

His face flamed, and he ducked behind the closed bar. Crouching, he edged along. He should find a seat. But the photographers were out in full force, filming the group on folding chairs beneath the pitched tent. The high-spirited socialites preened as though they relished their appearance on the reality TV show. If he didn't care about being spotted, he would have chilled and fit right in, perhaps even struck up a conversation.

Uh-oh. The band was swinging into an upbeat number announcing the bridal procession. Intent on letting Lucy see him, he got to his feet and propped himself out of camera shot. Or so he believed. The first bridesmaid made it halfway down the aisle when, out of the fricking blue, the lens veered in his direction. He slid behind a hedge that faced the house. He stuck his face through the cloying, sweet, white flowers that allowed him to survey things unnoticed.

Lucy appeared, shimmering from the shadows, in a color of pink that did something wonderful to her complexion, rendering it creamy and rose at the same time. Onyxes swung at her ears and matched her black heels. She, a living, breathing dream, held a bouquet of roses in her hands as she searched the guests.

He wanted to stand clear and say, "Here I am, adoring you."

The rest of the wedding caravan became lost to him. His eyes blurred with stinging water. His nose ran. Of all times for his allergies to give him grief. The bride, a beautiful redhead, and her groom stood together in the white-curtained pavilion. He failed to make out what they were saying on account of the bees *buzzing* in his ears. His head pounded. He couldn't quit sneezing. He would have to abandon his bunker.

Whatever you do, don't let those camera blokes catch you making a break for it.

He started to leave the wedding but thought better of it. Lucy counted on him to be her date. Even if it killed him, he mustn't leave her in a lurch. In his former life, he'd learned the ability of coming off as invisible during enemy assaults. This slipping by the photographers should prove a piece of cake. Wasn't the wedding service over? To be safe, he let minutes pass before he staggered from the darkness of the trees and into brilliant sunshine.

As smooth as smoke, he fell in with the twittering gang of well-wishers. His head swam, and he felt like an adolescent who just downed a bottle of rum. He huddled in the corner and propped his elbows on the bar to keep himself standing. Then he saw her, saw his queen.

She came toward him, her silk gown slit down the side, and he got a teasing look at her long, slender leg. The fact that she hunted for him made him wave his arms. He noted the people, the gents, the ladies, everyone looking at her as if wondering who she was. He realized for the umpteenth time that he was a lucky sod. It made his battle with the cameras bearable— more than tolerable. He'd face a firing squad for her.

"Liam?" Her voice held a shock factor. Her hands felt cool and soft as she clasped his chin as if it were her most cherished possession. "What happened to you? It looks like you were in a fight and lost."

He swallowed. "Hay fever."

"My poor baby."

His appearance gave him the excuse. "Do you mind if I sit the picture taking out?"

"Heavens, I wouldn't think of putting you through all that." She helped him to a bar stool as workers whipped around them, setting up the reception. "Just rest here and drink a little water on the rocks while I'm gone."

Grateful, he nodded. "I'll be A-okay."

His desire to sleep now weighed on him as he waited for her. His burning eyes fell shut. He didn't know for how long. It seemed like minutes when he felt Lucy shaking his arm.

"Dinner," she said. "Don't leave me for the rest of the day." She whispered in his ear, "And night."

"A stampede of bulls couldn't tear me from your side."

With a playful smile, she swiped her black gloves across his face. "Be still my beating heart."

They chose from a buffet. She went for fettuccine alfredo with asparagus tips. He, in a daze, dished up a vegetable Wellington. His nerves, combined with his constant search for cameras, kept him from eating more than a bite or two.

Lucy patted the back of his hand. "Are you okay?"

"My stomach's a little out of whack is all."

When they finished, the bride and her brother started the dancing off with Louis Armstrong's "What a Wonderful World." Soon, other couples were joining them.

What could he do? "Would you care to dance?"

Lucy, who had drunk a lot of champagne, took his hand. "Love to."

Having had his share of lessons, he knew his way

around the dance floor. He drew her into his arms and executed a decent two-step. No one would question, he didn't think, why he kept his face pressed against the top of her head. It hid his identity, and yet he could take advantage of getting up close and personal with the woman whom the cameras worshiped.

He'd never danced with her. She was amazingly graceful for someone who claimed to have two left feet. Perhaps all the champagne made her forget her self-consciousness. Well, she deserved a break for once. A night away. Still, he couldn't stop the fire that developed whenever he got caught in her orbit and moved with her into the shadows. Together they swayed alone in the dark.

"You're unbelievably sexy," he drawled in her ear. "Let me take you to bed."

The words were no more out than the hipster DJ spun an unrelenting beat. Couples unclutched each other for a fast dance. He almost shouted his desperation. But for the life of him, Lucy's bump and grind moves mesmerized him as much as the people moving in for video takes.

"It's Lucia in the flesh," a bloke hollered, and the cell phones came out as they had on Sandstone Peak, only worse. His girl was Lucia! The supermodel's footage would go viral in an instant, taking him along with her. His mouth tasted sour. He fought to keep his back to the cameras. But the photographers surrounded them. The cavalry had closed in, and he was losing the battle. He was going down dancing his fool head off. Liam Archer undercover no more.

In the distance, he heard someone saying, "Time to cut the cake."

The Lord be praised, he thought, just before Madison took his hand in hers and gave it a quick, firm shake. "You must be the poet."

Poet? He wasn't a bloody poet. He was an impostor, a dumbass phony now on full display. Somebody would surely start throwing tomatoes. "It's lovely to meet you."

"Get a load of Cary Grant," Madison said. "Honestly, dear, your voice gives me chills. I can't wait to hear you recite."

Lucy took her friend's arm. "You and Brandon have to stop by the teahouse. Liam's—he's so good at what he does."

What he does? He did nothing but sling hash. "Lucy's the one who delivers the Emily Dickinson with her special style." *Give credit where it is due.*

Brandon called from across the way. "Maddie!" He extended the knife handle-side in her direction. "You make the first cut."

Her smile to her groom radiated with happiness. "Liam. I'm delighted to have met you." She lifted a finger to Lucy. "We'll get together soon."

Chapter 20

My sorrow—I could not awaken
My heart to joy at the same tone—
And all I lov'd—I lov'd alone.
              ~Edgar Allan Poe (1809-1849)

The morning after. With a zinger of a hangover, Audrey stumbled into the kitchen. She reached for the teapot and the queen of anti-barf herbs, ginger. Ginger tea mended not only the stomach but the nerves. As she turned, her head whirling, she spied Liam tucked into the corner of the breakfast nook. What the hell? He clung, like a man before his maker, to her cell phone.

She dropped her cup on the counter, a sense of déjà vu destroying her logic. "What are you doing with that?"

His face, mouth agape, eyes wide, said, "Busted." He clicked off her phone, gave it to her, and stepped away, holding up his hands. "I needed to check on a problem."

She raised her chin. "Is it why you didn't come to bed last night?" She had gone into reverse, reliving scenes with previous boyfriends. "Are you keeping something from me?"

Left unsaid, unasked, was "Are you cheating on me? Are we over? Is that why you've been acting so damned aloof?"

Liam filled the kettle with tap water and fired up the burner. "You danced for the world last night. Caused quite a stir."

"Is that why you reached for my phone, Luddite?"

"I wanted to see, and, aye, your performance received ten million views on YouTube." His voice, she'd never heard it as judgmental. Was he trying to smile? It came off a sneer. "As usual, the media's crazy for you, luv."

She winced. What had she done? With a stomach more nauseated than before, she grasped her phone and unlocked the screen. Her heart twisted. Audrey had somehow gone full-throttle Lucinda, a wild child of the first order, hips a-swaying, arms above her head. Her performance wasn't bad enough. Liam, looking mortified, had tried uselessly to flee the cameras as they captured everything.

"Uh-oh," she said, "Lucia came out of hiding."

"It's a matter of time before the paparazzi show up."

She had earned his disgust. "I'm sorry."

"So am I."

Her emotions sank below the earth's surface. She'd driven him away just like her ex claimed she did all her men. He'd been standoffish since the day she told him about the wedding invitation. She questioned whether he had trouble with commitment. More on the money, was committing to her the actual problem? Even masquerading as Lucinda hadn't helped Audrey, the lost cause.

He motioned for Percy to follow him out into the yard. She followed them both.

"Liam?" He turned and appeared so unhappy she

had to ask, "Is there something you want to tell me?"

"Tell you?" The wind tousled his hair that glinted caramel and gold. "There are things I can't say." He gazed off in the distance with his gypsy eyes. "Sometimes, I think it would be better for everyone if I just return to London."

His rebuff confirmed her worst suspicions. "It's your choice." She wouldn't beg or grovel. Been there, done that. "You do what you feel is best."

He took her by the shoulders. "I might need to leave."

Heartbroken, she broke away from him and started back toward the bungalow. "Stay or go. It doesn't matter to me."

Oh, but it did, though she would rather die than say. Her modus operandi had risen again like the mythological phoenix. Because of it, fate had crossed her off the list of lasting love. She squared her shoulders and readied herself for Liam's eventual withdrawal. Somehow this breakup proved harder to take than the rest, devastatingly harder.

By early afternoon, the teahouse was filled with people. The press came in droves, which confined Audrey to the kitchen. An uncomfortable place to be since Liam and she weren't speaking to each other.

"Would you mind filling in for me?" she broke her silence to ask him. "I'll take over the cooking along with the crew."

He fixed her with a penetrating glare. "What do you want me to do?"

"Oh, I don't know. Wow the crowd with a poem, one the universe has been whispering in your ear." She couldn't resist the insult.

He recoiled. "I—"

"Maybe you don't have any poetry in you."

"Of course, I do. Sure, I'll recite. Why not?"

She watched him go toward the podium like he was heading to the gallows. He must be on pins and needles. And watching the way he took the mic in both hands, his breath quick as if he were trying to gather his courage, she hoped she hadn't been too hard on him.

He'd just opened his mouth to speak when someone called, "Aren't you the missing war hero, Liam Archer?"

Another man pushed through the blinding strobes and snapping cameras. "That's right. He's the same guy the UK is talking about."

A woman's voice rang out, "Come clean with us, Archer. Why would a counterterrorism analyst be hiding out in a teahouse?"

Then the questions blasted too fast and too loud, one after another. "Rumors are you're working undercover—is it true? How much time have you spent in Venice Beach? Did you need to get away? Are you here because of Lucia?"

Audrey's heart crashed to the floor when Liam didn't answer. She tried to make a break for it, but the paparazzi circled in front of her, behind her, surrounding her with their scorching lights and insane queries. Their smell of sweat and cologne nauseated her even more than before. An elbow poked her in the rib. King Kong stepped on her foot. Still, they surged closer, shouting more questions, robbing her of air, suffocating her.

****

From his position in the firing squad, Liam

observed Lucy. She put a hand to her mouth as the press hounds shoved their camera lenses in her face. He wished to be anywhere else than stuck in the crowd as she broke free and ran from the teahouse. He'd rather chase down a pack of gunners than elbow his way out to the street, his soul cratering.

The feeling that all of Venice Beach was crashing down on him hollowed out his chest. He couldn't hold on much longer. The seaside air prickled his skin as he called out her name.

"Lucy!"

He didn't need a GPS to figure she'd head to her boardwalk because the anonymity offered there was her sanctuary. Knowing her, she planned to blend in and disappear. With his long stride, he caught up with her when she crossed over to the beach twenty minutes later.

He reached for her arm. "Let me explain."

She shook him off, then surprised him with a cackle. "Get me some caramel corn. I could use some entertainment."

"Lucy…" He fumbled on what to say next. "This is a terrible mess."

She crossed her arms over her breasts. "Ah, I'd have thought you could do better that."

"First off, I haven't been playing you. Everything I told you, that I care about you, it's all true."

She snorted as if she didn't believe him. "Come on. Do you want to begin like that? You should try shooting yourself out of a cannon. That might earn you a round of applause from your ardent fans."

That's when he noticed. The surf bums, the jocks, the street performers—the entire Barnum and Bailey—

had fanned out around them, getting an earful. Liam rubbed the back of his neck, exhaling out all his air. "Let's take this show on down the road a bit."

She didn't bother to uncross her arms when she stormed through the brigade. "Here I thought you were enjoying your coming-out party. You've been preparing for this showdown. Now you don't have to act like you care for poetry or even care for me."

Her voice quivered, and he worried her rage would morph into tears. He fell into step behind her as she marched down the seashore, her spellbinding hips asway.

"I learned to love verse," he spat. "And I came to—to appreciate you."

She twisted around and stared at him as though he didn't add up. Like one of the many bills he'd seen her juggle. "Who are you, and what the hell is your game?"

"I've wanted to tell you. Name's Liam Archer." A pause. "Former commander of a task force designated by the Special Air Service to combat the war on terror." Another hesitation. "I was the glue that held the threads together, both on and off the field." A halt, bordering on half a minute. "After my last mission, when an innocent child was accidently killed, I ended up trading my military career for a stint with the Secret Intelligence Service."

"So you spy on people. Is that why you were so attentive? You wear down my defenses, tell me you want to be with me, then eagle eye everybody who walks through the door?"

"It's not like that. I mean, I tried my darndest not to notice you when I set up the electric equipment and wiretapped the phones."

She gave a nasty laugh. "Poor baby. My heart bleeds. You've been holding out on me, Luddite. All this time, you've had computerized gadgets up your sleeve."

She was mocking him. *Well, let her have her fun.* It was better than what she would do to him when he fessed up about her uncle.

He forged on. "Someone has been trading top secrets here in the teahouse."

"Really? An honest to goodness James Bond villain in Venice Beach?"

She'd go off her trolley, but if he didn't warn her, she wouldn't be on her guard. "I could be wrong. Let's hope I am mistaken. I want to be. But clues point to the traitor...and when I overheard some thug with—with Spade."

She threw her head back and roared with laughter. "The BS keeps getting deeper."

"I'm trying to tell you your uncle might be in cahoots with foreign adversaries."

"Are you out of your mind?" Her scoff had switched into the coldest sound he'd ever heard. "Did you seriously utter that just now? How could you accuse a man who's regarded you as a son of treason?"

"I got intel from Sam, and I eavesdropped on someone talking to your uncle, and it wasn't about the weather. I'm sorry. I don't mean to overwhelm you."

A cool craftiness evaporated all traces of warmth from her face. "You may be some mole-hunting, spy-catching character. But do you think you're the only one undercover in Venice Beach?"

"Lucy..."

"See, there's where you're wrong." She slammed

her hands on her hips. "I'm not Lucy."

"Okay, okay, Lucinda, then." And when she didn't budge an inch. "All right, Lucia."

"Try again, ace."

"Give me a moment…" Planet Earth fell out from beneath his feet. "What?"

"Here's a clue." The sun loomed high, and her shadow was very black. "The double syllables hang on the edge of the tongue as if a mixture of melancholy and hope before dawn."

He sucked in so much air he choked. "Audrey!"

"Grand slam, baby!"

"Since when?"

"Lucinda and I switched places six months ago. Yep, for half a year."

"You haven't been honest with me." Everything he always feared had come to pass.

"You think I played you the same as you played me? It looks like none of what happened in Venice Beach was real." Her eyes shut, and when she opened them, they shone with tears. "Go back across the pond, Liam James or Archer or shithead. Whoever you are, I never want to see you again."

Her mobile picked then to ring. It hardly ever rang these days. "Hello?" Her mouth fell open in alarm as she listened to the caller. Her glare bored into him. "Here." She passed him the phone. "For you."

With a sense of dread, he spoke up. "Yes?"

"Archer?" The voice sounded concerned for his wellbeing.

"Yes."

"It seems you're in a spot of trouble."

"Copy that."

"You are to return to London today. Please acknowledge."

"I am to return today."

The phone went dead.

Chapter 21

Myself when young did eagerly frequent
Doctor and Saint, and heard great Argument
About it and about: but evermore
Came out by the same Door as in I went.
                    ~Edward Fitzgerald (1809-1883)

A little after five the next morning, Liam Archer
opened the door of his flat on the bank of the Thames.
That closed-up stench clogged his nostrils. He tossed
his keys on the island topped with brushed stainless
steel. The sound of metal striking metal jarred all his
nerve endings. The sight of aluminum benches,
gunmetal slate floor, industrial gray everywhere
disturbed him even more. It looked like he lived inside
his combat helmet.

Filtering his thoughts, he positioned himself at the
window and looked out at the dull, overcast dawn. He
allowed his mind to lose itself in the blah nothingness.
Gone was the Mighty Pacific bringing its *kaboom* at the
break of day.

No, don't go there.

By eight, he took the tube to the south bank. The
techno music he used to blast from earbuds sounded as
comforting as needles in his ears. He surprised himself
by searching out Spade's style of bleeding-heart tunes
on his recently charged mobile.

He entered by a metal door that routed him through an entrance. If it weren't for Sam taking his wallet, he would be like most of the others in this high-tech piece of corporate England. Employees were swiping their identity cards through electric readers to gain access. But Liam must approach a reception area where a pair of uniformed women sat behind bulletproof glass.

He used the intercom system to state his intentions. They made him fill out some information passed through a slot under the window. The brunette slid him a plastic badge to pin on. Soon, a junior clerk led him to a lift that carried them to the sixth floor. He followed the sharpie, past the humming of air-conditioning ducts and employees hunched over PCs.

They wound up at the end of a long corridor. The lad gave the door a definitive rap, and the familiar voice fired off, "Come in."

Seconds later, Liam stood at Mark Perry's desk. The gray at Perry's temples was a recent addition to the fit, raven-haired man in his forties. A chocolate Easter egg wrapped in foil leaned against a photo of his kids and wife. A Mackintosh hung from a coat stand, and the officer had propped a squash racket inside the space for umbrellas. Liam remembered him from his SAS days when they had both been rookie fliers. Their mutual respect went way back.

That's why unease waved through him. Headquarters didn't summon him here to hand him a medal. He was totally screwed. What could he say? *I missed my flight because of a cagy bird. I stayed to protect a beautiful woman. I botched everything, mate.*

Perry gave his hand a warm shake. "Good to see you again, Liam."

"Thank you. Delighted to find you here."

"I've ordered your usual caramel macchiato with a double shot of espresso." He stared at Liam as he took a seat. "Your hair, you couldn't have it cut?"

"It was part of my disguise." He sat and sipped his coffee, his taste buds repelled by the sugary sweetness.

"Is there a problem?"

"I guess I got used to tea."

"We'll have some Earl Grey sent up."

"No, no. It has to be herbal and served with a certain formality." He sounded like a bloomin' dipstick. "No worries, I'm fine."

Perry folded his hands on his desk. "You missed your flight last September. I don't understand why. You don't have to tell me. It's a shame you weren't able to contact headquarters, though, because I doubt you are aware of the reason Operation Teacup came to an abrupt halt."

Liam shrugged. "I tried to call in but couldn't get through. I assumed they had denied my reentry based on my disobeying orders. By the time they contacted me, I had gotten involved in the espionage in the teahouse."

"The mission proved an embarrassing situation for MI6."

"I don't understand."

"We got a report of treason at the highest level and sent our best agents to investigate, but the information accrued turned out to be faulty."

"Could you divulge some details?"

Perry answered with a question. "Are you acquainted with the author, Johnny Spade, who writes spy thrillers under the pseudonym Constance Spring?"

"Yes, I am." Here it came, Spade's guilt by association or something more heinous. Again, Liam didn't want to hear the news. His stomach hardened, his mind dwelling on all his bleak suspicions.

"Are you familiar with a Dictaphone? It's a machine used by a few writers for recording their prose. They have been around since the early nineteen hundreds. Somehow, Mr. Spade's ham radio caught the high frequency bands at the right time of day, and parts of his novel ended up reaching the electronic receivers here in the UK."

"Blimey! So Spade's voice on the Dictaphone got picked up in London, and that single element caused all the ruckus."

Perry sighed. "We've been trying to put the unfortunate situation right ever since."

"I know the feeling," Liam said with a sigh of his own. His mind drifted to Lucy—um, Audrey. He had to tell her he had been wrong and how sorry he was over the error.

Perry laid his palms on the table. "The rest is difficult to say."

"Difficult?"

"Your work with MI6 was exemplary, meeting all our needs. Unfortunately, the press has somehow uncovered your secret existence, what you did for the military, and what you are doing for us. The notoriety of this has been damaging. We can no longer afford to keep you employed here, and that's a shame."

Liam should express his disappointment, but he was thinking of his boyhood, the sheep in the pasture, their bleating echoing from the cliffs. Thinking, too, of the hedges and the blackberries, ginormous and ripe in the spring. The robins singing their hearts out. No other sound. The wild thyme and the bluebells just starting to turn purple.

"Are you all right, Liam? Do you have any plans?"

All at once, he knew. "It's time I pay my father a visit."

****

—I was wrong about your uncle. I am sorrier than I can say. You have every right to be angry with me.—

Audrey reread the message. For the first time since Sunday, it didn't hurt to breathe. A text from Liam seemed strange. She hadn't slept over two hours last night. She kept replaying the previous months in her mind. Her partner. Her lover. The liar.

At nine that morning, Lucinda busted inside the doorway of the bungalow and put mothering arms around Audrey's shoulders. "Oh, Aud."

"I didn't get ahold of you," Audrey said, a sob surfacing. "I needed to be alone."

"I know, baby, I know. That's how you roll, but I'm here now. You go ahead, let out the plugs." Lucinda's voice soothed like a late-night radio DJ. "Attagirl. Niagara Falls has nothing over you. That's the way to wail the blues, sista."

Ten minutes into her crying jag, Audrey had recovered enough to say, "You had Liam pegged. He's been deceiving us all along."

"Somehow, it doesn't feel so good to be right," Lucinda said with a tired groan. "More to the point, we printed the headlines. I don't get it. I mean, are you kidding me? A secret agent setting up shop here? What the devil for?"

"It's a complicated story." One Audrey couldn't

quit going over. "He thought his country threatened by a traitor working out of our teahouse."

"That's so idiotic. Did he find any proof?"

With a rotten taste still lingering in her mouth, she recalled Liam's accusations. But this morning, he'd sent her the text clearing her uncle so his previous claims weren't worth mentioning. "There is one thing he admitted to." She opened a canister of peppermint tea and took a deep whiff to stimulate a little energy. "He told me he had set up spy equipment."

"Where?"

Audrey shrugged. "I guess we could eliminate the attic since there isn't any. No basement nor garage, but there is the shed. He left so fast he didn't have time to disconnect anything."

Lucinda opened the back door. "What are we waiting for?"

High stakes were what her sister thrived on. If anyone could pull off detective work with five-star finesse, it was her. But today, Audrey bolted through the yard with the same fiery passion running through her veins. She was dying to see if Liam's outrageous claims were for real. She closed one eye and scanned the rusty walls for any trace of 007 contraptions—not even a pair of binoculars.

Lucinda held up the trash can. "Somebody's been busy." She picked bird feathers out of the screen.

Audrey was too baffled to comment. The sight brought back all those confusing feelings she'd had for him in the beginning. She shoved a cardboard box away from the corner, and her spirits lit up. Who would guess a pair of recorders could cause such a stir inside her?

"Look at this." She arranged them on the dusty

floor.

"Now we're getting somewhere!"

Her sister sat across from her, and Audrey rewound the tape and hit play, surprised to hear Bennett's cocksure voice on one phone conversation after another. Everything he said was at full speed, like a rocket taking off. Nothing raised suspicion, though. The talk centered on his work. Never once did any of the discussions veer into a direction that made them question his loyalty. Quite the opposite. He was the first on the scene when a water main broke, directing traffic himself. He coached a little league team, for goodness' sake. His kindnesses and charisma had the sisters hanging on his words.

Lucinda uttered a stricken gasp. "That's enough. If I hear any more, I'll propose marriage to him myself."

"He's a catch all right." Audrey switched off the tape. "Too bad his heart, since he got dumped, centers on running for senate like his father."

"The damn fool. Running for office leaves him no time for falling in love again." Lucinda rolled her eyes. "Try the other recorder."

She did, and after a soft hiss, Olivia Ricci's lilting voice escaped into the tiny space. Why would Liam bug her phone? Audrey let out an exasperated sigh. Nothing to speak of, only the mayor making plans for an upcoming Easter egg hunt, her then scheduling an income-tax appointment with her accountant. She shook her head, almost ready to call it a day. Just for the heck of it, though, she reversed the tape farther and started it again.

"Liam Archer's gone thanks to you, Paul," Olivia was saying. "I've booked a room for you and a guest at the Four Seasons in Paris. Airline tickets and a bottle of champagne, Krug 1988, should be arriving at your address soon. It's all just a small token of my appreciation for all you have done."

"It was nothing I did," said a low male voice. "Your clout allows you access to classified information. No way can I blend in with the inner workings of a foreign government. You, *chéri*, deserve all the credit."

"True, but manipulating the press was right up your alley. You spoon-fed Archer's past to the scandal rags so that by the time the paparazzi got ahold of it, they descended on the teahouse like jackals. I have to admit. I quite enjoyed the show."

"And now you can pursue your covert activities without fear of getting caught. I think it's safe to say you're home free." A pause. "I've always wondered, why did you choose a location on the busiest street in Venice to conduct your business?"

"Who'd suspect a place called Tea and Poetry of being a dead-drop? Besides, it was there, with Monroe, I discovered my voice."

"But she never suspected?"

"No," Olivia said and uttered a sad laugh. "She'd have turned me in, and she wouldn't have understood, but she didn't grow up having to keep quiet just to survive."

The conversation ended soon afterward, and Audrey released a cry. "Olivia Ricci!" She seethed with mounting rage. She picked up a coffee can heavy with nails, then threw it so hard that when it hit, it caused a dent in the wall. Gasping, she added, "What kind of person would pass secrets to another country? Has she no shame?"

From outside, her sister sounded more preoccupied with talking on her cell phone than with what they had both heard.

A thought more terrible came to Audrey. "Olivia took advantage of Mama, then of all the rest of us. She's a sick creep who has been laughing behind our backs."

"Well, she won't be laughing much longer," Lucinda said from the door. "I got in touch with the police detective on Mama's case. He's coming here now. Soon, they'll have a warrant and a SWAT team at the three-story colonial-style mansion Ms. Ricci calls home. The only thing we insist on is being curbside when they haul her away."

A weight felt as if it had fallen from Audrey's shoulders. "Way to go. No wonder you are good at running the paper. You keep your head in a crisis."

"Thanks. And you know how to lead with your heart. Would you say that comes from composing poetry?"

"Maybe so. Or maybe it's because I've gotten the hang of being you."

"Me too, you." Lucinda blew on her short fingernails. "Has it occurred to you that if Liam had been a true Luddite, we wouldn't have the proof to catch Olivia Ricci?"

"No, not until you just said it." Audrey closed her eyes, gratefulness rising inside her.

"Did you also realize that when you fell head over heels for him, you broke your cycle?"

"What do you mean?"

"Sweetie, he's not a poet."

****

Liam rented a Land Rover, packed his gear, and traveled by himself on the narrow back road with its steep banks and hairpin turns. If Lucy were here, she'd freak. And Percy would die of fright. Oh God, he missed those two.

He searched the car radio for a beat fit for a buckaroo on a quest. *Bugger!* Andy Williams singing "Moon River" didn't cut it. He killed the music, not needing a reminder of the woman he needed to forget. He opened the windows. The high-pitched crescendo of the golden birds in the treetops soothed him. Sunbeams filtered down through the spruces and sparkled over the rhododendrons and the bog pools. That familiar sense of ruggedness, wildness, and self-will made him think of his father.

As far back as he could remember, all he'd ever heard was technology murdered his mother. This had driven Liam to become rebellious, so he'd gravitated toward anything with algorithms. He'd received a scholarship in, of all subjects to irk Dad, computer science. Words between father and son had led to marathon silences. On the day Liam left for college, amid a heated fight, his father had shouted, "I never want to see you again!"

The exact sentiment Lucy had expressed. If she hadn't, he might not be pursuing the right he gave up long ago. Now the terrain ascended to a grassy knoll where the Shetland ponies grazed inside walls he'd helped build when he was just old enough to carry the stones.

He left the Land Rover at the edge of the property. A breeze stirred in the top branches of the pines. The ducks, mallards they were, cried out as they flew over.

Two wind turbines and solar panels generated energy from the roof of the farmhouse. He took comfort in the billowing mist that clung to his upturned face. He'd dreamed of this while in the heart of war. When his mates had gone to battle and never come back, he'd dreamed of this, of coming home.

A sheepdog—a border collie he'd never laid eyes on—herded a couple stray lambs, then spotting Liam, the four-legged shepherd halted with a paw raised, ears perked.

"What is it, Gilly?" His father's voice boomed from the other side of the ridge.

Liam tried to call out, *Dad, it's me!* A short time ago, he had marched into enemy artillery. Tanks had fired at him. He had always been prepared for action, and yet he froze, his throat parched, unable to move a muscle.

As Dad climbed the hill, his windblown mane of pale hair came into view. His face grew clearer, tanned, and next, the tremendous span of his shoulders in his homespun shirt and trousers. His nose lifted, nostrils quivering as if distinguishing scents. Gray eyes hunted and snared his son where he stood.

"Archie, is that you?" he asked in a hardened tone.

Liam lowered his head. "Aye, Dad," he said, regressing to the Cumbrian dialect. He bent down, his legs weaker than he'd expected, and scratched Gilly behind the ears.

"Where are your fancy computers?"

"Don't know. Have you seen them?"

"If I had, you wouldn't be there."

This assault might go on till dusk without letup. "I thought I'd drop in," Liam said, as carefree as a lad on spring break.

His father raised a mittened hand. "Are you staying?"

Liam yanked his suitcase from the ground. "If you'll have me." He searched for a sign, seeking a miracle that would make Dad speak with—what, approval? Affection? He shoved his free hand in the pocket of his jacket. "It's been a while."

"Agreed." Dad turned and tramped through the tall grass. Against the mountain, his silhouette sprang to that of a giant with a shepherd's staff.

The interior of the house greeted Liam like an old friend. When the windows were lashed with rain and the view sheeted in fog, the lovingly crafted decor provided a refuge. The pinewood floors gleamed now in the afternoon sunlight. The quiet elegance and uncluttered open space pleased him. He'd always loved order.

He offered a white flag of a grin. "It's just as I remembered."

"As I recall, you couldn't wait to get away."

His father's bitterness had caused him to flee right after high school, but he put in, "I was a cheeky lad."

"That's not even debatable," Dad said in his lawyer's voice.

Damn. He shouldn't have come here. Liam wished for once his father would hold his fire. Foolish to hope time would mellow the sour disposition. Crazy to imagine the two of them talking like the previous grudges and misunderstandings hadn't poisoned the air between them.

"I suppose you're expecting some refreshment?" Dad didn't wait for a reply but thumped his staff on the floor and leaned it in the corner. "Come on, let's see about tea."

His father gathered several baked scones and a healthy allotment of clotted cream and set the table around a nook of no adornment. "Don't just stand there. Sit."

The homey display softened Liam. His father had taken over the cooking after Mum died, at first with resentment, but later with a passion and ingenuity he passed down to Liam. No matter what, father and son ate like kings.

Dad placed the pottery mugs on the table. The breeze from the open window ruffled his hair. When had the blond turned to silver? His neck had creased, and wrinkles lined his forehead. His father had aged without Liam's notice. He'd never thought of his father as growing older, not once.

"So you went missing," Dad said. "Disappeared, it seems, right off the face of the earth. Why did you surface here?"

"Who told you I'd disappeared?" Liam asked while Gilly nuzzled her head on his lap, and he dug his fingers in her silky fur.

"I got a letter from the government. They wrote you'd last been spotted in some beach town in California. They wanted to know if I'd seen you."

"How did you respond?"

"How do you expect? I told the absolute truth." He poured tea, his hand with an almost unperceivable tremor. "Shut them up as best I could. Said we didn't speak."

"I'm sorry for worrying you."

"I didn't lose any sleep over it. Why should I?"

Was that accusation or hurt Liam deciphered?

"It's not like you ever contact me."

"I wanted to…"

Mistake, dipstick, Liam scorned himself in no uncertain terms. Dad argued with every attempt at negotiation. But Liam had gotten up the gumption to come home. He wouldn't leave without a fight. "I tried to ring you last Christmas."

"If that doesn't take the biscuit." Dad hesitated. "What got into you?"

Liam spoke the truth. "I was homesick."

"What could you possibly miss about the forest?"

"You."

"Me?" Dad's brows lifted. "As I live and breathe, I never expected to hear that coming from you."

"There's so much to tell."

Dad frowned and cleared his throat. "Why not give it a go?"

He might as well try. "After college, I joined the military."

"Special Air Service courted you after you graduated top of your class."

With some difficulty, Liam kept his voice even. "Doesn't matter. I'm a civilian now." He dragged his hand through his hair to prove his point.

"Yet you still tuck your trousers inside your boots."

A dead giveaway that. "Here's something you don't know." Unless he had access to the news, and odds were, he hadn't. "I've been undercover in a Luddite teahouse where I got used to working without a computer."

"No, I didn't think you would give up—" Dad raised his fingers in air quotes. "—'The Screen.' Not for love or money."

"Just goes to prove that even Jeremy Archer can have a lapse in judgment."

Dad slathered his scone with cream and sat back in the chair. "I'm not going anywhere. Let's sort things out, shall we? How did you manage without your laptop?"

"When I met Lucy, she assumed I was technophobic, and I let her because I was on a mission. I pretended to shun computers, which cost me my freedom to advertise the enterprises we dreamed up together. At first, I resented the time I spent getting the word out the old-fashioned way. By hanging posters around town and approaching local businesses.

"But I fell into a routine and got comfortable with it all. I worked as a chef, taking from the recipes you taught me and adding some of my own. I can't say for sure when my mindset changed. Maybe when two teens couldn't hold an actual conversation. I told myself I was playing a role when I confiscated the phones that caused their verbal deficiency.

"Other things happened during the months I remained undercover. I saw the way poetry brought Alzheimer's patients out of their disease—if just for a while. One thing I never pulled off, though, was my ability to compose a poem myself. I wanted to, but it seems a person can't fake what is in the heart."

Liam worried he had gotten maudlin. "I'll show you her gift to me last Christmas." He pulled the chain that released the timepiece from his jeans, and he dangled it before his father's jaw-dropping face.

"What's this?"

"The Royal Navy of the British military distributed

these to their sailors during the Second World War. This baby was her grandfather's. Even with my cover blown, I didn't want to return to a digital watch."

Dad took it, weighing the disk in his hand, a smile spreading across his face. He undid the latch and popped it open with reverence. "She gave this to you?"

"She did. It was one of her most valuable possessions."

"And you let her go?"

Liam set his tea aside. "She told me to leave after she found out I'd lied to her about my identity. She said, 'Whoever you are, I never want to see you again.' "

"And you bloody listened?" Dad frowned in such a way that Liam realized his father was questioning his sanity. "You have always taken words much too literally. Sometimes folks say things they don't mean when pushed in a corner."

Had he misinterpreted his father's last words? Liam had swallowed his father's demand whole and took it as gospel, and that kept him from attempting to return.

He picked up a scone, seized a bite, and knew all the ingredients that Dad used: the butter, that hint of almond, and the burst of apricot. He closed his eyes and indulged in the warmth of the kitchen, the yumminess of the pastry, the familiar smell of Darjeeling tea. He scooped up some cream and bit off a piece, turning it over on his tongue and savoring the flavor.

Dad turned his wedding ring around on his finger. "This woman means a lot to you?"

"I can't quit thinking about her."

"What will you do about it?"

"Do?"

All the years of acrimony evaporated, and Dad appeared as young as he had been before Mum's death changed him. "Don't be like me and choose misery over happiness. Life is too short. Win her back, Archie."

"If only it were that simple."

Sometime afterward, Liam disappeared into the garden to pick veggies for the soufflé he planned to bake for dinner. The air was so pure here. Clouds scuffled along the mountain to the east. And he wished Lucy—*dang it!* Audrey. He wished she could see the sky at dusk, the stars at night. His father's advice etched itself into Liam's train of thought so that later that evening, he took out a pen. *Win her back...*

Not Lucy...but Audrey.

Audrey—just writing her name filled him with confusion and shame. How could he make her know he was sorry? If Liam had a second chance, he wouldn't have lied. But then the events leading to their getting together might never have taken place. Bugger, he should have known she was masquerading as Lucinda. He had been half-mad for her from the first. That the twins traded places had entered his mind, but he'd dismissed it as too farfetched.

Audrey—he should have defended himself when she discovered his identity. He hadn't told her who he was because it would have put her in danger. No, that wasn't the complete truth. He hadn't told her because he feared their affair would end as it had.

"What the hell was she supposed to think, you dumbass?" he muttered and threw his pen across the desk in his old bedroom.

Audrey—so much for his well-laid plans. His idea that he'd come back to England and all would be fine. Nothing had gone right because he had fallen in love with her. He loved her. The yellow legal pad awaited him. He didn't need some complicated instructional manual or even a magic wand to write. He just needed to think of her.

Audrey—the poetry he wrote came as easily as the flow of the river…

Chapter 22

In Xanadu did Kubla Khan
A stately pleasure-dome decree:
Where Alph, the sacred river, ran
Through caverns measureless to man
Down to a sunless sea.
                    ~Samuel Coleridge (1772-1834)

A text from Liam came in the morning, and Audrey snapped wide awake and studied what might lead to his first poem. It spoke of missing someone. How well she related. Should she respond? She hadn't when he cleared her uncle of all wrongdoing. His suspicions had been ridiculous and deserved no reply. Now, though, he'd reached out with the beginning of a verse. Could he follow through? Should she give him a chance? Her fingers hesitated so long they vibrated. A sign? She settled on a text of just three paltry words.

—Send me more.—

The next day he fired off a ditty about the moorland and hiking to High Stile Mountain, comparing it to Sandstone Peak. He wrote about simple things, such as conquering a recipe for Cuban flan, and took on serious topics such as the evils of war and what it did to a soldier. His poetry flourished, arriving like clockwork at ten a.m., six p.m. his time. Her pride in his work led her to recite some of it to Madison and

267

Lucinda.

One day, she read Liam's newest edition to Percy, who lapped it up, his chest huffing and puffing like a small dragon. He found a bald tennis ball and dropped it at her feet. The act signaled their daily war games in the jungle out the back door.

As she took charge and he romped, Uncle Johnny jogged into the yard and stopped beside her. Here it was, her golden opportunity. She shoved her cell phone in his face. "Liam's been staying with his father, and here's something I think you'll want to see."

Handing him a digital object crossed over to forbidden territory. "I've got a book to write," he said, his shock and distaste loud and clear. "A hundred things to research."

"Please, break your rule just this once."

He frowned but moved under the bonsai, and as his eyes adjusted, he assessed the screen, minutes passing with him scrolling—actually scrolling—before he commented, as if to himself, "The mood, the tone, the underlying meaning, it's all there."

"And his imagery sparks an interest, doesn't it?"

"I'll say. This narrative has an impact, allowing me to feel part of the ongoing story. Before this, Liam was a reciter. By returning to his roots, he's found his voice."

"You can't stop with just one." She was happy to discuss Liam with her uncle. "It's as if nature were speaking when he writes about the roe deer, dormice, and the tawny barn owl."

"He writes like the poets of the Romantic age."

"We have to book him for a reading at the teahouse."

Her declaration met with a disturbing silence.

"Well, that's a toughie," he said. "If you bring him back now, it might stop his flow."

She had to agree. "Liam has to hoard the creativity the forest brings to his work so that someday he can sell it. By the time he's ready for that, we can string two huge banners in front of the teahouse promoting his reading, plus posters and fliers—just like we did for you when you released your last book. We'll be better able to promote him once he returns—if he returns."

"You miss him?"

"You have no idea." She couldn't prevent the tears spilling down her cheeks.

He cradled her against his shoulder and kissed her head. "The feelings that you and Liam have is the *amour* I write about, the kind of love you cannot deny. There's no other choice. You must go to him, sweet pea."

"I can't just pick up and leave. Who'd take care of the teahouse? It's been hard enough without Liam here to cook."

"Don't forget I ran things when your mama traveled the world over for tea."

"You mean I tramp off to the UK by myself, show up at a moment's notice? All that bravado is so not me."

Uncle Johnny jiggled the loose change in his pockets. "You could have fooled me."

At the realization she hadn't been herself in months, her pulse jump-started. Lucinda wouldn't flinch at flying across the world. All this time, she'd been adopting her sister's character traits. What good were they if she couldn't spend fifteen hours in a plane?

Audrey had done it when she was a girl, before she had become so uptight.

With this in mind, she purchased an airline ticket, found Jeremy Archer's address, thanks to Google Maps, packed, made train reservations, and hired a driver, given by word of mouth.

The day before her big adventure, she called Madison's cell to say goodbye.

"What's up?" her friend asked.

"I'm going to Cumbria County to find my poet." Her words filled her with the same kind of butterflies she'd experienced when she first met him.

"Northwest England isn't your regular stomping ground."

Her legs wobbled. "I'll be fine."

"Shouldn't you call Liam and tell him you're on your way?"

"No." She swallowed to ease the jitters. "I might not get the nerve to see it through."

At four the next afternoon, with her stomach churning, Audrey carried her luggage to the door. Percy dragged his mouth down at the corners, and his panicked eyes scanned her face.

"I know you want to go, but here's the deal, bud. You wouldn't do well stuck in the cargo hold for eleven hours. I couldn't put you through that."

Her sister pulled up to the teahouse in the Lexus. "All aboard," she called out the window. Uncle Johnny gave Audrey a push from behind, while Percy rolled over on his back and blocked her path.

"I'll be home soon," she said, stooping to rub his tummy. "I promise you."

Lucinda talked as she drove. "I've been in the Lake

District on a photoshoot. Let me fix you up myself. That way, you'll shine even in stormy weather. Plus, if you're still on a budget, let me help in that department too. We'll spend time in London to make sure you have all you need to work it. Liam won't know what hit him."

Nobody else was like her twin. "Listen, it would rock for you to come along. But I just can't show up clinging to my sister. I've got to do this myself."

"Compute." Lucinda gave in with a frown. "I'll miss you, though."

"Who knows? I might be on the next flight back home."

Lucinda stopped at the airport drop-off. "Don't worry. Mama will keep an eye out. Nothing will happen." She gave Audrey a gentle shake of the shoulders. "You'll crush this."

But by the time she was thirty thousand feet in the sky, she wasn't so sure. Her destiny lay not only with the Boeing 747, but with the passengers from whom she sought reassurance. A boy, his face lit up blue from his smartphone, snickered at whatever he was streaming. A businessman read his email from his laptop, and an elderly lady flipped through pages of a romance novel. The calm flight attendant took food orders while Audrey kept a death grip on the armrests. Eating was out of the question. Not with her queasy stomach. She asked for a barf bag—a prelude to what lay ahead—the longest and possibly the last hours of her life.

By the time the plane touched down in Manchester, her body ached like she'd been up for days. She boarded the train and fought to stay awake. Through the slits of her eyes, she marveled at the stream of cottage lights along the dusky landscape. Soon, she fell asleep and didn't wake till the engine rumbled into the station. She searched the people milling about for her driver.

Doc had come recommended by a friend of a friend. No one knew his actual name, but he had been a doctor, who made house calls, in Ennerdale back when the locals were planting the trees and developing the land. At seventy, he'd hung up his stethoscope. To escort travelers in and around the remote valleys distinctive of West Cumbria gave him purpose. He loved people, and it showed in his face when he held up the sign with *Audrey* written in bold letters.

"Doc?" she asked and, when he nodded, added, "Hello there."

As he smiled kindly, his blue eyes crinkled at the corners. "Is this thy first time yonder?"

"Uh-huh. I guess I'm just a greenhorn."

"Prepare for a bit of a rough road." He opened the door of his Toyota Hilux for her. "No harm will come to thee, God willing."

Those words did nothing to ease the nervous stampede in her gut. She fussed with the seatbelt with the urge to raise her hands in the air and say, "What was I thinking?"

Soon, though, Doc was driving and pointing out the sights along the way. He entertained her with local history stories that made her laugh and kept her mind occupied. She didn't get why he'd forewarned her about the drive when the landscape remained level and green and looked so lovely she'd opened her window to see the scattering of clouds in the cerulean sky.

A half hour later, he turned off the highway. The trees here and the stretches of water surrounded by rock proved interspersed with bridges that appeared otherworldly. She couldn't help but swallow to moisten the dryness in her throat. When the road grew steeper and the turns sharper, she broke out in a cold sweat. Doc's tidbits on the Cumbrian people and places ceased to reach her. But then her ears were roaring with her fear.

She struggled to come up with a subject that would make her forget her predicament. "Doc, do you know Jeremy Archer?"

"Who doesn't? He's a local hero. Keeps to himself, but he'll show up to fight a battle when need be."

"Fight for what?"

"He fought in court against those trying to get permission to bury nuclear waste in West Cumbria."

"It wasn't safe?"

"A nuclear leak would pollute not only the ground but the Irish Sea."

Captivated, she said, "I'm visiting his son, but I don't have any history to reference. I'd appreciate any insight you can give."

"It is common knowledge. Most Londoners know Jeremy Archer from his successful law practice. But he'd been much more than a lawyer—he was an environmental advocate. To inform the world about the critical state of the earth's forests excited him. He would go as far as chasing politicians into lifts to get them to listen. But something in his head snapped when his wife died in an automobile accident."

"That's horrible." She sucked in a shocked breath. "How?"

"The steering wheel locked due to a computerized defect. A recall followed. But nothing could bring back the lives claimed, including Jeremy's bride."

"Is that why he moved here?"

"Aye. Jeremy bought hundreds of acres 'far away from the maddening crowd,' as they say. If I were thee, I'd stay clear of any computers. He's the epitome of anti-tech. I don't suppose you have any idea what I mean."

"Oh, but I do." She nearly broke into hysterical laughter. "My father when he was alive, my mother until she passed away, and my uncle—all Luddites."

"And thee?"

"I am not quite sure. I haven't used social media much these past months, which made me realize how addicted I had been to it. Being free of it allows more time to do what's important to me."

"Eh, we do well not to let technology rob us of our goals." Doc cocked his head at the cell phone in her lap. "And thee scarcely have need of thine. There's no reception."

She tried to turn it on. "But Liam texts me daily."

"He must care deeply to make the trek back to civilization."

Hmm, she could use the doctor's knowledge on another subject. "How much do you know about him?"

"Archie?" His broad face widened even more with his smile. "He had the chicken pox when he was three. Strep throat at five. A terrible case of poison ivy at seven. When he was ten, he asked for my help with a goose who had broken a wing. He watched over that bird, tended to its every need till it could safely go back into the wild. A pleasant lad, he was, earned a scholarship to Cambridge, but after he left, I lost touch."

She'd been so engrossed in their conversation that the grueling drive with its winding roads turned bearable. Still, when Doc said, "We shall be there soon," she let out a breath.

"Phew, I won't leave Percy an orphan."

"Percy is kin?"

"He was my mother's dog, and now he's mine." She paused, then added, "He is a Boston terrier named after Percy Shelley." Her chest suffered a pang, even though it had only been several hours. She'd entered some place strange. Without her dog—her baby.

Doc's baritone voice rose. " 'From the forests and the highlands we come, we come.' "

" 'From the river-girt islands,' " she added in delight. Together, they recited "Hymn of Pan." As they exchanged one line after another, her mind hardly registered the truck rounding a bend, loose rock crunching under the wheels.

Her first glimpse of the land beyond the woods made her half expect to find a white witch or a wizard as they passed horses, hens, and a pond with swans. Sunlight meandered across a stretch of purple heather, and ivy climbed the tree trunks and wound around fence posts.

She got out of the Toyota and strolled to where Doc was hoisting her baggage from the truck bed. "Thanks so much for all your help."

"Thee survived Mr. Toad's wild ride," he said with a note of whimsy. "Let me accompany thee." He pointed a finger. "Yon up the hill."

She took in the sight of the stark stone farmhouse, her nervousness returning. Still, she felt it necessary to say, "If you don't mind, I'd rather go it alone." She had turned into a daredevil, and she wanted Liam to know it.

"Be careful of the sheepdog. Gilly gets a bit territorial."

"I'll be fine."

But Audrey's insides quivered when Doc, her friend and confidant, drove away. Here she'd survived the flight, the dangerous drive, only to clam up upon arriving at her destination. *Nearly there, so get going.* She climbed halfway through the meadow and discovered herself surrounded by bizarre-looking sheep. Should she call out? What if Liam wasn't here? Her chest tightened another notch, and she forced herself onward.

Her feet clomped along the wet grass, then stopped before a ram with large horns curved like the number six. His eyes held a demonic sheen. She'd never imagined being stared down by an overgrown lamb.

Give it a little swagger. "Listen, buster. I have to get by."

His *baaahh* resembled a foghorn that almost blew her away.

Of all the stupid things, riling this monster sheep took the cake. This was bad. "Oh, let me through—pretty please."

Then she spied Liam atop an ancient, rickety tractor. He was plowing the adjoining field, the wind blowing his hair away from his amazing face. Happiness flooded through her.

She waved her arms and shouted, "Liam!"

He didn't see or hear her.

But the big bad sheep did. *Baaahh!*

She raised all five feet and ten inches of her and

lifted her shoulders so that the straps of her backpack dug into her flesh, and she swung both suitcases out to her sides. Her arm muscles would give her grief tomorrow, but the ram balked and headed away. Someone must be watching over her—someone like God, or the universe, or Mama.

Audrey skirted around the field and had gotten to the far side when a border collie ran in her direction, barking and snarling as if it intended on ripping her apart.

Oh no! She lowered her shoulders, lost her backpack, and dropped her bags in case she needed to run. But where should she go?

"Liam!" she cried. "Liam, help!"

He didn't respond to her.

She staggered backward as fast as possible on the slippery dyke. Then her espadrilles connected with space, the same as when she'd been on the ice rink. Her heart lurched the way it did when an elevator dropped from the top floor to the basement. The frigid water swallowed her into its dark depths, bubbles thundering past her ears. Her feet kicked and searched for a bottom that wasn't there. She swam upward through dead leaves, bark fragments, and yucky fish. At last, she broke the sun-dappled surface and took a much-needed gulp of air.

"Liam!" she shouted, the icy cold inducing shivers along her neck and shoulders.

Gilly carried on from the top of the cliff. Audrey went under again, the current strong enough to yank her downstream toward what could mean the end. She wouldn't get to tell Liam how much she cared. She'd wasted time, afraid of falling for a poet, wasted precious moments hanging back. It had been no way to live.

Ruff, ruff, ruff!

Treading water, she raised her chin to keep it above the surface. In the treetops overhead, a parrot, small and the brightest shade of green she had ever seen, edged across a branch, and his wings stirred like—well, like Kubla. An optical illusion?

She blinked, and the bird vanished, but all at once, the rushing current stopped. The canine, now a distance away, quit barking. Whatever the reason for this phenomenon, although her body shook with the cold, she found her voice once more.

"Liam, help me!" she cried.

Quick footsteps thumped the ground above. "Blimey, Audrey? Is that you?"

"Liam." She was quaking so hard she could hardly speak. "I had to find you."

"I'm here." He appeared and surveyed her whereabouts with a hand shielding his eyes. "Stay where you are!"

"As if I have a choice."

He disappeared, then sprinted off the bank, fell, torpedoing down, down, then popped up beside her, treading the water. "Audrey, what are you doing here?"

"You said I hadn't found the right poet. I wanted to tell you. Now I have."

"You have?"

"It's you!"

"By Jove, I love you."

"And I love you. To Jupiter and Mars…" Her teeth chattered. "Just one deal breaker…"

"What?"

It came out a rush. "I can't call you Archie."
He threw his head back and laughed. "Got it."

Chapter 23

The fountains mingle with the river
And the rivers with the ocean,
The winds of heaven mix for ever
With a sweet emotion;
Nothing in the world is single;
All things by a law divine
In one spirit meet and mingle.
Why not I with thine?
                    ~Percy Bysshe Shelley (1792-1822)

Tucked beneath the gables of the farmhouse, Audrey woke to the peal of her alarm clock. Her heart did a little skip-to-my-wedding-day jig. How she and Liam had pulled things off in only five quick days, she could only speculate.

Jeremy Archer had connections. She smiled, remembering the way he'd gaped when she appeared just inside his doorstep, her teeth chattering, clothes dripping. A soaking-wet Liam had whisked her by his father with "I'd like you to meet the woman I'm going to marry."

And that had been her showstopping introduction. Mr. Archer was a Robin Hood out to save Nottingham Forest from any foe. If she hadn't grown up with a man who fought for his beliefs, she wouldn't have been so at home with her future father-in-law.

Three days ago, she'd purchased a gown from a bridal boutique in Windermere—the same Windermere John Keats and Percy Shelley visited. Sweet Lord, she missed her Percy.

"Nothing is ever a hundred percent without the dog who loves you," she said, plucking her bouquet from the fridge in the kitchen. One daisy petal broke away as if to confirm the truth of her statement. She rubbed its velvety coolness between her fingers and imagined her sister.

"Get with the program," Lucinda, the one-track-minded fashion wonder, would say. "This is your red-carpet moment, the day of every girl's dreams."

And so Audrey pushed herself into the continuous motion manifested from her recent habits. She did her hair in Liam's favorite way on her. Loosely woven curls at her crown, allowing a tendril or two to slip down her neck. Her dress slid down her frame, the flawless grace of the material whispering with her every move. Too bad her arms weren't longer. Too bad a woman wasn't on the premises to fasten the button loops along the back.

If only Mama—and there it was. Today of all days, she wished for Monroe Powell's loving touch. Her signature calm, her casual nonchalance in creating the stuff of literature. "A shoe is a glass slipper and a glass slipper a crystal dipper in a bowl of champagne punch made for you…" Mama and her wondrous word games.

A breeze blew through the window, bringing an even stronger sense of her mother's presence. Audrey let herself go where her heart led her. As she had when she'd been on other adventures with her mother, she listened hard and heard the pop of a cork from a vial.

The pouring of steaming water into a teacup. She stirred, and the threads turned a golden yellow.

"Saffron," Mama said in her calm, clear voice. "Tea fit for my daughter. Experience how it rolls down the tongue, soothing the throat along the way."

Audrey studied herself one last time in the oval cheval mirror. Lucinda would approve. Her twin's spirit had never felt so close. They'd spoken a few days ago when Audrey was in cell-phone range. She'd sent a video to her sister so she could see the wedding gown, and Lucinda had gone starry-eyed and weepy.

"Make sure to hide your dress with something long," she'd said. "It's bad luck to let your fiancé see you in your dress before you take the jaunt down that glorious catwalk." And so now Audrey slipped on a floor-length black cloak.

The finishing touch of the hat made all the difference. The moment Audrey spotted the Victorian treasure of mesh and satin, she'd known it was right. It whisked her back to a simpler era, a time of tea and poetry.

And to make things close to perfect, Liam eased her into a horse-drawn carriage. There was something magical about traveling through a dark wood just beginning to catch the rose gold of dawn. Dew glittered on the greenery flanking the path. Red squirrels appeared as if to wish them well, then disappeared. The sunlight, filtering through the trees an hour later, lit the charming brick chapel and warmed her as her prince helped her out of the carriage.

He, the one she'd slain dragons to join, was dashing in tailored black. To her he looked like he stepped from the time of the poets of old. Pine needles snapped underfoot as they passed a deer and her fawn plucking wild apples from a tree.

Liam escorted her inside the red double doors, and the incense made her heady with its sweet aroma. The ornate carvings dated the architecture to at least a hundred years ago. Such permanence deserved respect and a fight-to-the-death spirit.

Liam adjusted his bow tie, taking her back to that red-letter day when he'd read poetry on the train. "Are you ready to become Mrs. Archer?"

"I am," she said, giddy with joy but struck with a sudden hiccup of the heart for those she'd left back home in her nitty-gritty kingdom by the sea.

He responded with his killer grin. "Let the celebration begin."

As if on cue, organ music flooded toward her, and two little boys in floor-length robes of carnelian lit the candles on the altar in the sanctuary. And the small church danced in light and shadow. Then her sister turned around and smiled from the front pew, and Audrey's heart skid to a near stop.

As they rushed into each other's embrace, she thought she'd burst with gladness. Then from both sides came Bennett Browning and Madison Gray, all dressed as if in the wedding—Bennet in a tux, and her sister and Maddie in matching dove gray.

Lucinda spoke first. "I hope you don't mind us wedding crashers, but we thought you could use some bridesmaids."

"You did this without my asking," Audrey said, her voice choked.

"I couldn't stay away," Madison said, joining in on the hugs.

Bennett pressed next to Liam. "You didn't think I'd let your groom tie the knot without a best man, did you?"

"Liam, were you aware of all this?" Audrey asked.

"I was," he boasted. "And I didn't utter a word."

Lucinda stepped back a little and lowered her chin. "I hope you don't mind. I know you said you wanted to do things yourself."

"Are you kidding?" Audrey gasped. "All of you being with us on our special day means the world to me. The only thing missing is—"

Somebody tapped her on the shoulder. When she turned, she found who she'd been about to name. Uncle Johnny. He was looking at her with a face so full of love she dissolved into his arms.

Dressed for the black-tie event, he said, "I wouldn't have missed walking you down the aisle for all the tea in China."

"Of course not." Her uncle didn't have his sidekick. "Did you board Kubla?"

Lucinda twisted her neck as if it were sore. "You don't want to go there."

Uncle Johnny crumbled a little. "Kubla flew off the day you left."

"What?" She remembered spotting a parrot that looked exactly like Kubla during the worst, most-frightening moments of her life. "Maybe it's not too farfetched to assume he somehow boarded Flight 257 when I did."

"He'll turn up," Liam said with conviction in his tone.

The introductory notes of the processional song, "All You Need Is Love," caused Audrey's butterflies to swarm within her. "It's time."

As soon as Liam and Bennett positioned themselves at the bottom of the steps before the sanctuary, the dearest women in Audrey's life, her sister and her best friend, began their walk. Left alone, she now removed her cloak and folded it across a chair.

Uncle Johnny lifted Audrey's chin. "You look beautiful, sweet pea." His eyes shone with fresh tears. "I only wish your mama—"

"She might not be present in sight, but she's here in spirit."

He swallowed. "I do believe you're right." The opening notes of "Wedding March" rang out, and he added, "Go turn the world on with your smile."

Then he escorted her through the chapel decorated by the sun streaming through arches of stained glass. "This is it," she said, seeing no one but the man, his hair grown out, gone curly, wild, and gypsy-like. Yes, she only had eyes for her prince, her one true love—her poet.

****

Watching Audrey, a vision in white, advancing toward him in the church that stood still in time was as comparable to Liam as watching her five days ago when he had proposed.

The river had stretched like a sheet of corrugated iron, with no people anywhere. They were totally alone with nature and their picnic lunch. She slid a spoon into her vanilla panna cotta he had kept on ice when she spotted the diamond that had been his mother's.

He slid it on her trembling finger, and she said, "If I were to hunt to the ends of the earth, I could never have found a ring as beautiful."

Liam would complete it with the hand-engraved wedding band. He'd stayed up most of the night thinking about her. Exhaustion should have caught up with him by now, but his adrenaline spiked when Audrey joined him before the bespectacled, white-haired pastor.

Liam blinked back the sting of tears. He didn't understand why emotion had caught up with him at long last, melting away his reserve. An aching joy spread through him like a flame. He had returned to a forgotten world. He'd found the magic key.

And he saw his mother laughing as she pushed him on a park swing. He saw her as she made pottery on a wheel in a little island of light, her expressive hands sculpturing the clay. He heard her as she recited nursery rhymes that would stay with him long after she'd gone.

Liam had blamed her for abandoning him. He hadn't understood her death and his father's anger. Was she just out of sight beyond some veil? Feelings trapped inside him all these years surfaced like bright and bold stars in the night. "Write from your pain," someone had advised.

In his youth, he had felt guilt's hold, believing he'd made his father unhappy. When a troubled teen, he'd turned the burden into rage toward his father. He'd wanted to rebuke all that his dad valued, so he'd gone to the opposite extreme. He'd studied computer science for the wrong reasons, but after living without technology, he realized some middle ground must exist for him to explore.

One thing for sure, his future lay with Audrey's in the teahouse where they had socked all their energy, all their passion. He felt a need there to keep Venice special, to keep creating poetry and tea for a new generation. Okay, they would return to their second home here in the secluded corner of England, bring their children and grandchildren, because, after all, everyone should have a getaway. Venice Beach, though, had become his Shangri La, God help him.

When the pastor said to him, "Do you have something to read?" his mind cleared. No reason to rely on the poem tucked in his pocket. Instead, he recited it from memory.

"Audrey—the double syllables hang on the edge of my tongue,

A mixture of melancholy and hope before dawn.

You, my love, are the disturber of my sleep, the catalyst of my dreams,

You who walk the landscape of my inner world through golden beams.

I must seek you or die from lack of my muse,

For your very name, my darling, I'll never lose.

Audrey, you are a daisy set to music inside a poem.

You are a spring rain with a clap of thunder,

Amethysts, torn from a rock in a Brazilian dome,

Those are your eyes, yes, that pull me asunder.

You are the magic north star leading me home."

He finished by saying, "I will love you always and forever."

She looked up at him through her tears. "And to think I once tried to silence you. I'm glad you didn't listen."

The rest of the ceremony became a whirlwind of lots of "Do you?" and "I do's." Until the pastor asked, "Do you have the ring?"

Liam seized it from his pocket and smiled as he

said, "With this ring, I thee wed…"

After the pastor introduced Mr. and Mrs. Archer, they headed back through the church. Audrey jubilantly waved at Doc, who had slipped in a pew right before the service.

Liam said, "I have a surprise for you just outside those doors." He clasped her arm. "I can't wait to see your reaction."

"Did you get us a balloon to travel the world? If so, I'm up to it."

"That's my girl." He passed her a sly grin. "You are the real Audrey? You didn't pull another switch just to keep me on my toes, did you?"

"You never know, dude."

"I know I'm the luckiest guy alive to have survived the double-trouble brigade."

****

She didn't think she could get any happier until she stepped into the blinding sunlight. The air smelled intensely of England, that particular woods-in-the-highlands fragrance she associated with Liam. It soaked in through her pores, through her nose, and caught in her chest. Her body felt weightless. She hesitated for a long moment, breathing it in, welcoming the calm it gave her, and realizing this moment would never come again. And that realization was what made life so precious. One day she'd write a poem about the past and its effect on the present.

Every person who meant the world to her crowded before her, and she embraced each one separately. But a sharp laugh broke her concentration, and another giggle, her sister's this time, gave her reason to wonder. She squinted to see through the sunlight as the group divided and pushed away from the path, granting her a look.

There beneath the trees in a patch of bluebells stood Sgt. Sam North. He nodded at her just once and moved in a sidestep that revealed two dogs, sitting tall and still as statues—Cleo, the war hero, and Percy, the rookie.

"Woohoo!" She tossed her bridal bouquet backward, gathered up her gown, and barreled down the path. "Oh my God, Percy!"

Her dog, the same one she'd almost handed over to someone who would love him, sat trying his darndest to stay put. His white-booted feet, trembling with excitement, betrayed him, but he didn't jump into her arms as he would have even a week ago.

"I can't believe it," she said to Sam, hugging him.

"A little training goes a long way, wouldn't you say, Mrs. Archer?" Sam nodded at Percy. "At ease, soldier."

She kneeled as Percy's eyes filled with adoration and joy.

"Did you know about this, Liam?"

"Let's put it this way. I knew when we met by the way you treated the little dickens. I knew by the way you treated me."

"What do you mean?"

"I've always been mad for a woman who has a soft spot for dogs and poets."

A word about the author...

Melody lives in Sacramento (the City of Trees). She writes romance novels. She's partial to poetry, sun, rain, strong coffee, and her writing room surrounded by books. Besides California, she and her late husband lived part time in a condo in Oregon overlooking the Pacific. That gave her a love for beach towns and whale-watching and sunsets—all the things that inspired the Love Is a Beach series. The writing process fascinates her, the alchemy of layering and developing characters, the tinkering with language. There's so much to treasure in the world: family, friends, and those random, everyday moments that make life grand. She hopes to give her readers all of that.

~*~

Find Melody online at:
https://www.melodydeblois.com/
https://twitter.com/Melody_DeBlois
https://www.facebook.com/melodydebloisbooks/
https://www.instagram.com/melody.deblois/
https://www.pinterest.com/deblois0181/